MW01268210

CONSUMED

BOOK ONE

By
Sara Wilson

Congrats Kaley and thank you for entering my contest. Hope you enjoy and second book coming soon. XOXO

PublishAmerica
Baltimore

Softcover 9781627725361
PUBLISHED BY PUBLISHAMERICA, LLLP
www.publishamerica.com
Baltimore

Printed in the United States of America

I would like to dedicate this book to

my friend Tammy Blumenthal

INTRODUCTION

Archer hated the fact that his father had brought him to this hole in the wall town to live that smelled of decaying pine. He even hated the fact more that he was going to have to go to public school with a bunch of humans while his older siblings were going to be home schooled. He was going to have to be forced to mingle with the low smelly humans when he was superior to them. He couldn't help but steam a little under the collar as he heard Wraith in his head laughing because Greed was whining on how he rather have Urobach teach him what he wanted to know. His two demons bickering back and forth inside him was his headache and his punishment because his father had volunteered to birth the four horsemen, however it would be another five or six years before he would inherit his horseman's power. So in the meantime he had to obey his father's choice, and set out to solve the riddle the stupid Oracle had told him. This made him steam more as he silently cursed his father for making him who he was and his mother who had left him to be raised by his father alone.

Sitting across from Archer was his older brother Kane, who was indeed escorting him to his human hell. Archer couldn't help but stare at his brother as he remembered the visit they had with the Oracle. Deep down, he hated the Oracle because her words were confusing. He was only thirteen for crying out loud, it wasn't fair to be subjected to what he was about to encounter. Glaring at his brother, he almost jumped when he spoke, "little brother, this is not what I had planned either, but we must do what we are told for now. We must prepare for what is ahead of us so we will be ready."

Archer knew he was scolding again, but he couldn't keep the whining out of his voice either. "How come I have to go to public school Kane while you, Lacy, and Price get to stay at home? Where is the justice in that because some old bat says my destiny awaits me in the human world? What did she mean by telling me that my greatest challenge was the fight within myself as I will have no control? None of the words she said made a lick of sense. Are all Oracles nuts like that?"

Kane laughed as the limo pulled up to the school. Already Archer felt the eyes turning to see who was coming to the school. No doubt in his mind none of them had ever seen a limo before. "Little brother I can't explain to you what I do not know. The Oracle left me with a weird riddle to solve myself, and I will in time like you will. I tell you what, when I figure mine out I will help you with yours." He smiled at him then, and for once Archer wished he looked more like his brother with his dark eyes instead of his bright green eyes. "Well little brother, have fun today and try not to get into too much mischief. You do remember where you need to go right?"

Archer laughed for the first time this morning liking the fact that him, and his brother were so close. "Yeah I go to the office and then they will take me to my class. Eighth grade and I only have one teacher. How am I to skip a class when I'm in the same class all day?"

Kane openly laughed, "I guess that you don't little brother, but I will return at three to hear all about your day. I want full details no matter what."

Archer got out of the car as his brother remained inside. He watched the car pull away as he noticed students heading towards the building as they looked at him. Most of them distanced themselves away from him so they wouldn't walk within ten feet of him. For a split second he wondered why humans would act that way, but then he shrugged it off and headed inside. The office was the first door on the right, so Archer entered to suddenly have the lady behind the desk stop what she was doing to stare at him. Unsure of himself for the first time, he noticed how quiet the voices in his head were as he spoke, "I'm Archer Stevens."

The woman smiled nervously as he heard Wraith in his head laughing as he was telling him that the woman was scared of him. For several seconds Archer wondered why this woman was scared of him, he just couldn't understand it. Greed on the other hand started to make demands for him to tell the woman to give him money. Figuring he would give it a try he told her to give him a pen. He couldn't help but smile smugly as she did in fact hand him the pen. Deep down if she was this easy to control, so would the others. They would all be sheep at his hand to command.

After Archer had what he needed to turn into his new teacher, he told the woman to stay. He was laughing with his demons as he exited the office and ran smack dab right into someone. He felt something sting instantly like he had been shocked. It was the weirdest feeling he had ever experienced since he had never felt a shock of energy like that before. Confused, he looked at who he had bumped into. The first thing he saw was the wild red hair that looked like a flame, and then he noticed that the hair was moving as slender white arms were picking up a book and a pen. Her voice was instant to as she continued to gather her things. "I'm terribly sorry I was running late and not paying attention to where I was going. I didn't hurt you did I?"

Archer almost snorted at that comment as he thought no human could ever hurt him until her eyes suddenly met his, and Archer's whole world stopped. In fact for several minutes Archer stopped breathing as he suddenly felt that here was the one human that could most likely bring him to his knees with her beauty alone. Her eyes were a rare shade of purple that was mixed with a brown, looking like amethysts. He had never seen anyone with eyes like hers before, making her one of a kind. Both his demons were suddenly yelling in his head making him snap to attention and focus. Greed kept saying mine and I want her, as Wraith demanded that he mark her and make her his. He had to mentally tell them to shut up so he could form words to speak to her. "No I'm not hurt, did I hurt you?"

She actually laughed at him making him feel self aware of himself as her smile made his insides melt. "No I am fine. I'm Allie McAlister."

Even her name was beautiful to him as he felt his heart skip a beat. Archer had to take a minute to make sure he wasn't drooling as she would peek at him from behind her hair looking like she was blushing. Could she be the one that the Oracle was talking about? She was also waiting for him to say something, and it took Wraith yelling at him that she was asking him his name even though she was batting those beautiful lashes at him making him lose focus as he just wanted to stare at her. The comments that followed what Wraith was saying snapped Archer to attention before he looked like a fool in front of her and embraced himself. Archer was quick to smile at her as he spoke, "I'm Archer Stevens."

Her face looked a little surprised and then she blushed more, making Greed moan in his head and demand that they keep her. "This is naughty of me, but I am late in escorting you to class. I volunteered to show you around today. I hope you don't mind that you have a girl escort and not a guy."

Again Greed was moaning in his head deep in pleasure as Wraith was telling him to take her home with them now. "I don't mind at all," Archer spoke the truth on how he really felt feeling pleased that she would be with him all day today.

She was smiling and blushing again as she spoke and Archer had no clue what she said. Wraith's voice was suddenly in his head feeling like he was shocked, "this is the one the Oracle was talking about. She is our heart." Those words confused Archer a little as he wondered how this girl could be his heart, she was human. Greed was still moaning as Wraith continued. "No one shall have her but us. She's mine. I want her."

"Mine," Greed repeated as Archer smiled at Allie without a clue on what she had just said.

Suddenly she frowned at him and Archer wondered what he had done. He even started to panic inside as he heard her voice. "Are you sure you are ok? I'm not normally a chatter bug, only when I'm a little nervous. If I am talking too much just tell me to shut up."

"Why would you be nervous? I'm just stunned that you are so open and easy to talk to," came out of his mouth too quickly as deep down he wanted to know everything about her. She blushed again and Archer felt the need to push her for more. Actually Archer really wanted to reach out and touch her again to see if she was real, but first he needed to make sure she was at his level. "I was wondering if you can help me solve a little riddle before we head to class." She smiled and nodded at him. "If someone told you change equals a heart to slay, how would you try to understand it?"

It was only a piece of what the oracle had told him, but he had to test her mind to know how to go ahead with her. "Sounds like someone will have a broken heart," she said instantly as her face looked so serious.

Archer paled as he understood what the Oracle's riddle meant. Not only that, but the girl's quick response made complete sense in his mind. This girl was his heart to slay. He would have to kill her for the horsemen to succeed. Both of his demons screamed out a no in protest. Wraith was instant to tell him that they needed to slay the Oracle and protect the girl so no one would discover that they had found her so quickly. Word could not get out at all that he had found the heart, or one of his siblings might do the deed and kill her. Greed was for once plotting on how to protect her as her voice finally got through to him with her slender fingers touching his hand. "Archer, are you ok? You went pale on me."

He shook his head instantly to reassure her, but he couldn't help but look at how perfect her hand in his seemed. She already had him wrapped around her finger and he was willing to bet that she didn't know it yet. "I'm fine Allie, but we need to head to class."

She nodded accepting his answer and led the way to class letting her hand slip out of his, as Archer watched her from behind missing the contact. His heart was still pounding as Wraith and Greed were plotting inside him. He couldn't let any of them figure out about the heart even his own family. If word got out about Allie, a piece of him would be gone along with Allie. He knew her death wouldn't be a quick one either. His siblings would love to torture her, and no telling what his father would do. The best plan was to make sure Allie and his family never crossed paths. He vowed with his demons to keep her safe no matter what the cost was.

CHAPTER ONE
FRESHMEN YEAR

Allie was excited as she got ready for school. Today was her first day of high school, and she would be able to see Archer again. Granted she did have a fun summer and spent a lot of time at the beach, she thought about Archer daily and all the fun they had last year. She even talked her mom into buying a gift for her to give Archer today knowing he would smile when he saw it. Allie was a little nervous that he would find the gift corny, but when she saw the shark tooth necklace it was screaming his name. Now all Allie wanted to do was get to her new school, get her classes, and hope she could find Archer because she had missed him terribly.

"Allie, it's time to go," she heard her father downstairs calling her bringing her excitement up a notch.

"I'll be right there dad," Allie called back as she scooped up her backpack and grabbed Archer's gift nearly giggling to herself. She was tucking it in the pocket of her backpack as she nearly ran down the stairs excited to start the first day of school.

"Slow down before you trip and fall, there is no fire behind you," her mother called out as Allie zipped to the door not being too careful.

"Sorry mom, but I can't wait to get to school." Allie responded back as she headed to the car not even turning to look at her mother as she spoke.

Allie's dad seemed to take his time as he was dressed for work carrying a brief case. He got in the car as it seemed like Allie couldn't sit still. Before he started the car he shook his head as he spoke drawing out his words like he was disgusted, "are you really this excited to get to school, or are you hoping to see that boy?"

Allie's smile was nearly ear to ear as she spoke. "Daddy, his name is Archer, and you have never complained about him before. Besides it's my first day of high school. I will have more than one teacher, get to meet new people, and get to see Archer."

Her dad actually rolled his eyes as he laughed. He even shook his head as they backed out of the drive however his voice was serious as he addressed her. "So do we need to have the talk Allie?"

Allie's cheeks went red instantly as the car moved forward. Dread washed over Allie as she could vision what her dad was about to forego. "Dad no, that's just awkward. Archer and I are best friends, nothing more than that. We are not in a relationship."

Her dad laughed hard this time as he snuck a peek at her face. "I was actually talking about curfew rules Allie now that you are in high school. They are much different rules than grade school however it seems that your mother must have talked to you about the other in which I am relieved."

Allie's cheeks were nearly as red as her hair. "Dad the way you phrase that is the same way mom did. I know boys will be different, but you raised a daughter with a good head on her shoulders."

Her dad smiled as the car pulled up to the high school. Allie stared out at all the people heading into the building. Only for several minutes did she have butterflies in her stomach, but dead down she told herself that Archer was here and everything would be alright. "Well here goes, wish me luck."

Her dad laughed as Allie opened the door and stepped onto the pavement. "Hey Allie," her dad called making her turn to look back at him. "Good luck sweetheart. Your mother will be here to pick you up at three."

Allie smiled at her dad and waved as she closed the door. Then she turned towards the entrance as she took a breath to take her first step. "I can do this," she told herself mentally and walked to the entrance.

Allie's first step was to get her schedule. The process took ten minutes to do, and she ran into a few people she knew. Heading to her locker, Allie ran into more people she knew and started meeting a few new ones, yet she didn't see Archer and was a little disappointed. Her day continued through her first three classes with no sign of Archer. Feeling a little bummed at lunch time she moved to sit outside only to spot Archer suddenly talking with two other boys. She moved quickly heading towards him glad to finally spot him. The two boys he was talking to didn't look friendly in Allie's eye and she wondered why Archer was talking to them.

She noticed one of the other boys turn to look at her as she got closer. His lips curved in a sly smile that made Allie think she needed to wash every square inch of her. The other boy then also turned to look at her, and he smiled at her but the smile didn't meet his eyes. Archer was the last one to look at her, and for some reason he didn't look happy as Allie came to a stop next to him. She smiled at him anyway as she spoke. "Hi Archer, I hope you had a good summer."

Archer was silent for a minute, but his two friends were openly looking at Allie up and down with their smiles getting bigger. In fact they looked like they wanted to eat her, that it gave Allie the chills a little. "Allie," Archer said with a scold on his face. "I thought I told you to stop following me around like a lost little puppy. Stalking is against the law, and you mentally need help. Beat it."

Allie was clearly shocked by Archer's statement that she stood there a minute with her mouth gapped open. He had never talked to her like that before that she couldn't understand why he was. His two friends were openly laughing, not caring about Allie's feelings at all. It took Allie another minute just to get over the shock before she spoke, "wow, I didn't realize that you morphed into a jerk this summer. Whatever Archer, if this is the way you're going to be I rather not know you."

Archer narrowed his eyes at Allie as she narrowed hers back at him for a minute. Then she turned and stormed away from him before he could see the hurt in her eyes. Never had Allie wanted to hit someone so bad in her whole life. Everything she remembered about Archer was gone. She didn't even know who that person was back there. Fuming inside Allie headed to her next class, who needed Archer Stevens.

Sitting in her seat for her next class, Allie couldn't calm her nerves. She also couldn't think straight. She was swearing in her mind while glaring straight ahead that she almost missed the girl talking to her. It took the little blond waving a hand in front of her face to make her blink and realize that she had snapped her pencil in her hand. "Are you ok?" The little blond asked her.

Allie had to shake her head to calm herself. "I'll be ok, just someone I thought was a friend became a jerk."

The blond gave Allie a smile and nodded her head like she knew what Allie was talking about. "Yeah I have been there before," she said instantly. "I'm Janice White," she said with a smile.

Allie felt her lips quirk up in a smile as she spoke realizing that she was letting Archer's behavior get to her. "Nice to meet you Janice, I'm Allie McAlister."

"So Allie, how would you like a new partner in crime that will get you in loads of trouble?" Janice seemed to tell her making her eye brows move like she was up to no good.

Allie actually started to laugh, and sure enough she got a hush by the teacher that started to lecture the class about talking during a lecture. This made Janice roll her eyes and start making faces. Allie had to look down at the floor or she would have started laughing again. The rest of the class was spent looking at the floor with a huge smile on her face. When class ended Allie discovered she had PE with Janice afterwards. They talked through the entire class getting to know one another, and found that they had a lot in common.

Allie only had one class left, chemistry. She went to class forgetting about Archer, and happy to have met Janice. Her smile left her face pretty quickly when she noticed Archer in the class. She tried not to even look at him, but that was hard when she found herself paired with him. "Can I have a new partner?" Allie was quick to ask the teacher not wanting to be anywhere near Archer.

"Do you have a problem Miss McAlister with Mr. Stevens?" The teacher asked her.

Archer actually smirked at her as if he loved her misery. The move made Allie grind her teeth and narrow her eyes at Archer. If he wanted to play games like this she would dish it back to him. "No I don't have a problem," she told the teacher.

The teacher seemed to nod and move on, however Allie was steaming inside as she thought this was the perfect Archer set up. Archer was staring at her with that little smirk that made her want to turn and rip it off. He then leaned in close and whispered in her ear, "oh poor Allie, it hurts my feeling that you didn't want me as a partner. Did I hurt your feelings earlier Allie? Truth hurts doesn't it?"

Allie closed her eyes for a minute as she took a breath to relax herself. She turned to look at Archer for a minute and ended up glaring at him. Instantly she decided she would play this game with him. She laughed and shook her head like nothing was wrong. "Yeah the truth does hurt, you're a jerk. As for my feelings, what feelings are you referring to? I never would have guessed that you thought I actually cared about you in any way. I just don't want a jerk for my partner that is going to accuse me of following him like a puppy to show off to his buddies instead of getting an assignment done."

Archer's eyes narrowed as he leaned in closer to Allie. "You don't want to play this game with me Allie you're not up to par."

This time Allie smiled at him all cocky. "Really Archer, you want to go there with me. Go ahead and try me, do your worst. I will take what you dish out and dish it back. Oh by the way I almost forgot, I have a gift for you. Hmm we will call it a declaration of my intent."

Archer looked confused for a minute as Alley opened her backpack. She reached in and grabbed the necklace she had insisted on her parents buying for him. She held it in her hand for a minute and then held out her hand when she really wanted to throw it at him. Archer was slow in taking her gift, and it seemed like he almost didn't trust her. Once he opened his hand, Allie dropped the little box in it that contained the necklace. Archer kept his eyes on Allie as she continued to glare at him. "Archer," Allie said with venom in her voice. "I hope you choke on it."

With the last word, Allie rose up right as the bell rang and walked out with her head high. Archer looked down at the box and opened it slowly. He noticed the shark tooth on the golden chain and started to smile. All summer long his demons had drove him insane thinking of Allie, and as it turned out, she had been thinking of him too. His smile grew bigger as he thought of the little war he had started Allie to keep her safe. This year promised to be fun for him, and he planned to strike next by dating her new friend Janice. Mentally he thought Allie didn't have a chance, and this would be a test to find out how long until she cracked.

CHAPTER TWO
SOPHOMORE YEAR

Sophomore year should have been something Allie was looking forward to instead she nearly wished that she could go to school somewhere else. Her freshmen year was spent constantly on her toes against Archer. It was a game of wits with him. The summer was her break, and she would spend it in the coastal cabin with her parents. The summer was also her escape away from Archer and her only chance to breath in relief. Two weeks into the new school year and Allie was counting down until summer again.

"Earth to Allie," Janice said while wearing her little cheerleader outfit.

Allie turned to look at Janice as she sat within the circle of friends of girls only. Allie was on a mental cool down after having crossed paths with Archer right before third period and during third period as well, so her thoughts were not with her. "Yeah Janice," Allie replied smoothly.

"Well you do me a favor tonight?"

Since it was a Friday night, there was no telling what Janice was planning. "Depends, what is up?"

Janice smiled as she sat next to her. "Do you think your parents will let you stay the night so we can go on a double date?"

Allie blinked twice as she thought who Janice would be going on a date with. "You're not going on a date with the guy Archer set you up with are you?"

Janice actually bit her bottom lip. "My parents won't let me go on a date with Matt unless I go with a friend too because then it is more of a group thing. Matt said he would bring a friend as well, and it won't be Archer. I know how the two of you don't get along, and as your best friend I would never subject you to it."

Deep down Allie thought maybe a night out meeting a new guy would be nice. Maybe it would get her mind out of trying to outwit Archer. "Hmm, well I have to ask my parents first."

Janice was quick to fish out her cute little hot pink cell phone. "Call them now. You can totally raid my closet in fact I think I have something cute that you can wear."

Allie felt dread sinking in as she took the phone. Why she suddenly thought this was a bad idea suddenly nagged in the back of her head. Still she dialed home to have her mother pick up the phone. "Hi mom it's Allie, I'm on Janice's cell phone."

"Is everything all right," her mother questioned her.

"Yeah mom, Janice was hoping that I could stay at her house tonight and go on a double date with her."

"Hmm," her mom said into the phone. "Who is the date with?"

"Janice is going on a date with Matt. He is bringing a friend with him so it is more of a group thing."

Allie's mom was silent on the phone for a few minutes, but it sounded like she was tapping her fingers on the counter. "Where are you planning to go?"

At this point Allie turned the phone over to Janice who was listening to every word between the two of us. "Hi Liz," Janice greeted my mom over the phone. "We are planning to see a movie, and then afterwards we will walk down to the ice cream shop for a treat before my parents pick us up there. We will be meeting the boys at the movie theater so no worries about us riding in a car with them." Janice seemed to smile big as she continued to speak. "Oh we will have a great time and Allie will call you in the morning."

Janice hung up the phone and looked like she was dancing with excitement. Her eyes also twinkled, "I will tell Matt it is a go when I see him next period. This is going to be the best night ever," she nearly sung into Allie's ear making her regret not coming up with an excuse not to go. However Allie smiled at her friend as the bell rang and she jumped up to head to her class with Matt. Then Allie frowned as she realized she had fourth period with Archer and her nerves were still shot from the last round she went with him. She had to mentally tell herself that she could get through the day, and she wouldn't let Archer get to her. Besides that, her day was almost over.

The day passed quickly for Allie, as she walked out of her last class with Melissa talking about the project next week. A sudden feeling made her feel like she was being watched, so she turned slightly to see Archer staring at her and Melissa. He smiled instantly like he was plotting and Allie suddenly knew that Melissa was on his list of Allie's friends to conquer. The whole action made her roll her eyes in his direction as she continued walking with Melissa to her locker fully noting that he saw that eye roll of hers.

At the locker Allie realized that Melissa had been talking the whole time and Allie had not heard a word of it. She felt a little embraced about it as Melissa told her to have a good weekend and walked away heading toward her locker. Shaking her head a little, Allie placed her things in her locker. When she went to close it, Rollin Davis was perched on the side of her waiting for her. "Hi Rollin," Allie said politely not understanding why the senior seemed to always keep tabs on her.

"Hello Allie. Did you have a good day today?"

His smile was nearly a leer as he stared at her, but it was always the same way he started a conversation with her. "Well let's just say I'm glad it is over. Excuse me Rollin but I have to go meet Janice."

Allie went to make her escape like she always did from Rollin, but he was quick this time to reach out and grab her arm to stop her. "Wait Allie, there is no need to rush off. Janice can wait a few minutes. I was kind of hoping that I might be able to talk you into going to the harvest dance with me next week."

Allie actually blinked. None of the boys in the school had ever asked her out before. "Wow, you caught me by surprise. Sure you want to go to a dance with me?"

Rollin's smile was cocky as he spoke, "oh yeah I want to take you to the dance."

Allie was about to respond as Archer's voice suddenly came from behind her. "Oh that is rich Rollin, who dared you to try to deflower the prune?"

Allie felt her cheek turn red as she turned to see Archer right behind her glaring at Rollin. "Archer," she said with distaste in her voice.

He was quick to look down at her and narrow his eyes towards her like he was judging her. "Allie," he said with just as much distaste as she had. Then he smiled at her, "care to tell me who your little friend with the brown hair is so I can get her number?"

His question pretty much told her that Melissa was indeed on his list to conquer next. She couldn't stop the eye roll as she spoke, "why don't I set the two of you up tonight Archer?"

"No I have plans tonight," Archer said instantly cutting her off.

"Allie, is Archer bothering you?" Rollin asked her before she could respond back to Archer.

Allie turned to look back at Rollin who was glaring at Archer. "Rollin," Allie said addressing him so he would look at her. "Let me get back to you about the dance," she said in the next breath when he continued to stare at Archer.

Rollin then looked down at her and the glare he gave her wasn't too friendly as he spoke, "I asked if Archer has been bothering you Allie?"

His hostel look made Allie swallow and step back towards Archer. Something about Rollin just sent the chills up her spine. "I'm not bothering her dumbass, Allie and I go way back, and she still gives me gifts to this day." Allie spun around to look at Archer ready to call him a liar however he was holding up the necklace she gave him last year of the shark tooth. "Did you not give this to me Allie?"

So many emotions ran through Allie's head at that moment that she was lost for words. After a moment her anger hit her. "Archer that is the only thing I ever gave you…"

"See Rolling," Archer said cutting her off from the lecture she was about to deliver. "I'm not bothering Allie or she would not give me gifts."

Allie snorted at his comment as anger ate away at her. "Oh Archer let me give you another gift then."

Without thinking she turned grabbed Rollin by his shirt and pulled him down to her. The move took him off guard as he was surprised, but he was even more surprised when she planted a kiss on Rollin's lips. Allie poured her anger into that kiss that made Rollin moan as his arms went around her waist. He even lifted her up off the ground so her feet dangled. When she pulled back from the kiss catching her breath, he set her down carefully. He was panting as his arms kept hold of her.

Then he smiled as his eyes turned toward Archer. "Thank you for the gift Archer it was worth it."

In Allie's mind Rollin didn't sound any better than Archer as she turned and looked at Archer. He had an eye brow raised like he wasn't even surprised. "Well you always liked kissing frogs Allie I'm not surprised that you kissed a toad this time. By the way if that was my gift can I get a refund? Cause that was like the worst kiss I have ever seen."

Allie was instantly furious as she pushed herself out of Rollin's arms to storm down the hallway. Deep down she hoped Rollin cleaned his plow to wipe the arrogant smile off his face as he laughed at her for storming off. Seeing red, Allie headed to where she would meet Janice forgetting about Archer and Rollin.

Archer waited for Allie to clear the corner. He knew Rollin had been stalking her, and would now deal with him. Rollin was arrogant enough to be leaning against the locker with a malicious smile on his face. "I'm winning the bet Archer I will be Allie's first."

Archer actually smiled at Rollin as he spoke. "No Rollin I don't think so." Rollin started to laugh at Archer as Archer continued. "She only kissed you like that to get me jealous, and guess what, it worked." He took a step towards Rollin who suddenly shot up ready to fight. Archer just smiled, "no worries, you won't feel a thing."

"Allie," Janice called to her as she stepped out of the building feeling like steam was rolling off of her. Allie tried to hide the emotions she felt as she faked a smile and moved towards Janice. "What took you so long?"

A breath escaped Allie as she spoke. "Rollin Davis asked me to the Harvest dance, but then Archer showed up and ruined it."

"Oh no tell me he didn't do that to you," Janice said next sounding all concern.

The two girls moved and got into Janice's mom's car as she pulled up. They climbed in the back continuing the conversation as they both greeted Janice's mom. "He did do it and to make matters even worst, I lost my temper and ended up kissing Rollin."

Janice actually laughed at that as she spoke, "so how was the kiss?"

Allie made a face. "Terrible. Rollin's breath was nasty from whatever he had for lunch, and I hate to admit it, but Archer was right, I felt like I kissed a toad."

Janice was openly laughing now. "I can't believe Archer called Rollin a toad. Did Archer leave before you did?"

Allie suddenly frowned, "no, and I hope Rollin cleans his plow. He was being an ass and deserves whatever Rollin deals out."

"Oh my god Allie," Janice said with so much mischief. "I can't wait until I see Matt tonight and get all the gossip."

Janice was bouncing in her seat as the car pulled up to her house. The girls got out slowly walking inside as it looked like Janice's mom was shaking her head at the two of them with a smile on her face. "Mom," Janice addressed her. "Do you mind if we leave early for the movie so Allie and I can window shop a little?"

Her mom openly laughed. "Oh Janice I know you too well. I know for a fact you're planning to count how many guys check you out."

Janice's cheeks turned a little pink as she smiled big. "Well there is that and the fact that the theater has the new dance party game and I figured it would be fun to shake it before the guys showed up."

Her mom laughed but nodded her head that they would be leaving early, in which made Janice jump up and down in excitement. Then she grabbed Allie's hand and raced to her room to get ready for the night.

CHAPTER THREE
A MOVIE

Allie and Janice arrived at the movies an hour early. They headed straight to the arcade to play dance party. Granted they were shaking it in the mini-skirts, they were laughing and having a good time not caring that others were stopping to watch the two of them. Best part was that a few guys would come up and place more quarters in the machine for them so they wouldn't stop. After a while Allie had to stop. She didn't have the energy like Janice did to keep up and she was thirsty. "Janice, I'm going to head to the snack bar to get a drink and some snacks for the movie before the guys get here, do you want anything?" Allie asked Janice as the song ended.

"I'm going to do one more, but will you get me some water," Janice responded.

Allie started to move away from the game to notice that a few guys were watching them. One of them spoke, "oh come on pretty girl don't stop now."

Allie smiled at them as she spoke, "sorry but I'm thirsty. My friend is going to do one more, fill free to join her."

The guy smiled at her but then turned to look at Janice. Allie had to shake her head as her friend started dancing again amazed at her energy that never stopped. Then she headed to the confession stand to get a drink. Waiting in line didn't take too long as Allie got a large coke and a bottle water. Her eyes roamed the candy stand and to her surprise she noticed Archer's favorite candy that he would eat over at her house all the time when they watched a movie together in the eighth grade. Not knowing why she requested the chocolate mints smiling thinking she was sure going to enjoy Archer's candy as she watched the movie.

Heading back to the arcade room, she noticed Janice dancing with Matt to the game. Both of them were smiling as they moved to the beat, and the look on their faces made Allie smile too. She had to admit, they seemed perfect for each other and she was glad that they were together. She watched them like the crowd did until the music ended then the two of them stopped to smile at one another.

Allie envied them for a minute, and then Janice turned looked at her smiling. She also had Matt's hand as she pulled him toward Allie. Her voice was instant the minute they reached Allie. "I'm so thirsty thank you Allie."

She took the water from Allie taking a drink, and nearly finished it off. Matt watched her with a smile, but then looked at Allie for a minute and winked. His eyes were back on Janice within seconds, as Allie actually wondered what movie they were going to watch and where Matt's friend was.

The thought happened too quickly as the world felt like it slowed down for Allie. Out of nowhere, she heard Archer's voice. "Matt I have the tickets, but the line for snacks is nuts."

"Archer," Janice nearly screeched in a panic voice as she looked at Allie with big eyes. "I didn't know that you were coming, Matt told me it was going to be Joe."

Matt bit his bottom lip as he met Allie's eyes. "Sorry Allie, but Joe got really sick. Archer was happy to take his place so Janice and I could go on this date. I really didn't want to cancel last minute."

Allie could hear her heart beating inside her as she could feel Archer standing behind her. She mentally cursed her rotten luck then she mumbled under her breath as she spoke. "Yeah I bet he was happy to take his place," slipped out too easily as she turned to face Archer hoping he had a black eye or something from Rollin.

He was smirking at her like he had planned every bit of this. Plus he looked as good as ever without a mark on his perfect skin. His eyes went instantly to the candy in her hand.

"Oh Allie after everything we have been through, you still remember my favorite candy I like to eat while watching a movie. That was thoughtful of you to get it for me."

Allie was grinding her teeth as her whole night suddenly seemed in the toilet. Yet she was willing to put up with Archer for Janice's sake. "Yeah no problem Archer," Allie said with a force smile as she handed him the box of chocolates while he smiled big at her.

"Umm, so Archer what movie did you get tickets for?" Janice asked unsure of how things were going to go tonight and casting Allie a nervous glance.

Archer kept his eyes on Allie. "I got us tickets for Hell's Gate. I figured a horror movie would keep you in Matt's arms Janice. However Allie I know you hate horror movies, you can always exchange the ticket for that kids cartoon."

Allie's glare became intent as she stayed focused on Archer. "Hell's Gate is fine Archer, besides I deal with you daily I think I can handle a movie that doesn't hold a candle to you."

Archer's lips tilted up in a smile, "challenge accepted Allie," he said in a soft whisper.

As a group they headed inside the theater, but to Allie's surprise there were no seats for the four of them together. "Matt why don't you and Janice take those seats as Allie and I sit in the back by the door incase Allie gets too scared."

Allie glared at Archer as she spoke, "maybe they want to sit in the back so they can make out Archer."

"Not at this stage," Archer stated clearly, as Janice and Matt both looked shocked by the two of them.

Allie rolled her eyes and moved to the back as Archer smiled at her and said something to Matt and Janice. Then he made his way back to her taking the empty seat. Instantly Allie felt cornered as the guy sitting next to her was already making out with the girl next to him. Archer on the other hand was staring at her with a smile that looked like he was winning. "Why are you really here? Earlier when you were spoiling my first invite to a dance, you said you had plans."

Archer's eyes twinkled as he spoke. "Hmm, I did say that I have plans. But now that we are on the subject, why would you consider going to a dance with the biggest player in the school? You would just be another notch on his belt of conquests. I always thought you were smarter than that, but clearly I was mistaken."

"My personal life is none of your concern Archer, and Rollin is not the biggest player in school, you are. Now tell me why you are here." Allie fired back at him.

"So you would have turned him down?" Archer asked avoiding her question.

Allie glared at Archer like he had grown a third head. "Archer why are you here when you knew as clear as day Janice was bringing me with her tonight?"

Archer stared at Allie for a minute as the theater went dark for the movie to begin. She was still staring at him as the previews begin. So Archer leaned in and spoke in a whisper. "Would you like one of the chocolate mints Allie? They always make the movie better."

Allie shook her head clearly frustrated with Archer as she sat back in her chair to watch the movie. Then she held out her hand for a mint, which had Archer holding back a laugh while placing a few mints in her hand. The movie started in no time, and for once Allie was scared. She was forcing herself to watch, but found herself jumping and turning toward Archer to hide. Then she realized that she was hiding into Archer and would correct herself as he wore a huge grin that was holding back laughter. Anger consumed her knowing that he was clearly enjoying her torture, so she looked straight at the ground hoping the noise wouldn't give her a nightmare. However she jumped the minute Archer took her death grip hand into his, holding onto it, and leaning in to whisper in her ear. "You're missing the movie looking at the ground. If you need to use me to shield the scary parts Allie, I promise I won't tell."

Allie turned a little too quickly, and it nearly brought her lips to his. Archer didn't move as their faces were so close. He also didn't let go of her hand. "Thanks," slipped out of Allie's mouth as she stared deep into Archer's green eyes actually feeling safe with him like she did in the eighth grade.

Archer still looked at Allie forgetting about the movie. Their heads were still close to one another that Archer literally had two inches before they would be kissing. He wondered if she would kiss him like she did Rollin. He wanted to feel her lips so bad on his as Greed seemed to be screaming at him to do it already. Giving in to his demon, Archer moved in closer to cover those two inches about to take Allie by surprise. He could smell the mint on her breath crossed with a smell of cinnamon. Her breath smelled so good that he closed his eyes devouring the smell as his lips were almost on hers.

A clearing of the throat broke up the almost kiss and made Archer turn his head totally caught off guard. His brother was standing next to him by the door, and was totally checking out Allie in more ways than one that was making Archer's skin boil. How dare his brother even be mentally undressing her like this when he didn't know her? Wraith was making himself heard as he kept telling Archer to punch Kane. Then the thought that his brother was here worried him because it exposed Allie in so many ways on what she meant to him. He was going to have to hide all of his feelings to protector her when he really wanted to kiss her. "Little brother we need to chat for a minute," was all Kane said before turning and walking out.

Archer was quick to turn and look at Allie. She was staring at him with a hand on her lips. She never looked more beautiful to him and never more shocked as she had to realize what almost happened. He had to wonder for a minute if she would have been kissing him back and if somewhere inside Allie if he was the guy she thought about when she was with someone else. "I'll be back," was all he said to her before he rose up and walked out not wanting to leave her side.

Kane was leaning against the rail. He was slowly changing as Death was slowly entering him. Plus his demon lust made him roam the hallways of hell in search of demons to enjoy. The look in his eyes wasn't lust, but someone else as he spoke. "What's her name?"

Archer didn't want to tell him anything. "Does it matter? She is just a weak mortal making the night more interesting to me."

"Something is off about her brother, I can feel it. Lust is afraid of her and death has an interest." Archer stared at his brother like he had no idea what he was talking about. However his brothers words alone made him fear that something would happen to Allie at Kane's hands. Kane then continued. "I can tell that she is pure, but something about her is nagging me in the back of my head. I might keep an eye on her."

Archer released a breath knowing he had to tread carefully. Plus he needed to make sure that Kane didn't watch her at all. "That girl in there is the one that matches wits with Wraith daily, and balances him. We're on a new level on wits and I plan to confuse her beyond all thoughts tonight. After I have her head twisted and confused I will let you know so you can toy with her too. It's a lot of fun. However why did you come find me?"

Kane smiled at him. Something about the way he was smiling told him he was looking at death and not his brother. "I cleaned up your mess little brother. I will not always be able to clean up your messes little brother so I advise that you learn to control yourself with the mortals. That poor soul looks like Wraith ripped him to pieces. This is the second time I had to clean up your mess without telling anyone why. No worries it will look like an accident, but I think you should tell me why you did it."

"This couldn't wait until I got home?" Archer questioned not liking the fact that Kane was here and so close to Allie to chew him out about his temper. Just who did he think he was?

"No," Kane responded arching an eyebrow as he waited for his answer not about to leave until he heard one.

Archer glared at him knowing he couldn't lie. Kane knew when someone was lying to him. So he decided on half truths. "At school today, I saw the girl I'm with tonight kissing the boy that met an unfortunate end. Greed got jealous and Wraith got pissed, and well I lost it after I was alone with him and he had to nerve to brag what he planned to do with her. Look I know I lost it, but now is not the time or place for this."

"That is very interesting little brother. Must be hard to control Wraith's temper and Greed's jealousy, maybe you should get rid of the girl and work on your control." Kane stated as he tapped his chin regarding Archer's words. "So tell me why you killed the Oracle then?"

Archer was grinding his teeth. No way was he getting rid of Allie, and the thought of it from his brother had Wraith simmering underneath his skin. He also didn't have time for the third degree right now. Right at this moment Allie was alone in a dark theater watching a movie she hated because it would scare her to death. He needed to satisfy Kane and make him leave quickly so he could go back to her and finish what he was about to begin. "I hate Oracles and their stupid riddles I had my own reason for taking that crazy bat out."

Kane gave him a cocky smile as he spoke. "The Oracle gave me a riddle too little brother, don't forget." Archer looked instantly confused not understanding what Kane was talking about as Kane smiled bigger knowing that he had confused him. Archer knew instantly that Kane was keeping something from him about the Oracle, and instantly he was worried about Allie. Kane looked thoughtful for a minute, but then seemed to be looking over Archer's shoulder. "Have fun little brother, your date looks like she is escaping the movie. Maybe she is trying to outwit you now by not letting you finish what I interrupted."

Archer turned quickly to see Allie slowly exiting the door of the theater heading towards the bathroom. He also noticed his brother had disappeared as panic set in. That was too close of a risk for Allie, and he needed to be more careful. Wraith was instantly in his head. "Let's kill him before he can hurt her, no one will know we did it."

"I'm not sharing her with him," Greed said instantly.

Archer took a deep breath as he mentally reassured his demons that Allie would be his alone and Kane wouldn't touch her. His eyes followed Allie heading into the girls room. He could tell from her body language that she was conflicted. She would also be thinking about him all weekend and what almost happened. That made him smile, but then he suddenly frowned. Kane was interested in Allie, and he planned to watch her too. Moving towards the bathroom, Archer took a seat to where he could see her coming out, but she would not see him. He wondered for a minute if she would return to the movie or run off.

Allie splashed the water over her face trying to figure out what almost happened. She used the paper towel to dry her skin that felt heated. Her heart was still beating fast as she knew she couldn't stay in the bathroom all night, nor did she want to go back to watch the movie. The arcade was open and seemed inviting, and Allie could play games until the movie ended. Thinking in her mind that this was the best plan to keep her mind from thinking about Archer, Allie braced herself before exiting the bathroom.

Luck seemed to be on her side as she walked out of the bathroom not seeing anyone in sight. She walked directly to the arcade not caring if Archer sat in the dark by himself watching that movie, or had left with his brother. A few kids were playing in the arcade engrossed in their games. Allie walked around looking for the right game that required all of her attention. For some reason the resident evil shooting game called out to her. She was instant to put two quarters in and get ready to fight.

Archer had followed Allie into the arcade room. He could tell she was looking for something to focus on to not think about what had happened. He smiled thinking it was clever of her to do, but he planned to spoil this too because he wanted her to be thinking of him. When he noticed she started to play resident evil, he was a little shocked. She held the little pistol in her hand like she knew was she was doing, and after watching her for a while, Archer would have to say she was very good at this game. Admiring her, Archer decided it was time to spoil her fun. He walked right up and grabbed the second player pistol. Before she said a thing, he dropped his quarters in and joined her game. Within seconds things heated up as the silent head game began. It was a matter of out doing the other in scoring, that everything else didn't matter. Not until he heard Janice. "Oh my god you two are in here playing video games?"

The distraction cost him as Allie scored the last point winning the game. She laughed her victory as she looked at her friend that was glaring at the two of them. "Is the movie over already?"

Janice rolled her eyes, as she walked closer. "It ended like ten minutes ago and Matt and I had no clue where the two of you could have disappeared too. This is the last thing I expected the two of you to be doing."

Archer remained quiet as Allie spoke, "well, I had to go to the bathroom, and was a little scared. Archer was nice enough to make sure I made it there without some psycho attacking me. Afterwards, I just didn't care to go back in, so we decided to play a game or two. If this was the last thing you expected, what was the first?"

Archer was a little shocked that Allie had lied to her friend so easily. Not only that but she painted him to be sort of a hero. Now he felt confused as she turned and looked up at him with a twinkle in her eyes. He would be wondering all weekend why she told her friend that, and then he realized that was her paybacks for that kiss that didn't happen. His smile was instant as he looked at her. "Clever Allie, very clever," he whispered to her, and then followed her as they left the theater chatting with Janice.

CHAPTER FOUR
FROGS AND FIRE

Too much had happened since the movies that Allie felt like she was on a cliff about to be pushed. When she returned to school on Monday, Archer and Melissa were suddenly dating. So Allie's science class was Archer this and Archer that. Coarse it made her sick, it had nothing to do with the frog her and Melissa were dissecting. However the rumor mill started that Allie had a weak stomach, and it seemed like all hell had broke loose. Every time she passed by one of Archer's friends in the hall way, they would make a rib it noise before they started laughing.

Frustrated and in gym class, Allie couldn't help but pound the tennis ball with the racket. Janice who was on the other end of the ball dodged it before she spoke up, "damn it Allie. Will you please stop trying to kill me?"

Allie completely stopped and looked at Janice as she noticed her friend looked a little scared and worried. She was instant to walk to the bench and take a seat as she dropped the racket and brought her hands up covering her face. She knew Janice walked over and took a seat next to her, but Janice let her relax for a minute. Allie started to spill. "I don't get why he hates me so much. Why does he enjoy torturing me?" Allie looked to her side at Janice, who moved her hand up to pat her back. "We were the best of friends in the eighth grade Janice. He was always at my house watching movies and having dinner with us, and then high school started and I am public enemy number one. What did I do?" Allie shook her head. "Now all of his friends make the rib it noise when I walk by, and all day long that is all I ever hear. It's driving me insane."

Janice seemed to huff a breath as she spoke. "Let's start with what happened at the movie theater on Friday night. I know you were lying to me covering for Archer, but I didn't want to press you in front of him. Something happened between the two of you, and now it looks like he is trying to make you jealous and get under your skin. From the look of you right now, I'd say it is working." Allie stared at her friend as Janice seemed in thought. "Look, just go up to Archer and his little group and tell them to knock it off. If they want to be jerks avoid them. Go find a boyfriend girl," Janice said with a little smile that made Allie smile too.

Then Allie frowned as she looked at her friend. "I haven't seen Rollin since he asked me to the dance and Archer interrupted it. What if he chases them all off?"

Janice rolled her eyes. "Then we will put a girl ban on him, and chase off the other girls from dating him. Besides I will give Melissa and him another week tops before Archer ends it because he can't get a rise out of you." A laugh escaped her mouth at that instant. "Everything revolves around you with him. When I dated him for that short time period, he was more interested in you seeing us together. So just walk up to the new lovebirds and well tell them they look wonderful together and that you hope everything is going well for them. I bet he will dump Melissa the next day."

"Janice," Allie said instantly shocked by her friend. "I like Melissa, she's a nice person. Archer would crush her and never think twice about it."

"Well that is because he can be jerk," Janice stated clearly.

Allie smiled and shook her head right has the bell rung for them to change out of their gym clothes. The girls rose up as one walking into the locker room. They were quick to change as it would be lunch time soon. Only one more class before lunch, and the dreaded thought that Allie had it with Archer made her a little sick. They didn't mess around as they exited the gym and headed for their classes. Allie even stopped at her locker placing her bag inside knowing she would claim it before lunch. She just hopped her class went by quickly without Archer giving her too much grief.

As it turned out, Allie's class went by quickly even with Archer in it as he didn't say one word. It was a nice change as she stopped at her locker and got her bag before moving to where her group sat for lunch. Allie got a little distracted as she sat when she noticed Archer and his friends sitting not too far away watching them with smiles. They never sat outside, so she knew something was up and it would explain Archer's silent treatment in class. Allie begun to hear the rib it almost instantly the minute she saw them. Deep down she knew they heard it too as each one of them darted a look towards her group with a smile. "Can you hear that?" Allie asked Janice.

Janice had a scold on her face as she nodded. Allie rose up instantly looking right at Archer. "Where are you going?" Janice asked Allie instantly.

"I'm going to ask him to stop it," Allie replied back to her as Allie moved away from her group and towards his.

Joe was the first to notice Allie's approach and instantly made a face of being caught doing something. Allie stopped right in front of Archer blocking the sun from his eyes, but having it highlight her hair. "Wow Allie your hair looks like it is on fire," Archer said instantly as he looked up and smiled at her.

Allie wasn't smiling, she was controlling her temper. "Alright Archer you have had your fun, now I would like you to knock it off. It's old and annoying now."

Archer continued to smile as he spoke, "knock what off Allie?"

Allie caught herself from snorting as she spoke, "knock off the rib it Archer. I didn't get sick from dissecting a frog I got sick hearing about your love life."

Every single one of Archer's friends seemed to be turned the other way, either staring at their shoes or the sky. None of them looked at Archer or Allie. The smile left Archer's face as his eyes narrowed. His words sounded like he was angry. "I have not made one rib it here today, and neither has anyone else. So you better walk away little girl before you blame me again for things you think you hear."

Allie should have turned and walked away, but she was steaming. Instead she took a step closer to Archer and narrowed her eyes at him. "We can all hear it over there Archer, and suddenly you and your little special group are out here laughing it up."

Archer stood up instantly so he was looking down at Allie and she had to crane her neck up to him. He gave her an evil smile as he spoke. "Allie," came out all smug. "I think you need to clean out your ears because you're not listening. It's clear that you got your panties in a bunch, but maybe if you weren't such a prune you'd have a boyfriend, and not moon over me."

"Oh I'm a prune without a boyfriend that is rich coming from you. Coarse you think I moon all over you, but here is a reality check Archer since you have your head in the clouds; I'm the only one that will stand up to you. I see through your bull, and I always will. By the way when you break Melissa's heart, and I know you will, my foot is going to be shoved where your sun don't shine."

Archer was biting his tongue so he wouldn't laugh at Allie as she turned to stomp off. "Hey Allie," Archer said drawing Allie's attention. "Rib it," came out with a smile as she stomped her foot down to return to her group.

Laughter came out of Archer's mouth as Allie reached down for her bag in her group. She couldn't be out here with him or else she was going to head towards violence. "Allie, calm down," Janice said to her as Allie picked up her bag hearing several rib its.

Glaring at her bag, Allie slowly opened it as the rib it got louder. Then before she could blink a huge ugly frog leaped out and onto Janice. Janice was instant to scream as she swatted the frog off of her and Allie dropped her bag. In shock Allie watched several more frogs exit her bag as the girls in her group scattered away from her bag. Allie was instant to look back at Archer who was holding his sides trying to hold the laughter in, but failing. Allie was beyond words as she left her bag on the ground and turned walking away.

In a daze Allie roamed not really paying attention to where she was going. She was shocked that somehow during her gym class or even while her bag was in the locker, Archer had dumped frogs in her bag. It took a minute, but then her temper kicked in, and she kicked the trash can that was suddenly in front of her making a loud bang noise as it started to fall over. Allie watched it as it started to fall that she was surprised when a hand caught it and set it up right. Her eyes followed the hand up to the guy with the dark eyes and the lip piercings. His voice was instant too, "first time I've ever seen a girl destroy school property, it is quite clear you are upset, but this is not the way to go about it."

Allie stared at the guy thinking she had never seen him before. He had the whole Goth punk thing down to a tee with the bracelets with the spikes on it to his dark clothing. She blinked realizing she was being rude, "I'm sorry I don't normally act this way."

"Oh I know you don't Allie, well you normally don't until Archer sets you off," he said with a smile making Allie wonder.

She shook her head as she spoke, "I'm sorry I can't recall your name."

He laughed then and his eyes twinkled letting Allie know that they were a dark blue. "It's Aaron, but we have never been introduced. We have math together, well I sit in the back, while you sit in the middle and Archer sits to your right. You realize you two are funny to watch, it's almost like a game of who can out do who. I'm rooting for you because I think you can out do him."

"Well thank you," came out of Allie's mouth too easily. "So are you friends with Archer or know one of his friends?"

Aaron laughed a little but then made a serious face. "No way would you see me hanging with any of them. They lack my style," he said with a wink at Allie.

He's flirting with me came instantly to Allie's mind making her blush a little. Her lips tilted in a smile, but then the frown set in. "I can't escape them even if I try. I will have to head to my next class sometime and my favorite person in the whole world will be there waiting for me."

Aaron looked serious for a minute. "We can always skip Allie, want to try it?"

Allie found the offer to be very temping. "Where would we go?" Allie found herself asking.

"Somewhere fun," was how he responded as he jester for Allie to follow.

Not knowing why and most likely the most foolish thing to do, Allie followed Aaron. They walked without saying a word to the parking lot, and then he stopped at a black ford mustang. He unlocked the car and opened the door for her, "Shall we go get a smoothie at Delights? I think we should skip the rest of the day, and then I will take you home." Allie nibbled on her bottom lip unsure if she should trust Aaron so openly. He actually laughed like he knew what she was thinking. Suddenly he pulled out a cell phone from his pocket. "You can text your friend if you want so someone knows where you are."

Allie was reaching out to take the phone when suddenly she heard Archer right behind her. "She's not going with you Aaron, and in fact I think you need to leave."

Aaron raised an eyebrow as he stared at Allie waiting to see what she would do. Allie automatically rolled her eyes as she turned to actually see Archer there just glaring at her. She released a breath as she shook her head, then she looked at Aaron who spoke before she did. "Another time Allie," was all he said as he closed the door and walked to the driver's side to get in and drive off.

For several minutes, Allie refused to turn and look at Archer. Once again he had showed up ruining her chance talking with another guy. After the minutes had passed she slowly turned to face her tormentor. He was staring at her pretty intently. Plus Allie could tell that he was mad and just about to explode. Not knowing why, she just started to speak. "Save the lecture Archer, I know what you are planning to say. You'll start off with Allie how can you be so stupid as to get in a car with someone you don't know. Then you will add on to it by telling me that it literally surprises you on how stupid I can be sometimes that you're amazed I know how to tie my shoes. I don't need to hear it Archer, I just need you to leave me alone."

Allie was going to walk away and back towards her next class, but Archer grabbed her and held unto her like he was hugging her. Allie felt all awkward from it, that she was shocked by Archer's words. "Promise me Allie that if you don't know someone that you will not go off with them no matter how mad you are at me. If you haven't seen them before and they know you, don't trust them." He pulled back as he looked into her shocked eyes. "Promise me this Allie."

Allie was dumbfounded. She blinked several times thinking she heard him wrong. If she didn't know better, she would think that Archer didn't want anything to happen to her. That thought alone made her chest pound as he seemed to wait for her to respond. "Fine I promise but only if you will stop picking on me when I tell you to stop. You make me so mad sometimes that I can't think straight."

His lips tilted up in a smile, "deal."

Archer was still holding onto her and Alley had to wonder why. "Archer will you let go of me?"

Archer looked thoughtful for a minute. "No," he said instantly making Allie look dumbfounded at him. "Since you were so ready to skip the rest of school, let's go. Besides I rather race go carts or something and the Castle is open, maybe some miniature golf too."

Allie bit down on her bottom lip unsure of herself. So Archer let go of her to peel her backpack off of his shoulder to hand to her, except he didn't hand it to her. "After Janice ripped me a new one because a frog peed on her white shirt, which is too funny, I promised her I would find you and tell you I was sorry. The joke went too far. However if you want your backpack with your next class book in it, you're going to have to come with me."

Allie made the face like she was judging the pros and cons. Then she spoke, "looks like you are not giving me much of a choice."

Archer smiled knowing she would be safe for the rest of the day, but he knew she needed more protection now. His mind was racing on why his brother would send one of his tracker demons to snag Allie. What were his plans for Allie, and how long had Aaron been watching them? Archer's free hand still was holding Allie, so he slipped it down to her hand as he held it in his. He found it a little strange that her hand was so warm and wondered if maybe she hit something with it. However it did not stop him from leading her to his car to escape the hell he called school.

After an hour of go cart racing and miniature golf, Allie felt like she was hanging with the old Archer that she remembered. She was having a lot of fun that she found herself in front of a little shop that sold jewelry. Granted it was next to the Castle, Allie couldn't remember seeing it when they pulled up. Archer was next to her instantly looking in the same window. "Interesting, I didn't notice this little Wiccan shop. Want to take a peek inside?"

Allie smiled at Archer as the two of them walked in. However both of them stopped when they noticed a little old lady sitting at a table pouring some tea. Her voice was instant too, "I've been waiting for you two to make your way in here. The tea is fresh come have a seat."

Archer stared at the witch amazed that they still existed. Normally they died at an early age when they would pass their power to the element of their choice. The fact that one was here reminded him that the time was coming shortly and the

War was about to begin. Then Archer noticed something else, this witch was blind. "Are you sure you have been waiting for us?" Archer asked instantly.

"First sit, and then I will answer your question." Archer shrugged as Allie moved to take a seat. The woman smiled as they sat. "The answer to your question is yes I have been waiting for you. I've been waiting for one girl that is pure and one boy that would be with her not so pure."

Allie actually giggled that it made Archer turn to look at her. He narrowed his eyes at her for a minute but asked the witch a question. "Ok so why have you been waiting for us?"

"Hmm," the witch said instantly like she was in thought. "Oh now I remember, I need to give something to the both of you. A gift I was told."

Both Archer and Allie looked at each other with a raised eyebrow, and then both of them almost started laughing for having the same expression. They clamped down on the laughter as the woman rose up and went behind the counter to pick up two boxes. She walked slowly back to them and took a seat. Then she placed the two boxes in front of them. "Well don't just sit there dumbfounded, open your gift."

Shaking their heads, both Archer and Allie opened the boxes. Inside Archer's box was a ring that he slowly pulled out feeling confused. He could feel power coming off the ring as he looked at the amethyst. He knew instantly it was a healing stone of an element, but why was he receiving one? "Wow this is too beautiful to except as a gift," Allie said instantly drawing Archer's attention.

Archer turned his head to see Allie holding up a ring that was similar to his but smaller. "Nonsense," said the old witch. "It's a healing stone," she told Allie as her head turned toward Archer. "It will protect you." Archer frowned at the witch as she smiled at him. "Both of you place it on your index finger it will protect the both of you."

Allie did so with a smile. Archer could tell she liked the ring. Shaking his head, he placed his on as well knowing it would never work on him. The witch smiled big at him as she spoke again. "Would you two like to know your future?"

"No," Archer said instantly as Allie said yes.

The witch laughed at this as she spoke. "Hand me your hand dear so I can read your future." Allie did so with a smile, but suddenly the woman's face seemed to take on a look of being swallowed by darkness. This made Archer lean in closer to watch her, but the woman reached out and grabbed his hand making him jump. Her grip was strong too as her hands shook. Then she suddenly let go dropping both of their hands. "It's time for the two of you to leave."

Allie looked a little disappointed as Archer spoke, "what did you see?"

The witch placed a hand over her chest as she spoke, "One riddle for you boy. The heart is your breath that you need. Yet all will try to destroy it, even you. So when the time comes do you put your heart first or your duties?" It was the same line the Oracle had told him years ago right before he killed her. Chills were instant as this witch knew, but the woman looked right at Allie and spoke as well. "The same is for you girl. The heart is your breath that you need. Yet all will try to destroy it, even you. So when the time comes do you put your heart first or your duties?"

The witch rose up instantly walking to the back of the shop not looking at the two of them. Her old heart was pounding as she felt a warm hand touching her. A voice was inside her head instantly telling her thank you. Tears escaped the witches eyes as she spoke back with her mind, "you're welcome my angel, but why must they be tested the most?" The voice was in her head again as it told her because of his sins. This made the witch cry harder as she spoke back with her mind. "I will pray for them in the upcoming battle, and tonight I will cast an old druid protection spell for them both to activate the protection stones." Again the warm voice was in her head telling her thank you.

Allie and Archer looked at one another with mirrored expressions not knowing what to think about the witch. Then they rose up and walked out of the store in silence. Allie voice was instant as she spoke, "would you mind taking me home now Archer?"

Archer knew she was confused by what the witch had told him. He just nodded his head not saying a word. He was also confused on why Allie would have the same riddle. It made him wonder about Allie and if this was his fault for wanting to be around her.

CHAPTER FIVE
UP IN FLAMES

Archer had dropped Allie off an hour ago, but his mind was in turmoil. He didn't say a word to her on the drive home, and he was thankful that she didn't say anything either. When they pulled up to her house, she looked at him. Just the way she looked at him, he could tell that she was deep in thought. Then suddenly she did speak. "Thank you for this afternoon Archer, it felt like I was hanging with the old you. I hope Melissa doesn't get mad at you for skipping out with me today. You two really do make a cute couple."

She went to get out, but Archer reached out and stopped her. He was about to say something when he realized what she said about Melissa. "I don't think Melissa and I will be working out. I will break it off gently so I don't get your foot up my ass. Allie," Archer started to say when he thought that maybe he shouldn't. However it was nagging him that the last thing the Oracle had said to him was the same the witch had told both Allie and him about their futures. "Never mind," he said instantly shaking his head deciding that he would not bring this up with her. "This afternoon was fun, shame we can't do that every day. However I do have a rep to withhold of driving you nuts."

A laugh escaped Allie's mouth suddenly as she opened the car door. "Ditto Archer, I look forward to tomorrow when we can start driving each other nuts again," she told him as she walked to the door.

Archer watched her walk to her door admiring the view. Then he pulled out and headed to the park to think. It got him nowhere as the day had gone by too quickly and now the night greeted him as he pulled up to the family estate. For several minutes he sat in his car reflecting the day events so he could clear them out of his head before he entered the house. He closed his eyes for a minute as he took a breath, but jumped suddenly as his car door was suddenly opened and he was tossed out like a rag doll. Archer hit the wall against the house sending dust down over him. The action made him cough, but his eyes darted up to his brother Kane who was glaring at him with Aaron and Fury. Wraith was quick to show himself inside Archer as Kane smiled at him. "Little brother, you stopped Aaron from doing something today, why is that?"

Archer kept his eyes on Kane as he dusted the dust off of him. "Why was Aaron spying on me brother?"

Kane's smile looked like a snarl as Archer noticed Fury's tail starting to show its flame. "Aaron wasn't spying on you, brother. I assigned him to the girl you took to the movies. It's interesting that she doesn't fear you and mind control doesn't work on her."

Archer's heart was suddenly pounding in his chest. He needed to keep a level head even though Wraith was making a battle cry in his head. Aaron then spoke to him. "I found it interesting that the two of you have battle in a mind game for over three days, and I will say this about the mortal, she is your match in every way but one." He moved closer as he continued his taunt. "She's mortal and would have made a nice meal."

Fury smiled as his tail of fire moved behind him. "She's a major distraction keeping War from emerging we can't have that in this stage. I can pay her a little visit tonight as she sleeps. One little sweep of my tail and she will go up in flames."

Archer's demons were leaking out as he started to lose control over them with the threat over Allie. Within seconds Greed spoke through him sounding like a hissing growl. "If you go near her Furfur, I will rip off your damn tail and shove it up Xaphan's butt as I throw both of you in hell." His words made both demons hiss as Greed used their real names.

"Oh little brother," Kane said drawing his attention. "You're losing control of demons now over a mortal. That's a weakness that is not allowed. However I will take care of Allie personally, she will not feel a thing, but it will look like an accident."

Archer felt like he was about to explode as his heart stopped knowing that Kane was going to kill Allie. Then suddenly he felt calm as he felt something inside him stir. The voice that spoke was not his own. "Are you afraid of her brother, a little mortal?"

Kane's eyes went a shade darker as Fury and Aaron looked at him strange. Fury smiled from his angelic face as he looked at Archer. Aaron's black eyes seemed to change to a dark navy blue as a smile tilted his lips as well. Kane's eyes narrowed as he spoke. "I fear no one brother. However the mortal girl known as Allie will not see daylight."

Archer felt the laugh leave his lips before he spoke confusing Kane. "Careful brother with her, it might be you not seeing daylight. She is stronger than she looks."

With that Archer turned and walked into the house as Fury started to laugh. Kane gave a sharp look to Fury as the demon smiled as he spoke. "I'm going to watch War, it's been too long, and about time he started to merge."

With that Fury followed after Archer as his tail melted away into his skin. Aaron stood next to Kane awaiting orders as Kane stared at the door. After a minute he spoke. "If Allie somehow lives through the night, I want you to befriend her. Something is off with her and I can't put my finger on it. For War to leak out of my brother and not worry about her like that, but warn me, makes me wonder what War has planned for this girl. Tonight will be her first test. Now go and watch my brother, I don't want him to warn her that I am coming." Aaron nodded at Kane as he followed in Fury's footsteps. Kane watched the demon leave and then melted into the darkness looking for Allie.

Allie was staring at the ring that the old woman gave her as a gift. The amethyst looked natural and big as the silver held it to the ring. It was beautiful and it wouldn't come off. Allie smiled as she shook her head climbing into her bed. This had been a strange day, and Allie knew that come tomorrow Archer would be back to the ass he always was. Slowly she reached over and turned off the light as she felt the ring suddenly heat up on her finger and then cool down the minute the light went out. It felt strange but then again Allie thought that maybe it was from lack of sleep. She closed her eyes and let sleep claim her.

Kane stayed hidden in the shadows as he watched Allie fall asleep. In the dark with the moonlight hitting her, she looked like she glowed. Her hair looked like fire against the white pillow that it made the nagging feeling about her bother him more. His demon Lust was mentally stripping her. The demon was begging for him to touch her and make her crave him. The thought made Kane smile as he would love for her ivory skin to be touching every inch of him and those ruby red lips to be wrapped around his throbbing member. He could understand why his brother was enthralled with her.

About to step towards her and let Lust take over, Kane felt Death stir inside him. Wisdom and cruelty squashed Lust's feelings as his eyes moved to the outlet by her bed. His thought was that it would be so simple and no one would know better.

Allie knew she was dreaming but it seemed so real. She was standing by an old warehouse in the dark. She could hear music playing and the sounds of someone working out. Not knowing why she moved to the door of the warehouse and opened it up. Slowly she walked in as she felt she needed to be silent. Her legs moved her to the dark corner as she saw a guy punching a duffle bag. Allie felt herself blink as she noticed he had the same hair color as she did. He then stopped and turned suddenly looking in the dark corner where she stood. Allie sucked in a breath has she noticed he had her eyes, but he couldn't see her. "What are you looking at?" A voice said making the guy turn towards the other man that Allie had not seen before. "You need to focus Adam not day dream."

"Someone is watching me I can feel it," Adam replied as the other guy moved towards him.

Allie blinked at the man that stood next to Adam. He was built and seemed unreal beautiful with shoulder length blond hair. However Allie jumped the minute his hand lit on fire and the man moved it in the shadows were she was at. "No one is here," he told Adam.

Adam's eyes landed right on her as it seemed like he could see her. "Who are you?" He questioned.

Allie said her name, but no sound came out of her mouth. "No one is here Adam, you are talking to shadows. Maybe we are doing too much training and you need a day of rest."

"No," Adam stated clearly. "I can see her. She has my hair color but it is past her shoulders with my eyes. Yet I can't hear her."

The man's head suddenly turned in her direction yet he still couldn't see her. He was searching the shadows for her. "Focus on her lips and try to read them. Find out where she is."

Allie looked afraid from the man's statement as her eyes darted back to Adam and she shook her head clearly afraid. "You can trust me. Where are you?"

Allie felt like she could trust Adam, but her eyes darted to the other man with him. She didn't trust him at all and she could tell that he was getting upset with the fact that Adam wasn't pulling more information. Allie shook her head as she looked at the other man. Adam spoke instantly. "She doesn't trust you Jehoel. I told you that your mannerism is scary."

Jehoel then nearly growled as he spoke, "well then she needs to wake up because she must be in danger if she is reaching out to you for help. All humans seek an element for help instead of waking up and helping themselves." He then turned looking in the shadows. "Do you hear me girl, wake up!"

Allie bolted up in her bed to nearly gag on smoke. She was instant to cough as she realized that her bed was on fire with her on it. She couldn't even feel the flames as she was sure they had to be burning her legs. Panicking she rolled off the bed with the burnt blanket, killing the flames on her. However raising her head up she noticed every inch of her room was in flames. The ceiling was starting to peal and fall on the floor making the fire bigger. Allie couldn't see an escape through the smoke that was making her cough louder and stealing her air. In fact the smoke was choking her making it hard for her to move much less see.

The shattering of a window made Allie blink as she could feel the breeze, slowly she crawled towards it knowing it was her only hope as the fire enclosed around her. Her body was weak as the spot she was just in was suddenly covered with fire from the ceiling. Reaching the window, Allie reached up hoping to pull herself up. Instead she felt the instant pain as glass entered her hand making her cry out. Tears blinded her eyes as she brought her hand down to cradle it against her chest. She was shaking as she moved her other hand to pull the jagged glass out. Breathing heavy Allie closed her eyes as the smoke ate away at her the heat covered her like a blanket.

Not knowing what death felt like, Allie was surprised that she felt like she was floating. Her eyes were too heavy to open, but she could hear voices. The first voice sounded amazed, "she's breathing."

Allie tried to open her eyes again, but she didn't have the strength. She felt her hand being turned and then something wet drenching it. She even felt something poke her, but the sting only lasted for a little bit. Then she felt herself being lifted again as something was placed over her face. Fresh air came so suddenly that Allie gasped to suck it in. Her eyes fluttered, and Allie saw her mother looking like her world was falling apart. Her father was holding her with a smile and tears in his eyes. Then she saw the glowing hand touching her mother, and followed it up to the man behind her that glowed. Her eyes moved to his as a smile touched his lips and he acknowledged her with a slight bow of the head. Allie closed her eyes with a smile on her lips as she was sure she was dead.

Allie must have been sleeping as it seemed the nightmare she had ended, but a voice woke her up. "Liz I heard about your daughter, I hope she is improving."

Her mother's voice was instant as she sounded surprised. "Mel, I didn't expect you to come, you didn't have to. Why would you risk coming here?"

"Course I did Liz. I will not leave you alone at a time of need. My offer still stands Liz my feelings have not changed for you."

She heard her mom sound like she was defeated. "I made my choice long ago Mel, I will not leave him now, it would destroy him."

"It's destroying me Liz. We were meant to be together. Come to me tonight Liz, no one will know."

It was silent for too long that Allie tried to peal her eyes open thinking she had to be hearing things. Tears flooded her eyes as she blinked then open. "Mom," came out like a hoarse whisper.

Allie blinked again seeing her mother loom over her. A smile touched her lips instantly. "Hi baby," she greeted her as she woke. "How are you feeling?"

"Thirsty," Allie again tried to say as her throat hurt. "Who is here with us?"

"It's just the two of us Allie. I'm going to get the doctor. They wanted me to get them when you woke up."

Allie watched her mom leave the room. Her head hurt suddenly as her room looked like it exploded in flowers, yet this wasn't her room. She blinked a few times as things slowly came back to her and reality set in. Somehow Allie knew she had survived the flames in the fire, but she had no clue how she got out of her room, and some of the things she had seen which she couldn't explain.

CHAPTER SIX
FROGGING

"These are cute Allie," Janice told Allie while holding up a pair of knee high boots.

"Yes they would be cute on you, but we are here shopping for me remember, and those would look silly on me." Allie told her friend with a twinkle in her eye.

Janice put the boots back on the shelf as the two of them moved on in famous footwear trying to find Allie something besides the sandals she was wearing. Today had been the first outing for Allie since being released from the hospital and Allie was told not to do too much too soon. Allie had to admit that she was tired as she didn't realize how tiring shopping was and it was her friend that seemed to be moving them from store to store. So far from this little shopping trip Allie had three pairs of jeans and three shirts. She needed shoes and undergarments, and somehow the undergarments shopping with Janice sounded like it was going to be torture since they saved it for last.

"You look a little tired there Allie," Janice stated as she looked at her friend with some concern. "Why don't you just get some sneakers and we will go sit in the food court for a bite before we hit up Victoria Secrets."

"Now that sounds good," Allie admitted as she felt a rush of energy moving her so she could rest and eat something. She also just grabbed the first pair of sneakers that she found in her size.

Within ten minutes the girls were sitting in the food court. Three bags were next to Allie sitting on the floor as Janice sat the nachos in the middle of them that were mainly just for Allie. Too quickly Janice sat slipping her diet coke just watching Allie. "I swear we need a better selection here at the food court. It's all junk food, and they have zero healthy food options. I don't know how you can eat the spicy nacho without it going straight to your hips."

Allie smiled at her friend ignoring the comment that Janice was always watching what she ate, "Did they give you the extra spicy hot sauce too?"

Janice rolled her eyes but pulled out the packets from her pocket. "These will ruin the nachos," Janice stated before taking out the small container with the hot peppers and setting it on the table.

Allie smiled as she pulled the nachos closer. She didn't respond as she opened the packets and dripped the sauce on top. Then she dumped the hot peppers on with a smile before she placed one in her mouth and moaned as it tasted so good. Janice was just staring at her weird as Allie swallowed and spoke, "This is wonderful, want to try one?"

Janice shivered as she shook her head. "I think I will pass." Janice said as Allie popped another one in her mouth. "How can you eat that without drinking something after each bite? I would have downed a diet coke and be working on my third one after one bite. I can smell how hot that is from here and it makes me want to gag."

Allie laughed as she spoke, "it's not really that hot Janice. All you smell is the peppers and your mind tells you that there is not enough you could drink to cool the taste. It's your senses judging too soon, you really should try it. Who knows you might like it."

"I think not," Janice said as she sipped the diet coke turning her head to look at the people in the food court.

"Can I try it?" A male voice from the left of Allie said.

Allie turned her head to see the punk style guy sitting at the table next to hers with another guy that looked bored but should be a model. It took her a minute to remember his name as her voice sounded surprised. "Aaron, I haven't seen you since..."

He smiled at her as his eyes twinkled. "Yeah sorry to hear about what happened to you and glad to see you about but are you and Archer dating?" Just those words and Allie could hear Janice almost gagging on her diet coke. "When you choose him over me I thought you two had some sort of secret relationship, and I will admit I was a little hurt that you left with him instead. I was hoping that maybe within time, next time you would pick me."

Allie was shocked as she felt Janice kick her under the table. She turned to look at her friend that gave her a look like she had some explaining to do. It made her find her voice quickly, "no we are not dating, no way no how." Allie took a breath as she continued changing the subject and avoiding his last question. "Go ahead and try one," she offered some of her nachos.

Aaron reached over and took one. Allie watched him as he placed it in his mouth savoring it. Then he smiled. "Your right it is not hot at all. This is actually very good. You surprise me Allie, normally all girls shy away from something like this." His eyes moved over to Janice. "I'm Aaron by the way. I have Math with Allie and Archer. You're the cheerleader right?"

It dawned on Allie that Janice was staring at the other guy at the table with Aaron. He was looking directly at her as she seemed trapped in his stare. However she answered him, "yeah I'm Janice, but who's your friend?"

Aaron seemed to move in a little closer to Allie as he spoke. "This is my cousin Fred, but I call him Fury. He has a bad temper and wanted to people watch today because it is entertaining to him. He's from out of town, so I'm kind of entertaining him."

Allie smiled at Aaron as she ate more nachos feeling like she had nothing else to say. So she watched Fred and noted how dark his eyes were. "So dark eyes run in your family," Allie somewhat asked Aaron.

This made Fred turn his attention to her and narrow his eyes as he spoke, "my eyes are green thank you."

"A dreamy green," Janice seemed to agree as Allie noticed that she was nearly drooling on the table looking at him.

Allie rolled her eyes as she spoke, "sure they are green, a black green. Whatever Furfur, it's not like I'm trying to offend you just because I asked a simple question. I know Aaron's are a dark navy, but they still look black from the distance."

Aaron wasn't moving and Fred looked shocked by Allie's comment. Then he started to laugh as he spoke to Aaron. "Amazing she was able to guess that with sarcasm." Then he turned at looked at Allie. "So tell me Allie why are you so different from everyone here, what makes you so special?"

Allie narrowed her eyes as she tried to control her temper. Fred reminded her too much of Archer with that comment and she didn't need to put up with it from this stranger. "Well this has been fun," she stated as she stood up. "I'm ready to continue our shopping Janice. Somehow it's getting to be a little crowded in here."

Aaron stood up suddenly and grabbed her hand. "Allie wait, don't be offend he doesn't know how to interact with people too well. He lacks manners, and has never learned respect."

For several minutes Allie stared up at Aaron as he gave Fred a dirty look, but then looked directly at her. "Then I'm glad you're not like him. I will see you at school Monday Aaron. I really need to finish up shopping for the basics. Besides I'm still not use to doing so much, and will need to go take a nap when this is over."

Aaron smiled at her as I spoke. "I can't wait until Monday, but might I be so bold as to ask if you will eat lunch with me?"

This time Janice spoke. "She would love to."

"Janice," Allie said sharply as her friend smiled big at her before she took a sip of her diet coke.

"Deal then and I'm not letting you back out of it," Aaron stated as he raised her hand and placed a kiss on it with a twinkle in his eyes.

Janice made the awe noise, but Allie found herself staring right into Aaron's eyes as his fingers caressed her hand. Slowly his hand left hers as he turned and started to walk away with Fred following. Allie watched them until they disappeared around the corner. Then she turned and looked at Janice who had a huge grin on her face as she spoke. "I don't care what you say. He's too cute to let slip through your fingers, and as your best friend, I won't let you. Besides you can date someone, and then we can go on double dates where I don't have to worry about you fighting with your date. Let's go shopping before I ask you twenty questions about you and Archer taking off together and you get all moody on me like you are now since I said yes to that lunch date for you."

Allie huffed but turned to follow Janice out of the food court. She'd figure out on Monday what to do about her lunch date as they headed to a Victoria's. However something about Fred and Aaron nagged at her. She didn't trust herself to be alone with Aaron, and she didn't know the reason why.

Around the corner, Aaron watched them. Fury spoke first. "She's wearing the same ring on the same finger as Archer, other than that I have no idea how she could of survived that fire. Did you get a good look at it when you kissed her hand and held onto it?"

Aaron smiled as he looked at Fury. "I did. It's a protection stone from a druid witch, but not any druid witch, the fire witch. She was the only one that lived the first battle that saved all of these cattle from us. What I don't get is why she chose to protect War and this girl. Normally she only protects those that she wants to survive, and they always do. Do you think that maybe this time she favors us? Do you think that our time to rule will be soon? I wonder when she turned evil."

Fury seemed to be scratching his chin in thought. "The witch is tricky she has always been that way. Everything she does, she does for a reason. Allie is not human you know, I can feel it. No one should be able to guess my real name unless they carry our blood. Kane was right something is off about her, and I should really look into her background." Fury actually snorted as he was thinking. "I have to be missing something about her however I don't know why I can't put my finger on it."

Fury disappeared as Aaron looked back to the shop Allie and her friend had just walked into. He couldn't help but smile as he saw it was Victoria Secrets. Allie had a secret, and he was determined to find out what it was, however it would wait until Monday at school.

"So when did you and Archer take off alone," Janice asked as Allie picked up a pink bra after just entering the store.

Allie looked at the bras not wanting to have this conversation with Janice, but she knew Janice would hound her until she was satisfied. She also knew she couldn't avoid it. "The day of the fire right after lunch, right after you gave Archer a tongue lashing I guess. That was where I met Aaron, he was luring me to skip with him, and I was tempted to do it when Archer showed up."

Allie didn't continue as she found her size and moved on to a different rack. Janice nearly cornered her. "Oh I know you better than that, and I know exactly what Aaron said moments before. You and Archer left school together skipping. Now spill the rest."

"Not much else to spill Janice we went and played miniature golf. He knew he stepped over the line, and so did I. It was like reaching a peace offering and just taking a moment to get along and forget we are enemies. He took me home afterwards, and you know what happened next." Allie tried to explain to her friend as Janice narrowed her eyes.

Janice looked a little confused as she spoke. "Ok then, so why do you two have the same ring?"

Allie was instant to look at the ring on her finger. No matter what she tried, she couldn't get it off. "The ring was a gift from a little old lady that owned a Wicca shop next to the miniature golf course. We were peeking in the window and Archer thought it would be fun to go inside. So we did and the woman acted like she knew us. She gave us the rings and refused to let us refuse them."

"Well damn, that kills what I was thinking about them." Janice said looking disappointed in Allie's explanation.

"Ok I will bite what were you thinking?" Allie asked her friend wondering what she had dreamed up.

Janice smiled big as a laugh escaped. "I was hoping that the two of you had a secret and that your little feud at school was a farce. I even thought that the rings were promise rings to each other. Call me silly but I guess I'm an old romantic."

Allie started to laugh at her friend as she spoke. "That's ok I like my old romantic friend, but seriously you read too much into it."

Janice laughed this time and in no time they had picked out some things for Allie. They had only walked out of the store and turned the corner when Allie nearly collided with Archer. Allie couldn't believe her luck about running into him here at the mall. This was the last place she should have run into him. He looked like he was in a rotten mood too as his hands came out to steady her instantly. Her eyes went directly to his and for a minute she thought he looked glad to see her. His words said something completely else, "damn Allie watch where you're going and stop spying on me. Plus do me a favor take a bath once in a while. You reek of ash and sweat."

Allie's mouth opened in shock and then she jerked herself out of his grip as she noticed his little circle of friends. "As if I would take the time to spy on you, more likely you were spying on me you perverted creep."

"In your wildest dreams half pint, however I bet you fantasize about me watching you. I bet you wish you were some of the girls I dated and see yourself as them. Is that all your sick mind thinks of Allie, grow up already you're not even attractive?"

Allie's temper flared. "You know what you knew I was going to be here. Don't think I lack the intelligent to know that Matt knew that Janice was going shopping with me today at the mall. You just couldn't refuse, you must have been going through Allie withdraws and decided why not get your ego going. Well I hope you enjoy this you damn stalker."

Allie turned and went in the opposite direction Archer was in. Archer was quick to grab her arm and spin her around sending her bags in her hand to the ground. His grip held her in his arms as he stared directly in her eyes focused on her alone. For several minutes neither of them spoke as their glare was heated enough to melt a freezer. Allie was sure it was Janice that cleared her throat as the suspense had to be killing her. Allie noticed instantly how Archer's body suddenly tensed as he spoke, "I'm not a stalker, don't ever call me that again."

He then let her go as he turned walking away from Allie leaving Allie stunned. Archer didn't look back either as his mood didn't feel any better even though Allie looked better than before. Once again he had wanted to kiss her as part of him was relieved that she didn't have one mark on her perfect skin. He was about to walk out of the mall forgetting his friends when he heard his sister's voice. "Oh brother, care to tell me who the human was that pushed your buttons and made Wraith want to punish her with his tongue?"

Archer turned quickly to see Lacy walking with his friends. They were puppets in her hands as easily as they were for him, soldiers for them to command how they saw fit. He smiled at his sister as he spoke wondering how much she had saw, "a mortal that Wraith likes to torment on a daily bases. She has been missing from school for a week, and he was a little excited to push her buttons."

His sister shook her head with a smile. "I'd say she out witted Wraith and now he is stewing over his mistake. But who cares mortals are cattle for us to direct. How do I look?"

His sister twirled around as he noted she had a new hair style and new clothes again. She really let her demon have whatever it wanted. "No one holds a candle to you dear sister, everyone bows to your beauty."

Archer took a slight bow to his sister that had her laughing. Her words next haunted him a little. "Good because I'm going to make your little mortal lick my toes soon as she will become my little lap dog. She'd be a fun project."

Lacy walked pass Archer with a smile on her lips as Archer stared at her. Greed was instantly in his head telling him to get his sister a pet and nowhere near his Allie he wasn't going to share with her. Wraith on the other hand was thinking of ways to murder his sister. It took a lot for Archer to control them of acting on their threats when he agreed with them. Somehow he was going to have to watch Allie more without her noticing it, what he needed was a spy to stay with Allie. "Matt, your sister needs to become Allie's friend. I have to keep her busy so she has no time for my sister to befriend her. With luck my sister will get bored with the idea and move on." Archer could only hope his sister would get bored with the idea. He would also have to sick some demons on her to help her forget.

CHAPTER SEVEN
SOMETHING DIFFERENT

Math was a little strange to Allie as she felt like she was being watched and needed to be on her toes. Keeping her head forward, Allie dared to look to her left to see Aaron two over and two back just staring at her. His lips even tilted up in a smile making his lip ring sparkle knowing she was sneaking a peek at him. It was most likely sending him the wrong signal if she smiled back, so Allie schooled her face. Feeling a more heated glare, Allie turned her eyes slowly to her right. At first she saw the same ring that matched hers as the finger it was on was tapping against the table very subtle. Then she snuck a peek at Archer to see that he was indeed staring right at her like he could burn a hole right through her. It was clear that he was mad at her for something, but Allie had no clue what as she noticed he caught her staring at him. He was even quick to mouth what at her. Thinking quickly at being caught by him too, she was just as quick to gesture to his tapping, but it only made Archer smile and continue to do it knowing that it bothered her.

Getting annoyed, Allie wanted out of class to escape. She wasn't exactly healed enough to be dealing with this level of stress that she use to be use to. Archer's tapping was making her focus on him instead of her work. She also wanted to escape Archer who was driving her nuts on purpose, and she was hoping to get out of the lunch date with Aaron without hurting his feelings too bad. Looking at the clock she noticed she still had ten minutes left to go insane. Then suddenly a plan formed in her head. Allie rose up from her chair and walked to the front where Mrs. Evans was sitting reading a book while the class worked on the assignment. Mrs. Evans was a nice lady around her mother's age, but somewhere in her history something had left the teacher with heartache. It showed in the way she dressed and her hairstyle that seemed from the early nineties. It wasn't like she had the famous mall bangs, but her hair popped out like Fran from the Nanny. Allie needed to make this conversation as short as possible, or else Mrs. Evans would go on about something she didn't need to know about. Allie was quick to tell her she wasn't feeling well and if she could go to the nurse's office. Mrs. Evans gave her a look of concern knowing what had happened to Allie last week. She was also quick to write a pass for Allie, and as Allie walked back to get her things she couldn't help but smile. This was the best plan ever in her mind as Archer suddenly gave her a funny look like he knew what she was up to and Aaron actually frowned as if he did too.

Focusing on the door, Allie walked to it without looking at either guy knowing she had out smarted them both. Her lips were slowly curving in a smile as she reached the door. Then suddenly she heard Mrs. Evans speak, "wait a minute Allie, Archer will walk you to the nurse's station."

Allie froze as it felt like her plan had slowly crumbled. She slowly turned in shock at Mrs. Evans not believing her ears correctly. Archer on the other hand wore a smile as he gathered his things and moved towards her. His smile turned pretty evil as he stood next to her and opened the door for her to exit as it seemed he had out thought her to get the higher ground. Allie released a breath as she exited the room a little steamed for having a plan fail that was so perfect to begin with. Facing forward Allie started to march down the hallway knowing that the nurse's station was on the other side of the school. She was so mad at herself, that Archer's soft chuckle made her stop and look at him. He was clearly amused. "Why are you laughing?" Allie asked him instantly annoyed that he was escorting her.

Archer smiled as he stopped next to her and looked down. "It's amusing knowing this was the best idea you could have come up with to escape having lunch with Aaron. Doesn't matter anyway, he will come check the nurse's station once the bell rings in about seven minutes. So I wonder if that is really where you are heading or if you have somewhere else you're planning on going."

"It's none of your business Archer where I was planning on going, so keep wondering." Allie stated as she passed Archer so he was behind her where he belonged.

Archer was quick to catch up as Allie marched around the corner. "So I take it that you didn't want to have a lunch date with Aaron and that is why you plotted this as an escape."

Allie came to a complete stop as she wondered why he was even asking. "Why do you care who I have lunch with?"

Archer was instant to stop and just stare at her. He raised his eye brow as he heard Greed telling him once again that she was his. "I don't care who you eat lunch with as long as it is not Aaron."

Allie rolled her eyes at him, "Oh do tell me what is wrong with Aaron."

Archer cringed for a minute as he felt something inside him stir. He knew jealousy too well and would lie through his teeth if it would keep Allie away from any male. "He's friends with my brother and the two of them have a bet going on over you since the movies. We might no longer get along Allie but still I wouldn't want my worst enemy to be subjected to my brother's bets."

Allie was looking at Archer strange as she tried to figure out why he cared at all. Her eyes narrowed at him as her head tilted to the side for a minute letting her temper get the best of her. "That was your doing, not mine on the friendship." Allie then shook her head at Archer as he looked a little astonished. She also started walking again as she spoke, "go back to class Archer I don't need you to babysit me."

It almost happened on cue next. Allie was walking away with her head high when she felt something sting going up her legs. She was instant to fall feeling the pain that last seconds, but she never hit the ground, Archer had caught her. "Are you really that clumsy to let your anger lead you that you would fall?" Archer asked her as he looked bewildered with an emotion that Allie didn't know if it was anger or fear.

Allie didn't reply because she couldn't explain what had just happened. It was the weirdest feeling, but suddenly she though going to the nurse's office was best. "I need to get to the nurse's office Archer I'm suddenly not feeling well."

Allie looked up into his green eyes, as he stared down at her with his arms still around her from catching her fall. "Tell me what is wrong Allie what is wrong with you?" He nearly demanded of her as his stare became heated.

Allie blinked several times before she spoke, "leg spasm. I must be over doing it. The doctor warned me this might happen. I guess I'm lucky the fire didn't burn my legs when the blanket was on fire, but still they were covered in flames."

That was as far as she got before Archer was suddenly checking every inch of her legs with one of his hands. Allie was shocked as he seemed to be looking for any mark on her skin that she didn't move. She was nearly relieved that she was wearing shorts, but even then Archer was man handling her legs that it was bizarre behavior. "Archer," Allie nearly yelled at him. "Just what are you doing mauling my legs?"

Archer stopped looking for any flaw to her perfect skin as he heard the tone in her voice. He didn't like the fact that she had a side effect to the fire Kane had caused. It took him a minute to control Wraith from hunting his brother down and beating the hell out of him. He needed a distraction, and a big one. Without saying a word, Archer started to get up with Allie in his arms. She was instant to hang onto him pleasing Greed. He ignored her protests as he started to walk with her through the hallways. Wraith loved the fact this was a punishment to her. Almost to the nurse's office the bell rang, and students started exiting their classes. Allie was now embraced as she hid her face into Archer's shoulder. She was praying no one she knew would see her. However luck wasn't on her side. Janice's voice was a little too close. "Oh gosh what happened to Allie?"

"She ruined her exit in an argument with me with one of her leg spasms. This just shows I'm the better person by taking her to the nurse," Archer stated as Allie looked up at him right at that moment to see the smirk on his face.

"You can put me down now Archer," Allie stated as clear as day.

"Nope," Archer stated back as he continued walking her right inside the nurse's office ignoring the look on Janice's face. He even spoke directly to the nurse as Allie stared up at him thinking who this person was and what had happened to Archer. "Don't let anyone bother Allie. I'm taking her to the back to lie down."

He continued walking until he had her in the back room that was the most private. He was gentle as he laid her down. Allie was really just staring up at him confused beyond anything. In her mind she wondered if she had heard him correctly boss the nurse around whom Allie didn't even get a look at. "Archer," Allie started to say but Archer was quick to place a finger over her mouth to silence her.

Confused more, Allie watched Archer slowly pull his finger away. His green eyes sparkled as he stared at her. Then slowly he started to lean his head down to hers, and Allie thought this was it, Archer was going to kiss her to confuse her more. Inch by inch he got closer and Allie couldn't move away. She was trapped as she could smell the Axe body spray he was wearing. His lips were inches from hers as Allie felt the need to connect those few inches and let their lips touch however, Archer spoke ruining the moment. "Your skin still smells like ash. You really need to bathe more often Allie, and maybe dip yourself in a tub of perfume. Then you can come within a ten mile radius of me." Allie repealed away from Archer clearly shocked. He had a huge grin on his face knowing he had the upper hand. "Oh gosh Allie I hope you didn't think I would stoop so low as kissing you. That would be like kissing my feet after I went barefoot walking in pig crap."

Allie growled as she narrowed her eyes at Archer. This made Archer smile bigger because it really showed that he was getting under her skin. Allie was so mad that she felt like her skin was heating up as she closed her eyes and tried to calm down. Slowly she spoke trying to keep the anger out of her voice. "Archer you can leave now, besides isn't there somewhere you need to be?"

Archer openly chuckled. "Oh yeah, I think it is time to date another one of your friends, but I'm enjoying picking on you at the moment."

Allie turned on her side so her back faced Archer. She was silent giving Archer the cold shoulder, but Archer found his eyes moving right to her backside wanting to touch her or curl up next to her. Both his demons wanted Allie that it was getting harder for him to control them. Archer's only fear would be that he would give into them, and then he wouldn't know what they would do to Allie. Slowly he forced himself out of the room not saying anything else leaving Allie wondering. He gave the nurse who was one of his father's subjects a mental push telling her that no one gets to see Allie as long as she is in here. The nurse nodded to him in understanding as he walked out the door to suddenly have Aaron in front of him. His voice was instant, "you're a bit protective of this one. Are you afraid I will eat her?"

Archer smiled feeling a bit cocky as he spoke. "It's a new game to Wraith keeping you away from Allie. I got to give into my demons sometime or they will drive me insane, and then what will become of this place, besides Wraith is enjoying this game. By the way the nurse is a Gala demon and one under my control. I told her to rip apart anything that tried to come near Allie while she is in that office. By all means Aaron please attempt it, Wraith really wants a show."

Aaron narrowed his eyes, but then also smiled. "You're not around her twenty four seven to protect her Archer. One day you will slip up and that will be the day I pounce."

"Hmm," Archer said all calm and cool. "Maybe I should gift Allie with a pet that will be with her twenty four seven to keep you away. Maybe a little demon of her own, that will keep you away." Archer smiled bigger as he looked at Aaron's confused face. "Oh and I know exactly how to give it to her so no worries she will have it by the end of the day."

Smiling Archer walked away as Aaron stared after him. Aaron could feel the spell around the nurse's station preventing Aaron from entering. Having a Gala demon close by was a smart investment on Archer's part. Soon he would find a way to get close to Allie. Until then, Aaron walked away waiting for another day to strike.

Allie lay on the cot knowing Archer had left. She just stared up at the ceiling wondering many things about Archer. Her mind was a mess as she wondered how he could be nice one moment and so mean the next. It took everything she had not to cry in front of him. She felt the chill almost instantly dance across her skin making her sit up because she could feel someone watching her. She looked around feeling confused, then suddenly in the corner she saw the boy from the dream she had before the fire. His eyes looked right at her as he smiled at her, almost like he was glad to see her. He started to speak, but nothing came out. It looked like his lips were moving, but no volume. Allie was quick to shake her head not understanding him. She even told him out loud that she couldn't hear him. He seemed in deep thought and then it looked like he was talking to someone else asking for something. Within seconds she saw a notebook and a pen being handled to him. He started writing on it and then turned it to face her. The question was a simple one. It asked her if she woke up in time and if she was ok. Allie nodded her head and spoke, "I woke up on fire my room was in flames. I made it out without a scratch but the smoke nearly killed me."

He seemed to nodded his head again as he flipped the page and started to write again. His next question was almost a meet and greet. It stated that his name was Adam, and what her name was. Allie blinked wondering if she was really having this conversation. "I'm Allie, nice to meet you I guess," came out feeling funny.

He seemed to repeat her name and nod before returning back to the notepad to write something else. His next question asked her where she was at. Allie blinked several times confused on this question and why he was asking it. Her response was short. "I'm at school at the nurse's station."

Adam gave her a weird look but then pointed at the where again. Allie was about to answer when the nurse walked in. "Allie is everything alright I thought I heard you talking in here."

Allie head shifted to the nurse taking in the white jacket with the blue jeans and then back to where Adam was who had suddenly stood up in shock. He even had a dagger in his hand as he looked at her and it looked like he mouthed for her to get out. Allie's heart started to pound as she saw what was happening. She had to be losing her mind as she looked at the nurse and tried to hide her fears. "I think I should go home for the day, can you call my mother to come pick me up?"

"Sure dear," was the nurse's response as she left the room seeming like she was worried about her.

Allie was then quick to look back in the corner Adam was in. He was still there with the dagger in his hand looking at the door, and then slowly looking at her. He looked shocked and Allie could tell his heart was racing a mile a minute. He was quick to pick up the notebook he had dropped, and started writing. His words were simple as they asked her what city and state she was in because she is in danger. Allie closed her eyes thinking maybe her mind was making her see this Adam that didn't exist. However deep in her mind she wondered what if he did. Her eyes darted to the dagger he still held in his hand and Allie shook her head, she would not tell him no more.

He looked a little taken back as the note book dropped down. Then he shook his head and turned the page to write something down. His next words surprised Allie as he wrote that the nurse is a demon, she will kill you. Allie shook her head in disbelief. She had to be losing her mind because the nurse was kind to her. She closed her eyes and counted in her head to ten. When Allie opened her eyes, Adam was gone. The nurse was suddenly back looking nothing like a demon Allie would see in a horror movie as she spoke, "your mom is on her way Allie. If you want to head up front she will be there shortly."

Allie nodded as she gathered her things and stood up. She felt a little dizzy at first, but shook it off. She headed out of the office and towards her locker to empty her bag. She wasn't so sure how she arrived at her locker so quickly, but she felt like she was in a trance. She shook it off as she opened her locker to have several different types of frogs leap out onto the hallway floor. Allie stumbled back in shock over the frogs as it looked like three dozen different types of frogs. Then she heard the laughter from the corner and turned to see Archer and his friends there. Allie grinded her teeth at the prank they had just played on her not caring about anything but their entertainment. Archer so smug walked towards her picking up a toad as he approached her. "Go ahead Allie kiss the toad and see if he turns into your prince."

Allie narrowed her eyes as she looked at the toad and then back at Archer. Without thinking she reached up grabbed Archer's shirt and pulled him down to her level. Her lips were inches from him that she could smell the minty taste in his mouth. He looked taken off guard too as Allie spoke so close to those lips that looked like she was about to kiss. "I can't bring myself to kiss a toad like you Archer. I already know that you are no prince, so I will take my chances with the toad in your hand."

She let go of Archer as she took the toad from his hands. He was shocked as she tossed her backpack inside her locker and walked away with the toad in her hands. Archer's smile slowly formed on his lips as he watched Allie's backside. His plan worked perfectly as he knew Allie would take the toad home with her and let it go outside her house. That toad would protect her from Aaron or any other demon from trying to hurt her. The other toads and frogs slowly started to disappear as Archer looked back at his group of friends. Matt stared at him as the others looked lost. This plan was actually Matt's, but then again he trusted his demon to call more than any other.

CHAPTER EIGHT
HERE COMES THE RAIN

Weeks had passed since Archer had placed frogs in Allie's locker. However math class seemed the same as it was since that day. Aaron was two seats over and one back staring at Allie like she had a secret. So far Allie had avoided their lunch date with excuse after excuse. She was running out of excuses. Archer was on her right tapping his finger ever so slightly that it made her look right at his hand to notice he was tapping it according to the seconds in the clock. Allie looked forward at Mrs. Evans that sat at her desk writing something. Her grayish blond hair was swept back in a twist as her brown eyes studied what she was reading then continued writing.

Hearing the pitter patter of the rain outside told Allie that her little lunch group would be moving inside, yet today she had no desire to join them. She actually wanted to stand out in the rain and let it drench her. Well she did if she could make the shiver leave her body from Aaron's stare. Looking down at her complete paper, Allie had to admit she was bored. Her eyes darted to the clock to see ten minutes left of class. She could actually understand why Archer was tapping he had to be done too. Looking back at Archer, Allie noticed that he was just staring at her. Not knowing why she opened her notebook and wrote in it that the toad is still alive, and showed it so Archer could see it. Archer was quick to get out his notebook while wearing a blank expression. He then wrote in it asking her if she was having lunch with Aaron today.

Allie was quick to shake her head in a no, which caused Archer to slowly smile. He then wrote in the notebook if she was avoiding him. Allie made a face as she thought about it. In a way yes she has been avoiding him, and she couldn't really explain the why. She was quick to jot down a guess so in the notebook. Allie noticed the dimple in Archer's left cheek as he tried to hold in the smile that was forming on this face. Deep down this conversion was bound to bite Allie on her butt. If Archer was nice it would be minutes before he ruined it and became mean.

Allie wasn't surprised when Archer covered what he was writing and then folded it nicely. He handed the note behind him and Allie watched it make its way to Aaron. Not knowing what Archer had wrote she watched Aaron's expressions go from neutral to suddenly mad as he crumpled the paper. His eyes landed right on Allie as he mouthed have lunch with me today, stop putting it off.

Allie was stunned as she faced forward looking at the clock. She wondered for a second why Aaron was so insistent. The thought made her curious, and Allie was not normally a curious person. Allie was then quick to write on the paper to Archer what the bet was. Archer looked confused for several minutes, and then it dawned on him what Allie was asking. He smiled instantly as he wrote the bet was to see if he could eat you.

Allie was more stun than before. Her mouth dropped open making Archer just stare at her. If she wasn't so shocked by his statement she would have noticed that the way Archer was looking at her was with desire. His eyes were trained on her lips. Shaking it off Allie looked back at the clock to notice only two minutes was left. She silently placed her notebook in her bag, and then her other things right as the bell rang. She was slow to rise up as others started to exit the class. She realized suddenly Aaron was blocking her path when she looked up and met his dark blue eyes. Anger surged through Allie as she didn't think. Her hand came right up and slapped him across the face hard. Aaron looked shocked as anger stirred in his eyes from Allie hitting him. However Archer's voice held laughter has he spoke, "yep, I told you Aaron that Allie would slap you silly by the end of class. Coarse it would have been an extra bonus if she would have kneed you in the balls as well."

Allie spun to look at Archer who wore a smile as if he was pleased. Allie never felt so bad in her whole life over her actions. She looked back at Aaron and spoke instantly, "I'm sorry Aaron, I really am sorry." With that, she darted pass him and out the room not looking back.

Aaron watched her leave knowing that she was upset and he knew who made her upset. He actually started to laugh as he looked at Archer. "Nicely played Archer, you were right she did slap me silly. She has quit a hit too, but the question is can she take them just as well. Mark my words, one day you will go too far with this girl and the result will cost you."

Archer glared at Aaron as he turned to walk away. His eyes narrowed as Wraith was pushing him to follow Aaron. In fact Wraith wanted Archer to pound his face in, but he was controlling his anger. Then he smiled as he walked out the door. He knew Aaron would go look for Allie, but Archer knew right where Allie was at.

Allie sat in a little cove by herself outside. She was tucked against the building, so she was staying dry as it sprinkled out. With her knees against her chest, Allie leaned against the wall looking out watching the rain. She knew her friends would be wondering where she was, but Allie really needed a minute to pull herself together. So lost in thought, a new voice startled her. "It's beautiful and quiet out here, but I don't really care for the rain."

Allie turned her head so quickly that she nearly twisted her neck. A boy sat across from her nearly mirroring her position. Bad part was she had no clue how he had got out here without her seeing him. It seemed like he just appeared as Allie took in his shoulder length blond hair and bright bluish purple eyes. She also noted that his pants looked like a soft white as he had flippers on his feet and a light tan tank. "Are you cold," Allie asked him since he seemed so under dress outside with her.

He actually smiled at her as he spoke, "nah, a little muggy out don't you think. I'm Nathan by the way. Real name is Nathanael, but please don't call me that, it's too long."

Allie smiled this time back at him. "I'm Allie, and pleased to meet you."

He stared at her for a minute as it seemed like he bowed his head towards her. "So why don't you tell me why you're out here and not inside with all of your friends?"

Allie shook her head because she must have been easy to read. "I needed a moment to pull myself together without everyone wondering why I wasn't talking. I let someone get to me and I acted when I shouldn't have."

"Hmm," he seemed to nod. "Regret is something we all go through. Every action has a reaction, but sometimes the reaction leads us into the next CHAPTER."

Allie blinked at him thinking he sounded much older than he looked. "So tell me why you are out here when you don't care for the rain?"

His lips cracked into a bigger smile as he leaned towards Allie. "I saw this girl sitting on the bench in the corner by herself and wondered if she needed someone to talk to. I figured someone as pretty as she should not be out here in this yuck by herself."

Allie blushed from his comment as she smiled and looked down. She turned her head towards the hallway windows to notice Aaron just staring at her. He also looked to be on a cell phone talking to someone. "Looks like the one I hurt found me," Allie stated clearly as she turned and looked back at Nathan.

His eyes moved to look at Aaron in the hallway. Allie noticed that his smile turned evil like he was sneering at Aaron. "Now that one deserves to be hurt, and if you can continue to do so, I will be smiling for the rest of the year."

Allie rolled her eyes as she spoke, "that sounds like something Archer would say. What is wrong with Aaron that every guy seems to not like him?"

Nathan actually laughed as he spoke facing Allie again. "He's evil and you shouldn't trust him. In fact if my friend

Adam was here, he would set him as a personal goal to get rid of him."

Allie sat up instantly as the image of the boy she saw named Adam came to her mind. Nathan was looking at her funny, and Allie started to shake off the thought as she spoke, "why would he do that?"

Nathan had his head slightly tilted as he studied her. "Do you know Adam?"

Allie shook her head as she didn't need to explain the Adam she knew came from a dream of some kind. "No I don't know Adam. I just wonder why everyone thinks Aaron is evil."

Nathan's expression hadn't changed as he spoke, "hmm, maybe I should ask Adam if he knows you. He is always up to some new mischief so I wouldn't be surprised. The one you call Aaron is not who he seems, in fact that is not his real name. You should never be alone with him. Public places are best."

Allie couldn't stop the snort as a laugh escaped her mouth. "You sound like a parent Nathan. That would be something my mom would tell me because she wants me to be her little girl forever."

Nathan frowned at her words as he spoke, "every parent wants to keep their children little forever. We hate to see them grow up and make mistakes, but we still love them."

Allie gave him a strange look as she spoke. "You sound like you have a child Nathan. It must be hard being a teenage parent."

A laugh escaped his mouth as he spoke. "What if I told you that I am much older than I look?"

A creepy feeling drifted over Allie almost instantly as she spoke, "then I would ask why you were here?"

She watched his teeth run over his bottom lip as it seems like he was debating. Then he smiled as he spoke. "I'm making sure that the demon watching us right now doesn't corner you when you're alone and clearly upset. Demons fed off of that. Also to let you know that you are walking a fine line as it seems you're in the wolf's den. You're holding up good, in which I am proud. Also something important, your heart is here, but can you protect it?"

Allie stood instantly looking at Nathan. Either she was losing her mind, or he was insane. Maybe she was insane. Her words came out sounding scared as she spoke, "what the hell does that mean? Just who the hell are you to give me such a message?"

Allie was panicking as Nathan's eyes stayed focused on her. "Calm down Allie, everything will be alright. You will understand it in time, but it is too soon." His smile returned as Allie continued to stare at him. "As for who I am, I am Nathan,

I told you this. To give you this message is to protect you. My vow is to watch over you and make sure nothing ill happens to you, you're very special. Besides even now they are testing your limits and you're not even ready for that. Soon you will be." Allie's heart was pounding as she stared at Nathan. He continued, "If you are wondering what I am Allie, I am many things to you. Most important one is that I am your guardian angel. Your heart is heading this way, time for me to go."

Allie blinked and he was no longer sitting there. Trimmers raced up and down Allie's body as she felt like she couldn't breathe. She was hyperventilating thinking that she was seeing things. Archer's voice made her jump and nearly come undone. "Allie! You need to tell your nagging friend I did nothing to you." Archer stopped his sentence as Allie turned towards him and he saw fear in her eyes like she was about to fall apart. "What's wrong with you?"

Allie's body was shaking badly from what she just saw, but she was working on controlling it because she didn't want Archer to see her like this. This would be something Archer would use against her. "It's nothing, I just need to be alone," escaped her mouth with a tremble.

Archer seemed to be looking at her funny. Allie couldn't tell what he was thinking as many emotions crossed his face, but then he surprised her. Ignoring her words, Archer moved closer to her. He took her hand in his and led her back to the bench. Without saying a word, he pulled her down next to him and placed his warm arms around her, just holding her. In a way it felt like he was protecting her, that it confused Allie more as she wondered why Archer was doing this. "Archer," Allie said into his side.

"What Allie?" He replied back to her as he continued to hold her.

"Why?" It was all she could say as she felt like crying.

Archer was silent for several minutes and then replied with, "because." He didn't say anything else. He just continued to hold her until the end of lunch.

CHAPTER NINE
STORMING

It was a little after six by the time Archer had got home. He was worried about Allie, and had watched her in the shadows ever since lunch. He still couldn't get the look out of his head when he saw her so afraid yet trying to act brave. Something had happened to Allie while she was outside by herself in the rain and he mentally swore if it was a demon, he would kill them.

Not paying much attention, Archer started the climb up the stairs to his room. His hand had only touched his doorknob when he heard Aaron's voice. "We need to talk."

Archer spun to see Aaron leaning against the wall. He raised his eyebrow up as he spoke, "what do we need to talk about? You're my brother's spy, and trying to steal my toy."

Something about Aaron didn't look right as he came out of the shadows. He was acting timid and if Archer didn't know better he would say he was as scared as Allie was at lunch. He even wouldn't keep eye contact with him, which was unusual.

Something was wrong. Archer was about to comment on it when Aaron spoke, "I saw everything at lunch today."

The thought that Aaron had seen him holding Allie made Archer see red. He was instant to grab Aaron by his shirt lifting him off the ground and slamming him into the wall. Aaron met his eyes surprised as Archer spoke nearly spitting venom, "what exactly did you see Aaron?"

Archer felt Aaron shiver, but he refused to let him down until he heard it all. Aaron spilled his guts as quickly as possible. "I saw the girl with an angel, but not just any angel. I couldn't hear the conversation, but they both looked at me, and I recognized the angel. It was Nathanael, the ruler over fire and vengeance. He sneered at me telling me to come out and play. He wanted bloodshed. Then he said something to her, and I noticed she started to freak out. You came out within seconds and he disappeared, but he didn't go that far. I was surprised that you of all people gave her peace of mind. I could tell she felt safe with you, but the angel was watching the two of you closely with that sick smile of his. He looked at me with that same smile as he spoke in my head telling me what the girl was to you." Archer's heart was pounding at these words because if Aaron was saying them there was more to the story. His concern over Allie increased within seconds as Aaron continued. "He knew that the girl was your one true weakness and the only one that gave you strength. Without her, the elements will destroy you first when the time came and you would let them. He is planning to kill her tonight Archer, and if he doesn't Kane and Fury will because I did not have time to tell them the rest. You have got to stop them."

Archer dropped Aaron quickly as shock took over. His heart was pounding so hard that it was thundering in his ears. He had left Allie only five or ten minutes ago, after he knew she would be inside her home safe and not leaving for the night. He thought she was safe. She should be safe, but there was never any telling with the odds stacking against her. She now had three people trying to kill her all because of him. Turning around quickly, Archer ran down the stairs, he needed to get to Allie now. He wasn't about to let her die.

Allie was still trying to shake off the weirdest day of her life. She had to imagine the whole thing. Angels and demons could not exist, but she could not explain Archer. He did nothing but held her when she needed it most, and he was the last person she had expected that from. However once again Archer had succeeded in making her think of nothing but him, just when she thought she had him figured out, he threw her a curve ball.

Trying to distract her thoughts, Allie worked on making her room spotless. So busy cleaning it took her a minute to realize that her shoe had split open. Taking a seat on her bed, Allie studied the shoe knowing she couldn't wear these shoes tomorrow, and she didn't have a spare pair. Frustrated, Allie went in search for her father since her mother was not home. She found him reclining in his chair reading the paper while the news was blaring. For a minute Allie smiled at her dad with his black socks, tan dress pants, and white tee shirt. He was wearing his glasses as he read and it reminded her of a Norman Rockwell picture. "Dad," Allie said instantly drawing his attention and making him turn to look at her. "We need to go to the store tonight, I need shoes."

Her father frowned a bit as he spoke, "it's storming out Allie can it wait until the weekend?"

Allie held up her shoes showing that they were now destroyed. "All I have is a pair of flippers, and I can't wear them if it is like this tomorrow."

"Well we could call your mother and have her pick up a pair before she gets off work."

"Dad," Allie stressed. "Last time I told mom my size she came back with the wrong size, and something that would only go with a dress. I just need a new pair of sneakers it should only take us thirty minutes tops. We are ten minutes away from the closest shoe store."

Her dad actually chuckled. "Last time I took you shoe shopping we were there for an hour and ended up with five pairs. Well let me get my shoes back on and a shirt that doesn't make me look like a slob. Maybe we will get some take out too just encase your mother is too tired when she comes home."

He started to get up, and Allie rushed to his arms giving him a big hug. "You're the best dad ever," she told him as a smile spread across her face.

"Sure say that now that you are getting your way," he teased her as he fluffed her hair. "Better go get your flippers on and bring an extra pair of socks. I'm sure you will want to wear your new shoes out of the store."

Allie squeezed him again before heading back to her room to get her flippers. Somehow her dad made everything feel right to her. He was indeed her rock after a bad day, which brought her once again thinking about Archer and how he just held her at lunch time. No one had seen them and he never gave her a reason either. It felt like he was protecting her, but she didn't know from what. "Come on Allie lets go before this storm gets worse," her father yelled from down the hallway.

Allie grabbed her coat as she exited the room. She dashed toward her father that looked handsome as he smiled at her. He even had an umbrella in his hands as they made their way to car. He was always the gentleman as he walked her to her side of the car with the umbrella and opening the door for her. Allie climbed in as he shut the door and made it to his side getting behind the wheel. "Thanks dad," Allie said with a smile.

He smiled at her and started the car up. They pulled out of the drive and started the trip into town. "So tell me how your day at school was Allie," her father asked her.

Allie looked over at him as he stayed focused on the road, but she had always been truthful with her father. "I'd like to say it was a typical day, but it was weird."

Her father snuck a peek at her but then darted his eyes back to the road as twilight sunk in. "What happened?"

"What always happens," Allie nearly moaned. "Archer," came out as one word.

Her father actually smiled. "I have to admit, I would have laughed too with all the frogs in the locker. The time and planning on that is amazing that he came up with it, but I'm proud that you didn't fall apart. That toad in the front of the house almost seems like it is protecting the house. We haven't had ants or any spiders in the house at all."

"Well today he succeeded in confusing me dad. I did something bad today dad. I slapped another boy because I believed Archer and his lies. I felt so bad I told him I was sorry. I went and sat by myself at lunch, and to be honest I was having a pity party of one." Allie left out the part about Nathan. She was still trying to think if she imagined it or not.

Her father didn't comment as he seemed to be waiting for the rest. "Archer found me, and I expected him to tease me or something, but you know what he did. He embraced me giving me a hug, and then held me until the end of lunch. When I asked him why, he responded with because. I'm so confused with him. One minute he hates me the next he acts how he use to, like my best friend."

Her father smiled but kept his eyes on the road. "Honey, Archer is having a hard time with his emotions. He went from you being his best friend to suddenly I can't be best friends with a girl, and do you know why? It is clearly because he sees you as more than his best friend and doesn't know how to go the next step."

"What are you trying to say dad?" Allie asked him feeling confused. Her dad turned to look at her with a smile of knowledge of his face. However something out the front window caught Allie's eye. "Dad lookout," Allie screamed.

Her dad turned around to see the deer that was suddenly in the road just staring at them as he jerked the car to the right. The deer impacted the car as the car swerved in three hundred and sixty circles as it went off the side of the road and sailed right into a tree. Allie felt the impact as her head suddenly felt like it was pounding. Her whole body hurt as she reached over for her dad. The airbags had not deployed as they should of, but her dad was bleeding. His eyes were closed as he lay over the steering wheel, and Allie started to panic as she tried to get her seatbelt off. The stubborn seatbelt wouldn't unhook. She was screaming her father's name as suddenly she smelt the flames minutes before she saw them begin in the front of the car. She didn't hear her door being ripped open, but she felt something rip into her side as her seatbelt suddenly was cut. Then she felt two strong arms wrap around her pulling her out of the car. She turned towards her savor to plead to get her dad before the fire took control. She saw the huge white wings flapping and Nathan's face right before the explosion sent both of them flying. Allie's head hit hard and darkness swallowed her up.

CHAPTER TEN
SLEEPING BEAUTY

Archer could only stare at Allie lying on the hospital bed looking so pale against the white sheets. Her red hair looked like a living flame that he ached to run his fingers threw it. He had read her charts several times to distracted himself from acting on his impulses to find out she was in a coma, yet was breathing on her on. He had even read the police report and knew Allie only survived by a miracle. If she didn't get thrown from her car, she would have shared the same fate as her father and Archer would literally be in pieces.

Archer sat next to her on the bed and took her hand in his as he stared down at her. He used his power to keep nurses and doctors away during his visit. Allie's own mother was downstairs right now in the cafeteria having lunch with someone, so Archer only had minutes with Allie without anyone knowing. Not knowing why, Archer reached out and brushed her hair back out of her face tucking it behind her ear. His fingers trailed down her cheek in a caress not liking how cold they were. He was near tears wishing she would open her eyes just once so he could gaze into her amethyst eyes that always seemed to sparkle. He leaned down breathing her in thinking she still smelled like cinnamon to him. His voice was soft and gentle as he spoke in a whisper near her ear. "Wake up Allie, I can't live without you."

Archer's face was inches from hers as he now stared directly at her face, so close. His eyes focused on her eyes willing them to open, even a slight movement underneath the lids. Then his eyes trailed down to her cherry red lips, and for once Archer just wanted to feel them on his. He wanted to know if they were as soft as they look. Not caring if this would be the first or the last time, Archer leaned down and slowly began to kiss Allie's lips in the softest of caresses. At first he couldn't believe how soft her lips were reminding him of cotton candy or even a rose petal. He knew that if she was awake and kissing him back, he would not be able to stop kissing her, he didn't want to. He slowly started to pull back thinking at lease he got to kiss her just once. He now knew how soft those lips were, he just wish she would have kissed him back. Then the strangest thing happened as he started to pull back feeling hopeless. It seemed like Allie had lifted her chin up and was taking in a huge breath through her nose. He could see the rapid eye movement as it looked like she was trying to open her eyes, yet they seemed too heavy for her to do so. He couldn't tare his eyes away as he watched her slowly open her eyes and stare at him until she blinked and spoke in a scratchy voice. "Even in my dreams you're here to pick on me amazing how I can never escape you." A smile touched her lips as Archer continued to hold her hands in his as he looked down at her feeling the smile on her lips grow on his.

"Where else would I be my sleeping beauty, this is where I belong." Archer whispered to her as his own smile tugged on his face knowing she thought she was dreaming and his reference would hold meaning to her.

A laugh escaped her mouth, but a cough followed it as he noticed Allie wince taking the smile right off his face. He didn't like the fact that a simple gesture hurt her. He even wondered where her pain was. "Good one Archer," she said after she stopped coughing. "So how do you plan to torture me in my dreams? To be honest I don't know if I can fight back. I feel like I went through a ringer, and I hurt all over. You will have to come back when I feel better."

He made a face like he was deep in thought. Realistic he knew she didn't remember what had happened. She thought she was dreaming and he wondered how she would handle the truth. He lifted a hand out of hers and brushed her cheek as he spoke. "I guess then I will wait until you have your strength back, but until then I really want to kiss you Allie."

Allie laughed again, which caused her to wince more as she moved her hand to her side. Archer was instant to gaze at her side and pull the covers back looking for her pain. She was wearing a hospital gown, but she was holding her side like she was in too much pain and the simple gesture would fix it. He was instant to lift the gown hearing her protest at his action, but did nothing to stop him because she was too weak. Her side was wrapped in a bandage and he could see her blood leaking through it. Panic ate at him as he was instant to look back at Allie's face as she seemed paler than before but still smiling at him. It was no wonder she thought this was a dream, she must be slowly dying. "Allie I will get someone in here to take care of your side, but promise me that you will not die on me."

Her lips tilted in a smile as she spoke softly. "I won't die Archer, if I did who would you pick on, and who would be brave enough to fight back?"

He watched her close her eyes slowly like she was tired and Archer sprang into action as his demons demanded him to fix her. He called the closest nurse to come in the door and look at her side. He needed to make the bleeding stop before he lost it and his demons took over. He made himself invisible as he watched the nurse check Allie's side and then hit the panic button to bring others in. Soon a whole team came in and sprang into action on Allie removing the badge. Archer sucked in his breath when he saw what looked like a knife wound with a few stitches. Anger rolled over him thinking that someone stabbed her on purpose and the hospital doctor didn't stitch her up good enough. When the doctor came in asking what had happen, the nurse explain that she tore the stitches. He seemed shocked as he looked at the stitches. Then he smiled and spoke. "That means she woke up and we need to make the stitches stronger. Let's stitch her back up since the wound doesn't look infected, and nurse, go tell her mother the good news."

Archer watched the doctor stitch her back up making it look like it was never there. He took a deep breath as he could hear the nurse return and moved himself to the shadows just outside the room as her mother entered with the one she was eating lunch with.

Allie seemed to wake for the second time to hear the sound of voices. She could feel someone holding her hand, and someone else speaking not too far away. "Liz, just be happy she woke up. She will be in recovery soon you will see. Then she will be back to her normal self."

"It's my fault Mel. If I wasn't with you, they would have never gone out in that storm for any reason. They had to be worried about me, how can I live with the guilt? Every choice I make I always end up paying for it."

Allie felt the weigh leave her side and then the hand slip from hers as she heard the guy speak again. "Liz it is not your fault. She is a part of you and strong. She will pull through this and I will be here for you every step of the way."

Allie tried to open her eyes but it felt like she was using all of her energy just to do so. She only had her eyes open a crack as everything seemed in a blur. Even in the blur, Allie saw her mother being embraced as she was weeping on this man's shoulders that looked a lot like Archer. Feeling confused, Allie got her eyes to open more wondering why Archer was here. Her voice came out scratchy as she spoke. "Archer? When did you get so old and why are you here?"

Both her mother and the man looked at Allie, and that is when she realized that it wasn't Archer. She felt confused as she blinked at him and her mother raced to her side. He stared back at her with a strange look on his face, but then slowly smiled at her as if he knew a secret. Allie's mom was quick to speak. "I'm so glad you're awake, baby."

Allie was frowning as she stared at the man who held his smile. "Liz I will take care of the moving for you while you spend time with your daughter. You will not have to return back there." The way he said there made Allie think that it was somewhere dirty.

"Thank you Mel," her mother said while staring at Allie smiling with tears in her eyes.

"Mom," Allie said instantly as she realized the meaning of the conversation. "Why are we moving, and where is dad?"

She felt her mother stiffen instantly and the guy name Mel suddenly become very aware of it as his eyes narrowed at Allie for making her do that. Her mom even schooled her face, and Allie knew she was about to tell her something that was very bad. "Baby," her mother started, but Allie knew just by the look on her mother's face.

She shook her head instantly as the memory flooded through her. She was shaking her head. "No," Allie said instantly. "It wasn't a dream!" She was pulling away from her mother as panic set in and she was remembering every detail of what had happened. "Nathan didn't get to him in time, and I begged him to. This is my fault I should have just wore the flippers in the rain."

"Allie no," her mom said instantly trying to calm her as Allie turned away crying in her pillow.

Allie knew the man was still in the room with her, but she couldn't look at her mother or him to see their shocked expressions. Through her sobs she did hear him speak, "he won't take her too Liz, I will make sure of it."

"Thank you Mel," her mother said again before she felt her mother lean down and wrapped her arms around her to give her comfort. Her mother's voice was instant. "It's not your fault Allie. No one could predict what would happen. Your father was a good man, but he would want you to get better and be yourself again. We will make it through this Allie."

Allie was sick as her mother held onto her. Right at this moment, she just wanted to close her eyes and forget it all had happened. She would do almost anything to see her father again.

Archer could feel Allie knowing she just heard the news about her father. Part of him wanted to go back into the room and hold onto her being her rock. The other part wanted to snatch her and take her away from here forever to make her forget. He noticed the door to her room open, and then had the biggest shock of his life. His father had just stepped out of the room and he was staring directly at him with an arched eyebrow. With a quick hand gesture made by his father, Archer followed his father not knowing what will happen since he was discovered. Archer rounded the corner to suddenly have himself teleported into his father's office. Even more surprising was that his siblings were sitting there waiting. Looking at them he couldn't help but worry about Price who was just recently starting to host Famine. He had lost a lot of weight, and his eyes looked like they were starting to sink in. However he always seemed to be hungry. Lacy was also feeling the effects of Pestilence, and Archer was worried because she was spending time at the hospitals making people more ill. Her demon envy didn't help her either as it seemed to get off and making others wish they were her. His oldest brother Kane sat with a frown on his face. His eyes were a complete black now as Death was nearly all the way in control. Archer stared at him too long as Kane looked directly at him. "She lived little brother." He stated as if Allie had passed a test.

Before Archer could respond, his father did. "She is also off limits to the four of you. Her mother and I are very close, and an old enemy of hers has come back."

Archer blinked not understanding what his father was talking about. However Price spoke, "explain father. I do not like secrets."

"I know what the four of you have been up to, and don't think I didn't see the signs. Lacy I know you created that storm last night. Kane I know what you and Furfur did to lure that girl out and ambush her. Price I know you made the car explode so you could feed off the souls inside. Nothing you four do goes by unnoticed. However from this moment on you're not allowed to target her. The arch angel Nathanael is trying to get her, and like I said her mother and I are very close."

Archer stopped breathing hearing this news as Kane spoke not really caring about what was said. "How close are you to the mother?"

His father glared at Kane but Kane didn't shrink back. His father then smiled as it looked so evil. "Very close," he responded back not adding anything else. "You're all dismissed except you Archer," his father said in the next instant.

Archer watched his siblings get up and walk out of the room one by one, but Kane stopped in front of him and looked him directly in the eye. He lifted his hand up and placed it right over his heart. His words were soft as he spoke. "Little brother I now know. When the time comes I will reveal what the oracle told me, but you will not like it."

Archer watched him walk out of the room, then turned and looked at his father who was behind his desk gesturing for him to sit. He did so not knowing what his father was about to say. For several minutes his father stared at him, and then he spoke. "Allie is a beautiful girl, just like her mother. Would you mind telling me the relationship between the two of you?"

For the first time in his life, Archer felt tongue tied. How could he tell his father what Allie meant to him? He took a breath and tried. "She calms my demons, and they want to be around her. My first year here she was my best friend. All those times I told you I had to go over to my study partner's house to get the assignment done, was time I was spending with her. I didn't need the help I just wanted to be with her. As the years seemed to pass, I couldn't let her stay close with the other demons so close. I would push her away by picking on her. Some days she would best me, and others I would best her."

Archer released a breath about to continue as his father spoke. "She's your other half." He looked up at his father to see his shocked expression. Then he looked confused as he spoke. "You're not to meet her until the time of the ceremony when War claims her as his bride." Archer blinked at his father's words. His father looked lost in thought, but had a big smile on his face like he was putting the puzzle together. A laugh escaped his mouth as he spoke. "No wonder Nathanael is after her. War's bride will host the deadly sins and give birth to the next line of horsemen." His father looked giggly as he started to smile, but then the smile vanished. "Archer she has to stay pure until the ceremony. War's bride has always been a virgin."

Archer blinked at his father. His heart was starting to pound. This was all news to him. He didn't even know that he was allowed to have a bride, and the thought of it being Allie suddenly made him smile. Then the smile vanished as he thought that the ceremony wouldn't be until after he graduated from high school. It was going to be a long year and a half to make sure Allie didn't date no one, and harder on him to control his urges on taking her. His father spoke again not noticing his son's expression. "I want someone assigned to her to watch over her."

Archer spoke as he seemed shell shocked. "I watch over her."

"No I want another too," his father said instantly.

"Aaron has been watching her for Kane." Archer responded next.

"Perfect," his father said. "I will send him now to watch over her. You may go."

Archer rose up he needed a few minutes alone to figure out what to do now, and how to go about it. Allie was in a tender spot, but at least now he knew that Aaron would not hurt her.

Allie felt like she was dreaming again. The room seemed so bright that she blinked several times until a face was suddenly in hers. She jerked back instantly to wince as she felt the pain on her sides. Nathan's voice was instant, "easy Allie, I don't want you to tare those stitches again. I needed to check on you to make sure you were pulling through. Don't worry about your father he went to the right place I made sure of it."

Allie wanted to shout at him, but instead her lips curled in a frown as she fought the tears. "He's dead. How is that the right place?"

Nathan reached out and wrapped his arms around her holding her while she cried. His voice was settle as he spoke, "he's still with you Allie. He always will be. He loved you very much and he still loves you in death." That made Allie sob harder as he continued to speak. "Someone is coming, and they have vowed to protect you Allie. Such vows are not taken lightly by my kind, however I will still be watching over you."

Allie's tears had stopped as she felt him disappear in her arms, but sadness was eating away at her. She felt numb as she sat in her hospital bed letting sadness eat away at her over something she no longer had control over. She also noticed how much colder her room felt as she knew her mother was talking to the doctor about her release, and her mother had been busy for the past two days moving into a new house. Her door suddenly opened making her turn her head towards the door. The first thing she saw was a huge bouquet of flowers, and then they were slowly lowered as she saw Aaron's face. His voice was instant as he spoke, "I heard the news, and figured that you might need some company to cheer you up regardless how you feel about me."

Allie blinked a little surprised as Aaron walked in and sat the flowers next to her bed. He took a seat and smiled at her. "How did you find out?" Allie asked him as Nathan's words were in her head.

"It made the news," his reply was simple.

Allie felt the tears minutes before they started to drip from her eyes she had no control over them as she realized Aaron was the first to come before any of her friends. Aaron was quick to grab a tissue and wipe her eyes. He even took a seat on the bed next to her and wrapped his arms around her. "It's ok Allie, I'm here for you. I will help you through this. One day at a time."

Deep down Allie knew Aaron would too. She mumbled right into him knowing that he would be there when she felt like she would fall. "Thank you Aaron."

"It's the lease I can do Allie," he told her as he kissed the top of her head, and continued to hold her as Allie spotted Adam in the corner just staring at her with a strange look in his eyes. She went to speak, but he shook his head. His lips tilted in a smile as it seemed like he picked up a piece of card board. He wrote quickly and then faced it towards her. Allie read the words quickly telling her that she could trust him, the demon is assigned to protect her. It made Allie stiffen as Aaron spoke again. "It's ok Allie I'm not planning on going anywhere, and Archer will not chase me off either. Whenever you feel like you are going to fall, just say my name and I will pick you back up." His words made Adam smile and nod his head. He suddenly disappeared making Allie wonder why she was seeing him.

CHAPTER ELEVEN
A LITTLE RUMOR

Weeks had gone by, and Allie was still wearing all black. Archer was getting tired of seeing Allie in nothing but black. It made her skin look more like an ivory snow and her hair a major distraction of red flames. He wanted to see her in dresses again too, as she seemed to be struggling in her classes as if she couldn't focus on the assignments. Too many times he caught her just staring off at nowhere as he wondered what she was thinking. Her friends even tried to get her attention, and the result was that she would place her hand over her heart as if she was in pain. Archer didn't like when she did that, and he was at the point now to do something to make her stop doing it.

Aaron seemed to be with her constantly. He would coax a smile from her lips making Archer want to kill him. He found himself following them daily surprised that Aaron had got her into taking pictures. Deep down Archer was proud of the pictures Allie took. She had a natural talent at it as the school paper would use some of them and the yearbook staff was asking some from her. If this was helping her move along from her father's death, then Archer supported Allie in this. However his demon greed was constantly in his head not liking all the time Aaron was spending with her.

Today Archer was fed up with Aaron in general. He was making it a point to hunt him down and have a little chat with him. He found him alone standing against a wall listening in on some senior jocks conversation. Archer marched over to give him a real piece of his mind when Aaron looked up at him and motioned for him to be quiet. Just that alone had wraith ready to nail him for no reason until suddenly he heard one of the seniors say Allie's name. He stopped instantly next to Aaron and listened as everything inside him froze.

"The Allie chick is smoking hot. You notice when you talk to her that her hand goes right over her heart," one of the jocks said.

The ring leader seemed to laugh. "You know why, it's because she has a scar there from the accident. It's the only flaw on her perfect body however it will still be fun to nail her. Did she agree to come to the party?"

A different one spoke this time. "She said she would think about it, but we are working together on the year book, and I know I can talk her into it with the help of her little blond friend."

The first jock then spoke. "I want dibs on her. I'm sure she can use a good guy in her life, at lease for the night."

They were laughing at that comment as Archer started to see red. Aaron reached out and grabbed his arm drawling his attention to wait. The third jock then spoke, "How do you know about the scar, she is normally always in a button up shirt almost to her neck?"

"I got her alone and asked her why she does the heart touchy thing. I even made her smile. I might have the best chance of nailing her than you two," the leader seemed to laugh.

"You think she will bring that scary dude she has been hanging with?" The first jock said.

"Now that I don't get, she said they are friends only, but have you seen the way he looks at her? He's like a personal body guard trying to keep everyone away from her. I'd like to know what his plan is because I think he would keep her from some alone time with me." The third jock stated.

"Well the plan is simple, he is not invited, and we need to keep it that way. Just a few of us, and a few girls for us to enjoy," the ring leader laughed as he spoke.

The bell rang as Archer and Aaron didn't move, and the jocks left not knowing they were there. Aaron then spoke. "I had a feeling about them when they started to get all friendly with Allie. She is starting to come out of her shell a little, but someone like that might shove her back into it."

Archer seemed to be staring at nothing controlling his anger. He found himself no longer wanting to rip Aaron's head off but instead three jocks that wanted to deflower his Allie. He was slowly simmering as he wanted to hunt each one of them down and destroy them. "Does she have a scar over her heart?" Archer asked Aaron as he mentally thought Aaron better not know.

"To be honest I don't know. She has never said nothing like that to me, however I do notice that when she seems in deep though she does put her hand over her heart." Aaron told him point blank.

"I need to know," Archer stated as Aaron arched his eyebrow up at him. "I will find out today too."

"Ok I will bite, how do you plan to find out?" Aaron asked him knowing that Allie had been giving him the cold shoulder as of late.

Archer smiled sweetly at him. "I have my ways, and it might snap her out of her damn mood."

Archer walked off leaving Aaron there. He knew where Allie would be, and what he was about to do might bring her old self back.

Allie had just finished her science class and was heading to her locker. She was placing her stuff inside telling herself that as each day passed it would get easier. She mentally had to tell herself that her mom would date new people, but she couldn't fathom it being Archer's dad out of all people. She couldn't even look at Archer without thinking of that dream she had of him in the hospital, and then overhearing her mom talking to his dad. Her mind was in so much turmoil at lease Aaron had been there for her making her safe. She also had not seen Adam or Nathan since the hospital when they both told her that Aaron would protect her. Since then she felt more comfortable around him and he showed her so many new things to keep her mind on other things.

Placing her things in the locker, Allie turned to have Archer suddenly in her face. He towered over her as she backed up into the locker placing her hand right over her heart. Her voice was instant, "oh Archer you startled me."

His eyes were looking right at her hand as he spoke, "you've been ignoring me, or should I say avoiding me since you came back. Why is that Allie?"

At that moment, Allie wondered if Archer knew about their parents dating. "I've had a lot on my mind, it's nothing personal." However it was personal if he knew about their parents and the dream that she had of him.

His eyes were still on her hand covering her heart. "Why are you doing that?" He said while raising his hand up to point at hers.

Allie looked down at her hand realizing what she was doing. She dropped her hand instantly as she spoke, "I guess it is just a reaction I haven't been able to correct as of late."

"Liar," he stated as his eyes locked with hers. "A few jocks said you flashed them the scar that lies there, is that true." Allie's mouth opened in shock from his statement as Archer continued. "Why don't you flash me too since you enjoy doing it."

Allie reacted instantly as her hand came up and nailed Archer in a slap that echoed. He was stunned for a moment before he zeroed back in on her. "You hit me," he stated looking at her looking taken back.

"You deserved it for that comment," Allie told him as she unbuttoned one of her buttons making Archer wonder if she was really going to flash him. Then slowly she pulled out the chain that was around her neck. It was a heart locket. "I have no scar there, but I do wear this locket with my father's picture in it to give me comfort. Does that meet your curiosity you jerk?"

The look on Archer's face was one Allie had never seen before. He was instant to reach out and take hold of her locket. Allie was afraid to move as he slowly opened the locket to look at the picture. She watched him closely as he stared at the picture for a minute. Then his eyes lifted up and locked right into hers. For several minutes nothing was said between them as they just stared at each other. For Allie she found that she couldn't turn away from Archer as it felt like time had stopped. Archer was slowly lowering the locket back down, and the minute his hand brushed against her skin, Allie had the shivers. Still her eyes stayed on his as she refused to look away. His words however were wrong. "You need a picture of me in there too Allie, since I am always on your mind."

Allie was instant to snap out of the trance she was in as she brushed Archer's hand away and started to button the one button again. She was suddenly angry that he would suggest such a thing. "Well this has been a treat Archer like always, but I have better places to be."

Allie turned and closed her locker as she was ready to make her departure. Archer was not to be dismissed as he spoke. "How's your side doing Allie?"

Allie froze as she slowly turned to look at him. No one at school knew about her side. "How do you know about that?" Allie was quick to question him.

Archer smiled big and suddenly Allie was preparing herself for a big blow. He had to know their parents were dating. "Hmm, well I did come visit you at the hospital. You were a little out of it. You even admitted your true feelings about me."

Allie felt the blood drain out of her face as she remembered the dream she had about Archer. What if it was all true? "I don't believe it." She said so quickly as her heart started to pound.

Archer seemed to lean in closer to her. "You were begging me to kiss you Allie. I had the nurse come in to check your meds to discover you had torn your stitches."

"I would never beg you," Allie stated as her heart was pounding in her ears.

"You did beg for a kiss Allie. So admit it, deep down you want me." Archer said with a smug smile on his face.

Allie blinked as suddenly she knew she needed to get away from Archer. He was doing this on purpose to her. Taking a calming breath, Allie leaned forward towards him bringing her hand up and touching his chest. "Your right Archer, how can I refuse your charm," she said while slowly petting the front of his shirt right over his heart. "Every girl here loves it when you grace them with your time. They all beg for your attention and crave it." She looked up at him batting her eye lashes as Archer was smiling at her. "It is just a shame I choose a frog over you," Allie said in the next instant as she pushed Archer back to make her escape and start walking down the hallway.

Archer stared after Allie with a smile on his face. He missed her fighting spirit and was glad to see it back. He turned his head to see Aaron there shaking his head. He was also holding back a laugh as he spoke, "I got to admit that was good."

Archer was still smiling, "yes it was good. For a minute I thought she planned to seduce me in the hallway. So today Allie gets a point. However you need to find out if she is going to the party and where it is. If she goes it needs to be crashed or else I can't promise what I will do if one of them touches my Allie."

Aaron nodded at Archer and then moved in the direction Allie went. Deep down if Allie went to that party he was going to make sure he was there. Slowly Archer turned and walked in the opposite direction of them. His demons were calm with the idea of Aaron watching over his Allie, but those jocks were going to be introduced to them soon. Just rounding the corner, Archer nearly collided with Janice. She had her hands over her chest as she glared at him and for several minutes it made Archer wonder if she had seen what had happened. Her words confirmed it, "I swear your courting is all wrong. You realize she is clueless about your feelings."

Archer sucked in a breath as his first thought was to act like nothing had happened. "I have no idea what you are talking about Janice," Archer told her as he walked passed her thinking she was a nag. However her laughter made him stop and look at her funny.

She smiled at him making him think that Janice was far from human and it would explain Matt's attraction. She actually walked up and patted his chest for a second as she spoke. "Don't be foolish Archer I'm rooting for the two of you ever since the movies. Maybe she is the one for you, and you two are the ones that can save us all." Janice didn't say anything else. She walked away from Archer as he stared after her confused.

Allie took her seat in the last class of the day still feeling scattered brain after her run in with Archer. Somehow working on the yearbook made her feel better, and it let her take pictures. Now she was staring into space thinking that Archer really did show up to see her in the hospital, but the question was why. Lost in thought about it, Allie jumped when a hand covered her eyes and a male voice whispered in her ear a guess who. Knowing who it was because he sat next to her and had been way too friendly, Allie smiled as she spoke. "Hmm, it can't be Jessie, can it?"

His laughter was instant as he took a seat next to her wearing his football shirt. For the pass weak the senior had been flirty with her, and she couldn't understand why. He was a good looking guy and most likely had a string of girls following him around like a bunch of puppies, but yet it seemed like he had zeroed in on her. "So how is my Allie girl today?" He asked as he smiled at her.

For several minutes Allie thought about pouring her soul out and getting everything off her chest, but that would be awkward. So Allie kept it simple. "I had a run in with my arch enemy, who now has it in his head that I want him."

Jessie seemed to study her for a minute, and then he responded. "I'm having a hard time believing that you of all people have an arch enemy. You're way too sweet. You want me to gather a few guys and take care of him so he leaves you alone?"

This time Allie laughed. "No, Archer would see that as a turn on and continue to torment me."

Jessie blinked at her as he spoke, "Archer Stevens?"

"Yes that is the devil in the flesh," Allie quoted as she puffed air.

"So that is why the guy with all the piercing hangs with you." He chuckled for a minute. "You do realize that he is friends with Archer," Jessie told her.

Allie felt confused for a minute. "Aaron and Archer are not friends. If I remember right Aaron is friends with Archer's older brother. To be honest I don't think that they like each other. Besides Aaron is a saint compared to Archer."

Allie's comment had Jessie laughing as if he knew something Allie didn't. Allie couldn't help but start to fidget with the ring on her finger drawing Jessie's attention. "You know I have to ask about that ring. I did notice that Archer had one similar, so care to explain that?"

Allie stopped fidgeting with the ring she had not been able to remove since she put on. She looked at Jessie and spoke. "It's a rare chance that I was going to skip with Aaron, that never happened, and I ended up skipping with Archer." Jessie's face grew serious as he motioned for her to continue. "It was a day we drew a moment of peace and went to play miniature golf instead. I actually had fun that day and well, we went into one of those witchy shops next to the miniature golf place. The lady inside was so nice. She gave both Archer and I matching rings as she called them protection stones. I thought nothing of it at the time, but I'm starting to think that it works. Plus I haven't been able to remove it since I placed it on."

Jessie had a strange look on his face that made Allie instantly playing with her locket for comfort. Then he slowly started to smile and lean towards her as he spoke. "So are you going to come with me to the party?" Allie was going to tell him no, but he continued to speak. "I would be honored to have a girl like you next to my side. Plus I promise to behave and act the perfect gentleman."

Allie was about to ask why he wanted her to go with him when Rebecca came in and sat down. The little blond was as outgoing as Janice but she loved the party scene too much.

"Allie is going even if I have to hog tie her. Heaven forbid she will be sitting at home on a Friday night watching some crappy movie when she can be living it up. Besides I'm ordering her to have fun, or else I will show up and bring porn to watch."

Allie's eyes went big as Rebecca smiled big at her. Jessie spoke so quickly holding back a laugh that Allie's head was spinning. "So should I come pick you up Allie around seven?"

This was happening too fast for Allie. She was looking for any excuse now to get out of it. "I have to ask my mom if I can go, she frowns at me dating."

It sounded lame, but Jessie just smiled as he spoke. "I can win any mom over, so I will be there at six. I'm not letting you back out now Allie, I got a yes."

He was smiling as he started to work. Allie looked over at Rebecca who had a bigger smile on her face. Somehow it felt like she had just got set up as she glared at her friend. Taking a deep breath, Allie had to school herself that it was a date with a senior to a party. Nothing bad was going to happen, or so she hoped considering her luck.

CHAPTER TWELVE
THE PARTY

Allie sat in front of her mirror in her room looking at herself. She had yet to tell her mom she had a date and where she was going. Instead she was trying to decide if it was a good idea at all and wished that Rebecca didn't volunteer her for this date, she wasn't ready. She had changed her clothes at least three times not knowing what to wear. Right at the moment she was in blue jeans and a black button up blouse. It would be the best casual outfit without giving Jessie the wrong idea about her.

Without warning, her door opened and her mom walked in. "Allie there's a boy downstairs named Jessie, saying that you have a date with him tonight."

"Yeah I do," Allie responded. "The girls thought it would be good if I went out."

Her mother took a seat. She looked a little concern as she spoke. "I've noticed you haven't really been going out, and you're not on the phone as much. How are you coping Allie? Is the dating thing with me awkward for you?"

Allie turned and looked at her mother. She couldn't hide the sadness even if she tried. "I miss him mom, I can't get over the outcome and wonder if I could have changed it. Maybe I need to go out and have some fun to help me forget and live. I just don't know if I am ready for it."

Her mother gave her a smile but stood up and placed her arms around Allie giving her a hug. "I miss him too baby, but he would want us to keep living. You go out with that boy downstairs and have some fun. I will be here if you need me."

Allie felt the smile on her lips from her mom's encouraging words. She seemed to nod as the two of them walked out of her room and in the living room where Jessie was. Jessie was dressed in jeans and a white shirt that buttoned up the front looking more muscular on him. He was instant to smile as she saw him looking her up and down as if he approved of what she was wearing. Allie smiled back still feeling the dread that this wasn't right, yet deep down she believed that she needed to go through with tonight. She was quick to look at her mom, "do I need to be back at a certain time?"

Her mother was still looking at Jessie, but then turned and smiled at Allie. "Please be home by midnight." Her eyes darted back to Jessie as she continued to speak. "I hope that you have a good time too, but any trouble and I expect a phone call."

Allie nodded at her mother as Jessie spoke. "She's going to have a wonderful time and I promise to have her home by midnight."

It didn't take long after that for them to move out. Jessie was the gentleman and opened the door to his mustang for Allie. Then he was sliding behind the wheel and they were off to only who knew where. The car ride itself was awkward for Allie as silence was between them. She knew she needed to talk or else she was going to want to go back home. "So where is this party at?" Allie asked hoping it would ease the awkwardness.

Jessie's smile beamed at her as it looked like his eyes were twinkling. "The party is on the outskirts of town at Wayne's house. He's invited a few of his friends over."

"Oh, so will I know anyone else there?" Allie asked next.

Jessie seemed to shrug a little as he reached over and took his hand in hers to bring up to his mouth to place a kiss on it. "You never know," was all he said as he placed her hand back down, but held onto it making Allie look at their hands.

He went back to focusing on the road and a nagging feeling started to eat away at Allie. If there was no party when she got there, she was going to use the phone and leave. Something about all of this didn't feel right to Allie, but she didn't know if it was just her or not.

Thirty minutes later, Allie was relieved to see that several cars were parked in front of a house that seemed to have no neighbors with music blaring. It made Allie take a breath and relax a little. Jessie was instant to park and then jog over to her side to open the door. He even smiled as she got out of the car looking over every inch of her again. The minute Allie was out his hands encircled her hips and made her stop to look at him. He just about pinned her as her back was suddenly against the side of his car. He was looking down at her in an embrace Allie had never been in before as she looked up at him not knowing what to do. He even started to lean in like he was about to kiss her and Allie suddenly froze up and turned her head away. His voice was right in her ear. "What's wrong Allie? Am I not allowed to kiss you?"

"I'm not ready for that Jessie," Allie said a little too quickly as she heard the little laugh in Jessie's voice as he pulled back.

"Well maybe I need to get you something to drink first, and maybe we should do some dancing. Besides I can really shake it." He responded like it didn't bother him.

Allie turned and looked at Jessie surprised by his comment. "I'd like that," she responded as he took her hand in his and led them towards the party.

Jessie remained silent on the walk to the door, but the minute it opened it seemed like he was suddenly mister meet and greet. Allie recognized some of the football players from the team as they were giving him high fives and her sly smiles. Within seconds someone had handed Allie a drink that smelled a little funny. She knew it had booze in it, but mainly just held onto it. Allie also didn't recognize most of the girls there that seemed a little tipsy. Right away Allie was ready to leave, but Jessie had other ideas as he led her through the house to where most people were dancing.

For several minutes Allie watched Jessie dance as a small smile crept on her face. He really couldn't dance. It took Allie a minute before she placed one hand on his hip and started to lead him in dancing while balancing her drink. The drink was really in her way, so she went to move and set it down. However Jessie stopped her and shook his head as he leaned in and shouted in her ear over the music. "You can't set it down you have to drink it."

Once again Allie was looking at the drink wondering about it. She had tilted it up deciding to take a little drink to try it, when suddenly Jessie had tilted it up on her forcing her to swallow nearly the whole thing or be wearing it. Allie felt the instant head rush making her dizzy as Jessie was smiling at her and leading her away from others. It didn't seem like it took long, but suddenly Allie was outside and using Jessie to keep herself upright. "What was in that drink? My head is spinning." Allie was instant to ask.

Jessie smiled as he watched her. Then he tilted her chin up and leaned in. His kiss caught Allie by surprise as he didn't answer her. Instead she felt him thrusting his tongue in her mouth as his other hand went around her waist. A moan escaped her mouth has she tried to catch her breath, but Jessie wasn't stopping. It took every ounce of muscle to bring her hands up and push Jessie back a little. It was then that she caught her breath and spoke. "Jessie I don't feel so well, will you please take me home?"

The look that crossed Jessie face looked a little like anger. Then he smiled at her. "Allie I think you just need to lay down for a bit."

"No I really want to go home, I'm not ready for this, and I'm sorry about it." Allie said next.

"Allie I'm going to take you to lie down," Jessie said with a little more force as his hand gripped her wrist tight hurting Allie a little.

"Ouch Jessie, you're hurting me," Allie said next.

Jessie seemed to lose his temper next as he slammed Allie into the wall. "Quit being such a tease Allie. I know you want me, and now you will get me."

Allie's head was starting to throb as Jessie's hands and mouth seemed to be everywhere on her. She struggled against him but was really no match at all against him. Thinking quick, Allie brought her knee up and nailed him in the crotch. Jessie winced against her as he kept her pinned. Then he held off and nailed her across the face taking her breath right out of her. Stunned that Jessie was doing this to her, Allie felt the tears leak out of her eyes because she couldn't stop him from doing what he wanted. One minute she felt sick as his hands started to tear at shirt, and the next he was no longer there.

Allie blinked to wonder what had just happened, and ended up seeing Jessie lying against a different wall passed out. Then her eyes noticed the guy off to her right just looking at her. His dark eyes were piercing right through her, but Allie knew him instantly. "Are you ok?" He asked her as she stared at him.

Tears leaked out of Allie's eyes as she wanted to cry into a ball. Yet she responded, "thank you."

He moved towards her as Allie kept looking into his eyes. He stopped in front of her and lifted his hand up to wipe away the tears that were escaping. "You're welcome Allie," he said. "How about I take you home?"

Allie couldn't stop the emotion that took her over. Her arms went right around Archer's brother as she kept telling him thank you. He was hesitant at first, but then slowly encircled his arms around her as he spoke in a whisper. "You're the first to ever willing embrace me. I can see why you're special now. I wonder if my brother will care if I steal you from him."

Allie's head looked up to lock again in his dark eyes. "Please don't tell Archer any of this. I wouldn't be able to stand up to him if he knew. The things he would say…"

Allie didn't finish her sentence because he placed two fingers over her mouth. "My name is Kane, Allie. This will be our secret. Besides if my little brother knew about this, that block head over there passed out would not be breathing." Allie looked confused for a minute as Kane smiled at her. "Now let's get out of here. Why don't we stop and get you some tea to calm your nerves a little before I get you home."

Allie looked down at her shirt noting that it was torn at the bottom and a few buttons were missing. She was instant to try to fix it, which had Kane snorting a laugh at her attempt. She looked back up at him with big eyes as she spoke. "I look a mess and I'm not sure I should go anywhere but home looking this way."

His smile was instant as he spoke, "I have an extra shirt in my car you can wear. I keep it in there for emergences but it will be a little big on you."

Allie seemed to nod her head as Kane led her away from the party. His hand was resting on her lower back as he directed her away while an emotion he had never felt before seemed to root inside him. For once lust was not tempting him and death felt protective of this girl. It confused him as he placed her inside his black sedan. Then death kicked in as he walked to the back taking out the white shirt. He was instant to look at the party house and think burn. His smile grew as he saw the small flame start. Then he walked to the driver's side and climbed in before Allie would notice that the party was about to go up in flames.

Twenty minutes later, Allie sat in a Starbucks sipping some cha tea. Kane's shirt was big on her, but somehow looked cute on her. She felt better than she had moments ago, and seemed completely comfortable around Kane. Kane on the other hand seemed like he was in deep thought about something and remained quiet. "Do you need to get something off your chest," Allie nearly blabbed at him in a quick rush as she took a sip of her tea.

Kane's dark eyes looked up at her as a smile touched his lips. "Just something about you Allie that nags me in my mind yet makes me so calm. I suddenly have a strong urge to keep you safe and slay anyone that hurts you."

Allie stared at him for a minute as she sat her tea down. "I think I like you better than Archer." His head snapped up and seemed fully alert as she continued. "Something about you seems peaceful and calm to be around."

A smile touched Kane's lips as he stared at Allie. He was tempted to steal Allie from his little brother. Instead he spoke, "I need to go wash my hands I will be right back."

He got up and headed to the bathroom once Allie had nodded her head. Inside he took a breath as his demons seemed to be talking at once. Lust was going off on the oracle, but death was laughing. His mind was a mess as he was trying to figure out what Allie meant to him.

Allie sat alone for several minutes as she continued to sip her tea. She was trying not to think at all, because she didn't know what would happen if Kane didn't show up. Right at the moment he was her knight in shiny armor. Taking another sip, Allie almost jumped when she noticed Aaron's cousin Fred suddenly take a seat across from her with a smile on his face. Allie was quick to set her cup down gracefully without coughing or choking on her tea. "Fur fur you scared me, is Aaron with you?"

He actually laughed as his eyes seemed to be twinkling. "No Allie, I'm here with Archer." Dread hit Allie instantly as Fred smiled bigger at her. "We just walked in when I noticed you sitting here sipping by the smell of it some herbal tea. However I will comment on the shirt, I know it is not yours, so what happen?"

Allie's heart was pounding. She even started to look to see where Archer was. She noticed him instantly at the counter ordering a drink. She was instant to look down trying to think of anything to avoid Archer. However she wouldn't be able to if Fred was sitting across from her. "Ok long story short, I'm here with Kane."

Fred's smile got even bigger as Allie heard some girls across the way make ah noises. Granted Fred had it in the looks department, Allie was counting down until Archer would be there. "So where is Kane?"

Kane's voice came out of nowhere, "I was washing my hands why are you here and in my seat?"

Fred actually laughed as he spoke to Kane. "I just came from an awesome bon fire. I think it had a grand total of six fire trucks, guess all those kids were lucky to get out in time. Archer wanted a coffee, so we stopped in here, and then I saw Allie wearing your shirt. Can you blame me for taking your seat?"

"You're too nosey for your own good Fury," Kane responded as Allie realized he used his nick name. "Allie, are you ready to go home?"

Allie was more than ready to leave before Archer noticed her that she nodded. She got up rather quickly hoping to get lucky, but she wasn't. Archer's voice was instant, "why are you here Allie?"

Slowly Allie turned to face Archer. He was scolding at her that it made her a little angry. "None of your business Archer, last time I checked this was a free country."

His lips tilted up in amusement as he spoke again. "Ok Allie, so why are you wearing my brother's shirt?"

Allie noted how both Kane and Fury remained quiet. She had a feeling both of them were enjoying the show. "Again Archer none of your business," Allie told Archer without losing eye contact.

Archer took a step closer to her so Allie would have to look up at him. His green eyes were blazing has he seemed not amused by her answer. Kane's voice was instant, "little brother, I promised Allie I would take her home now."

Archer held up his hand to Kane while he glared down at Allie who was looking up at him glaring back. "I will take her home after she tells me why she is in here with her wearing your shirt."

It hit Allie then. Archer was jealous. She blinked twice not believing it, and then suddenly she was shaking her head slowly trying not to laugh. "Are you jealous of your brother Archer?"

Archer's hand came up and Allie could tell he was controlling his anger. The action made her want to taunt him more. However Allie just smiled at him until he narrowed his eyes. "Why would I be jealous of my brother Allie? You're nothing to him, just someone he took pity on for the night."

Allie was instant to gasp at Archer's comment as he wore a smug little smile. It made her narrow her eyes at him seeing the grin light up his eyes. "Hmm pity, shame he told me he should steal me away from you. Coarse anyone is an improvement from you."

His smile vanished instantly as he moved his eye contact over Allie's shoulder to stare at Kane who was holding back a laugh. Allie couldn't help but look at Kane as well. His smile was downright sexy as he seemed to be enjoying himself. Archer spoke again drawing Allie's attention, "Kane why is Allie in your shirt?"

Kane was still smiling as he answered. "Little brother, her shirt was a little torn, and I couldn't have her come here with me like that."

Archer's response was instant, "why was her shirt torn?"

"It's none of your business Archer." Allie said instantly as she went to walk away from him only to have him suddenly in her path and blocking her. "Get out of my way Archer, I'm not staying her a minute longer to listen to this."

Archer didn't miss a beat. He blocked her from going around him, and then swooped down and picked her up to carry over his shoulder. Allie was shocked as she heard Fury's laughter, that for once her mouth failed her. She couldn't speak as he carried her out of the coffee shop and then set her down against a car as he invaded her personal space and nearly molded her front. Her eyes looked up at his, but they were so very close that she could smell his cologne and the heat coming off his body. His lips were inches from hers as his eyes were locked on hers. His voice was instant as he spoke. "Who tore your shirt Allie?" Allie was about to tell him where to stick it, when he continued. "If you dare tell me to mind my business again, I will find a way to make you talk, and I will enjoy it."

Flashes of Allie's dream came in her head as she remembered him kissing her. She wondered at that moment what it would feel like for him to kiss her. His mouth was so close to her that she could smell the minty taste of it as she licked her lips nervously. His hand was moving up her side, holding her in place as Allie's heart began to pound. Then suddenly she answered him. "Why don't you go ask Kane since he pulled the creep off of me and got me out of there?"

For several seconds, Archer's green eyes went darker on Allie. Then he pulled back away from her, but did not let go of her hips. "You went to that party with Jessie."

"So what if I did," Allie responded instantly. "It's none of your business. Now get your hands off of me."

Archer moved so quickly that Allie was shocked. His hands gripped her hips and pulled her right into his body away from the car. His head came down and his lips were inches from hers that Allie really thought that he was going to kiss her. "Little brother," Kane's voice came out of nowhere making Archer freeze as Allie's own hands were on his chest to steady herself, "I promised Allie I would take her home, besides you might want to check out that bon fire with Fury."

Allie's eyes were locked on Archer's as he seemed conflicted. He even growled before he moved away from her as if she burned. "Take her home brother, but do not linger."

Kane smiled at the two of them as he offered his hand to Allie. She was a little slow in taking it as she felt drawn to look at Archer. Archer had turned away from her as Kane spoke, "have fun little brother, I promise not to linger."

Archer turned to see that Allie had moved easily into Kane's embrace as he led her to his car. He was counting as he realized he almost lost it and consumed Allie in a parking lot. She needed to stay pure, and if his brother didn't interfere, she wouldn't be. Taking another breath he heard Fury move up beside him as he spoke. "She has firer, I like it. So are we going to a bon fire that your brother started to clean it up or torture a few souls?"

Archer felt the grin on his face as he spoke. "Actually we will make sure they all survived. Then from this day forward little Jessie is going to start having problems. He's going to pray that he never touched Allie to begin with."

Fury was smiling big as it seemed evil, "well you won't mind if I slap him around for hitting her then will you?"

Archer's head nearly snapped in Fury's direction. "He dared to hit her, how do you know this?"

Fury was still grinning, but it looked evil. "Kane told me. Allie put up a good fight too and got in some good hits, but when he hit her, Kane lost it a little and knocked his ass out."

Archer was steaming. "Jessie is going to die in the most painful way tonight."

Archer strolled over to the driver side of his car as Fury started to laugh. His tail even started to come out, and he had to contain it so he could get in. Within minutes they were heading towards the fire that his brother had started.

CHAPTER THIRTEEN
UNFORGIVABLE ACTS

Allie felt like a zombie as she moved from class to class. She had heard the news in first period that Jessie had been in a fatal car crash, so the whole school seemed like it was in mourning. However the events of the night before and how he had acted, she just couldn't feel sorry for him. She had a slight bruise on her cheek from where he had hit her. Currently makeup was covering it up so no one noticed, but the slight touch made it hurt like hell. She just couldn't be around her friends today. They all knew Jessie and would be talking about it. Rebecca might ask her if the date happen, and then what would Allie say.

Sitting in third period again, Allie found herself wanting to lay her head down and sleep. She didn't care that Archer was glaring at her again, and Aaron was watching her closely. She just wanted to close her eyes.

Archer watched Allie lay her head on the desk and slowly close her eyes, he could see the bruise on her cheek as clear as day even though she had use makeup to cover it. Jessie deserved his painful death for doing that Allie, and Archer had enjoyed every minute of it. Looking back at Aaron, he could see the concern mirrored on his face about Allie. He had met Fury and him at the fire and had found Jessie still passed out. No one had known that they had removed Jessie, and no one had known where he was at or Allie. So the set up looked like he had took her home, and then lost control of his car as it went off the road to land in the back of a parked semi carrying explosive gases. He became a crispy critter, and Archer was satisfied with the outcome. However today as he looked at Allie, he knew she wasn't coping well. He was quick to push with his mind to Aaron to tell him he didn't want Allie here today. In fact he was encouraging Aaron to take her somewhere that she could have fun. Aaron looked at him a little shocked but nodded his head. The action made Archer feel better as he looked back down at Allie. Her eyes were still closed as she was exposing that bruised cheek to him. He wanted to kill Jessie all over again until suddenly he noticed a little blue light under Allie's skin running over the bruise. It made him lean in closer as he was not sure what he was seeing. While she slept, this little blue light moved faster over the bruise as he watched it start to shrink. He couldn't take his eyes off of it as it was slowly healing Allie. He even started to reach out to touch it wondering what it was when the bell rang suddenly making him jump and Allie wake instantly.

Allie eyes opened instantly to look at Archer who looked like he was about to touch her. Not only that, he was glued looking at her cheek. Allie was instantly embraced has he must of seen the bruise. She turned away from his shocked expression so quickly and started to get up that she nearly collided into Aaron, who reached over and took her bag. "Come on Allie today your eating lunch with me, and we are going somewhere fun."

It was a command from Aaron, but she never felt so relieved in her whole life. She just nodded her head and started to follow him. At the door she turned to look back at Archer. He still looked stunned, and Allie knew the next few days were not going to be easy with him. After last night in the coffee shop, she wouldn't be able to picture what he would do now that he had seen the bruise. So she turned and continued to follow Aaron knowing that he would keep her safe.

It took Archer a few minutes to get over the shock. He still had no clue what that light was that was healing Allie. He needed to talk to someone that did. Getting up quickly, Archer made his way to his car. He knew where he was heading. It took him about ten minutes to get to the little witch's house, but he knew she would be here home schooling her daughter. Archer didn't even knock when he got to the door he just walked right in like he owned the place, and he did. The witch was sitting on the couch with her daughter across from her.

The daughter had a notebook in front of her as her eyes looked all white and she was drawing something. Archer knew the witch's daughter was given the gift to be the next oracle, but something was off about her that didn't make Archer feel comfortable. The witch held up her coco skinned hand signaling him to be quiet. Archer was quiet as he took in the daughter's coco skin and earthy brown hair. Just looking at her it would be hard to tell what ethic she really was because she could pass for many. Then suddenly her white eyes turned to a rich emerald green signaling the vision was over. Her eyes locked on Archer has she spoke, "I saw two blue lights, but there should be only one."

The witch's voice was instant. "That is very good Ellie, you have done well. We have a visitor now, and he has questions."

Ellie seemed to get up and looked like she was going to leave when Archer spoke, "I just saw one of the blue lights."

Ellie's head snapped up and stared right at him, and then she looked at her mother who had risen up to look at Archer as well. It seemed like both of them were holding their breath. Archer was growing frustrated from it as he spoke, "tell me what it means."

"Are you sure that you want to know the answer to that?" The witch seemed to ask him.

That statement made Archer mad. "Would I be here if I didn't want to know? Someone I care deeply for was hurt and a blue light appeared healing her. Why did a blue light appear to heal her?"

It wasn't the witch that spoke, it was the daughter. "Does she wear the same stone on her finger that you do?"

Archer was instant to look at his hand and where the ring rested. "Yes she does so what."

"It's a fire protection stone, very powerful one too. Once on it can never be removed until death, but the question is why you both have one when there should be only one."

"I don't care for your riddles Ellie, I demand answers. Why was there a damn blue light healing her skin?" Archer said as Wraith was leaking through wanting to hit her for punishment.

The witch cleared her throat as she spoke, "Ellie head upstairs while I talk to the young War about what he wishes to know." Ellie nodded her head and walked up the stairs. Archer watched her noticing something was different about Ellie. He could almost smell it on her skin, but could not place it. Mentally he thought he should send Kane here to investigate. The witch spoke again drawing his attention away from Ellie. "She is still learning. I'm blessed to have a child that was gifted so."

"Why does the one I love have a blue light witch, no more riddles?" Archer nearly growled.

She gestured for him to sit and Archer did so even though Wraith wanted to explode. The minute he sat, the witch began. "Ellie doesn't understand her visions yet. She has another power that scares me deeply that I do not understand either. Her visions as of late have been about a boy that is the element of fire, but he is not complete. Almost like he is not the element of fire but the decoy to make you think he is. He has the blue light running under his skin, and lately he has been reaching out to another, another blue light. Ellie has not seen more on it or she is refusing to share it with me. The element of air is blocking her vision from me, and keeping the secret from me. He's been talking to her, and I do not like it. As for the blue light you have seen on your beloved, it can either be the ring healing her because she has some of our blood in her, or she has been touched by an angel. If the last is the case, then you should know that they plan to steal her from you. I just don't know when they will do it."

Archer sucked in a breath as he remembered Aaron telling him about the arch angel watching over her. "Do they know I plan to take her as my bride?"

The witch looked a little shocked by the statement, but covered it well as she responded. "They know all, and never doubt that."

Ellie was listening to her mother and the young War talk below. She heard Air in her head instantly. "My love what has you stressed? I can feel your heart pounding."

She was quick to answer back in her head. "War is here talking with my mother. I know who the element of fire is now. She has yet to come into her powers. They might be locked like mine. However it seems like War is concerned I think he is in love with her. He plans to make her his bride."

Air was silent for a minute as Ellie retreated quietly to her room. Then suddenly he spoke, "how can war love fire? They have always been mortal enemies."

"He doesn't know what she is, but I don't know what he will do when he does. This is dangerous because he plans to take her as his bride. The outcome of that can change the whole game plan she might turn on us and choose him. I need to focus on this and see if I can see the outcome. The red witch has blessed the both of them." Ellie stressed as she sat on her bed and looked up at the ceiling.

"Easy my love," Air responded to her. "We still have time, and the red witch never does anything without a reason. Fire and War might be the key we need to focus on to stop the destruction of humanity."

Aaron took Allie to a paintball field. Both of them were dressed in overalls and jackets to cover every inch of them.

They also had goggles on to protect them. Allie was grinning from this mainly because it was her idea to begin with as Aaron had a look of dread across his face. The place was crowded with grown men having a little too much fun as it seemed like a battlefield was going on. They were quickly placed onto teams for the next round, as they were both placed on the green team. However the blue team looked serious as they stared them down. Allie was the only girl on the team, but she smiled at the others as Aaron looked worried. He was also staring at one on the blue team that looked like he was glaring a hole into Aaron. Allie watched his hand gestures toward Aaron has he signaled that he would be taking him out first. Allie burst open in laughter drawing attention of most the blue team. She looked right at the one that had threatened to take Aaron out first and gestured back he would be the first to fall. Not only did she gesture to the rest of the team that they didn't have a chance, she laughed. Aaron was quick to whisper in her ear, "What are you doing? These guys are most likely pros at this."

Allie laughed more as she spoke out loud, "I'm a pro at this game none of them have a chance."

Aaron looked at her funny as it was announce that their game was to start next. He was wondering what had happened to the Allie he knew and who was sitting next to him. A member of the staff walked up to Allie and spoke directly to her. "Welcome back Allie, we are all sorry to hear the news on what happened to your father. I hope you're not here to let out some steam. I'm not sure we can handle some ego blows again. However, someone is leading the blue team that has wanted to challenge you a while back."

"Oh really who Roy," Allie asked as Aaron felt shocked learning a secret about Allie.

Roy pointed to the guy standing in the dark corner. He seemed to step forward into the light. Both Allie and Aaron took in his long black hair tied back in a pony tail and his handsome face. His eyes were piercing as they looked like a light amethyst that sparkled. Aaron was shocked to see the angel and suddenly very worried as Allie seemed to shrug like he was nothing. She had to be clueless to know what they were about to go up against. His eyes then turned and looked at Aaron. His eyebrow rose up as if he was questioning him. Aaron felt fear slide over him as he knew he couldn't protect Allie against him, and he wondered what the angel was planning. Allie snorted next to him as she covered a laugh. "Ok Aaron stay next to me, I will protect you from this group of bad shooters."

Aaron looked down at Allie like she grew a third head as she smiled up at him. Roy spoke next. "Alright you may enter through your doors now may the best team win."

Allie moved through the door quicker than the others as Aaron stayed close behind her. Something had changed while they were waiting for their turn. She could hear Aaron's heart pounding to keep up. It didn't distract her at all as she continued to move through the maze to connect with members of the blue team. She spotted the first one as he seemed to be scouting in the bush waiting for one of her team. Allie was quick to scout the area noting that he was alone, but the others were not far behind him. She crouched with Aaron next to her and pointed out the location of the blue team member. Aaron didn't wait he fired and took out the first person making Allie smile. They moved as a team with Aaron nearly on Allie's butt. When she spotted the guy that made threats to take Aaron out first, Allie showed no mercy. She nailed him twice before he realized it making him swear as he realized who had taken him out. Within seconds Allie had took out two blue team members as they moved closer to the blue team flag. She listened to the others call out once someone was down and the green team was heading to victory.

Aaron's heart was pounding as he wondered where the angel was and how come Allie was so good at this. They rounded the corner and he noticed the flag, but Allie stopped him from moving. Her voice was soft as she spoke. "He's here," came out as she smiled and started to search the tree line.

Aaron could feel the angel watching them, but he couldn't figure out where. Allie gestured for him to go left as she was going to go right, but he shook his head. He wasn't going to leave her. The action made Allie roll her eyes at him and then gesture to follow her. They had only gone a few feet when Allie stopped him. The angel was standing out in the open and looking right at them. This made Allie smile as she rose up and slowly started to walk towards him in the open and made Aaron panic. He was quick to raise his gun and fire at the angel, only to suddenly have a shot of paint nail him by the angel sending him sailing on his butt. He was shocked as he watched Allie dodge a shot and then nail the angel as he flew back to land on his butt laughing. She was quick to grab the flag and declare victory for the green team signally the buzzard to end the game.

Laughing she walked over to the angel and offered her hand to help him up. The angel was laughing too making Aaron feel confused. When he was on his feet, he stopped laughing and looked right at her. "You're better than I thought, but why are you hanging out with the happy trigger finger on the ground over there."

Aaron saw Allie's smile as she looked at him and responded, "He's one of my best friends."

The angel frowned instantly as he looked at Aaron. As Allie started to walk towards him, the angel looked like he was going to grab her. Aaron was quick to get up and race to Allie's side to stand between the angel and her. This made the angel cock his head but smile at Aaron, as Allie turned to look at Aaron. The angel then spoke, "I want a rematch but next time we bring our own team players."

Allie was laughing as she spoke, "what you want me to bring all my girlfriends out here and bruise all your friends' egos?"

The angel was laughing but then he looked right at Aaron. "Actually I was thinking his friends. My friends would really like that."

"Oh geez," Allie said as she rolled her eyes before Aaron could speak. "Well this has been fun, but no rematches with someone with a grudge."

The angel looked at Allie funny as she placed her hand in Aaron's and started to pull him away. The angel's voice was almost instant. "Shame Adam would love the challenge."

Allie stopped instantly and turned to look back at the guy she just beat. He was smiling at her as she slowly started to think she was going insane. He was smiling at her like she knew who he was talking about, but Allie shook her head not wanting to think a name was haunting her. Aaron was also staring at her and she could tell that he was worried. She spoke instantly. "I'm a little hungry, will you take me to lunch."

Aaron seemed to nod as the angel laughed. His voice echoed out as the two of them walked away. "She has you whipped, nothing but a lap dog little demon boy."

Anger simmered in Allie as she turned and looked back at the man that was taunting Aaron. She glared at him as he stopped laughing and really looked at her. A sly smile rode up on his lips as he said one word, "Allie." Then it was like he vanished making Allie stop and look for him.

The whole act made Allie uneasy as Aaron had stopped to look with her. Her voice was instant. "Where did he go and how did he know my name?"

Aaron spoke too quickly, "time we left Allie, this doesn't feel right." Allie nodded, she couldn't agree more.

CHAPTER FOURTEEN
SOMETHING SO SIMPLE

Archer was having a hard believing Aaron's story about Allie. It was even harder for him to believe that she beat an angel and he showed good sportsmanship. However Archer didn't like the fact that the angel dared to taunt her using her name and a vanishing act on top of that. Allie had to think she was going insane with all that was happening. He watched her from the distance as she seemed in thought about something. The whole thing made him frown. He hated Allie having to go through with all of this. He just wanted to take her and lock her up where she would be safe, instead he had to share her with all of these things here. Another year he told himself, as he watched Aaron walk up to her and lead her away from her group.

Taking a breath Archer continued to follow them. The football team seniors still had their eyes on Allie. It didn't even matter that they lost a player. As Archer followed them around the corner he spotted two of the seniors. The quarterback Josh

Webb was quick to step in Allie's path to make her stop. She did stop as Archer strain to listen to her voice.

"Hey Allie," Josh's voice brought Allie out of the fog she had been in all day.

Allie seemed to slowly pull out of it as she looked up to notice that he was in her path and nearly blocking her. "Hi Josh," Allie was quick to say as she was glad Aaron was next to her.

He smiled as his blue eyes seemed to twinkle. "How are you today Allie?"

"I'm ok we were just heading for our next class to study before the test. Well, talk to later Josh," Allie responded to dismiss him and get to her next class.

Allie fully noted how Josh was staring her down from that comment. For several minutes she wondered if he blamed her for Jessie's death. "So I was wondering if you had plans tonight," he asked her making her blink wondering what he was planning.

She was going to respond when Aaron did. "She has plans tonight and tomorrow. In fact she is booked up for the rest of the year, so go find another girl."

Allie turned her head to look at Aaron surprised to see him glaring at Josh. She looked back at Josh to see the same glare from him at Aaron. Then Josh turned that heated glare on to Allie. "How about I pick you up tonight at six Allie, and we go see a little movie?"

Allie felt speechless and a little shocked. She could feel Aaron getting angry next to her. Before Allie could respond it seemed like Archer's voice came out of nowhere. "She can't tonight Josh. Her mother has been secretly dating my father, and they are having dinner at my house tonight to break the news gently to us, except we all know don't we Allie."

Allie spun around so quickly nearly startled as her hand was instantly on her chest. Her locket was verily giving her comfort as Archer's glare was directly on her. Not only that but he looked mad about the whole thing. He then shook his head as he continued to speak. "You knew they were dating didn't you Allie? This explains a lot about your behavior over the past couple of days since you have been back."

Allie went to open her mouth to respond but ended up closing it. She was lost for words. This was all awkward as Josh spoke not caring about the speech Archer had just delivered, "hmm so what about tomorrow then Allie?"

Instantly Allie thought Josh was persistent. She even wondered why he wanted to go out with her. What was so special about her? "I'm sorry Josh, but I can't date anyone right now. Not even do something as simple as a movie. Jessie was the last one I went on a date with and well…"

Josh reached out and lifted her chin up as he stared right at her. "Tomorrow at six, and I'm not taking no for an answer." He then turned and walked away before Allie could respond.

In fact she was staring after him as Archer was instant to speak. "Wow Allie is that like your first date of someone asking you? Big player like Josh most likely won't even want to watch a movie but make out with you and then spread rumors the next day about how you are a slut. He's a great choice to date."

Anger surged through Allie. "Do you actually have a purpose on being here Archer? Shouldn't you be devouring one of my friends or something? Do you actually think I have control over who your father and my mother date?" Then she looked at Aaron and spoke before Archer could respond. "Do you have plans tomorrow at six?"

Aaron's lips tilted in a smile as Archer started to laugh drawing her attention. "Oh that is rich Allie. Best laugh I had today," Archer responded as he turned and walked off.

Allie stared after him for a few confused until she heard Aaron speak. "I'd love to be the chaperon on the date you don't want to go on. Should I bring my cousin too?"

Allie actually laughed as she spoke. "Yea would love to see Fred and the look on Josh's face when he sees him."

They both continued walking as Archer watched them from around the corner. He was relieved in so many ways. Josh would have her deflowered in seconds if he was alone with Allie, but with Aaron and Fury there, Josh wasn't going to have a chance. He couldn't help but smile as he thought of Allie in his home tonight having dinner with his family. She really had no clue that this dinner was the first step for her to be recognized as his future bride. He just hoped that it went smoothly as he pushed away from Allie waiting until she saw his home that would soon be hers. In fact Archer was counting down the hours until she would be there.

Allie couldn't believe the size of Archer's home when her mother pulled the car up to his house. The thing almost looked like an estate with no neighbors. To make matters even better, a man walked out to the car and opened both of their doors before they had a chance. Allie was stunned at the wealth because she never would have guessed it.

Her mother looked stunning in a navy dress that molded her every curve. Allie felt like she couldn't hold a candle to her mother, as she was wearing a dress her mother had got her of a deep purple that seemed perfect for her as it molded her top and then flirted around her legs. Her mother also took her hand and led her to the door that opened by itself. Inside the house itself, Allie stopped stunned by its beauty. Archer's home was beautiful.

The sudden bang made Allie turn her head to see a man struggling down the stairway. He looked weak with fever and illness, and Allie was instant to move towards him. Just has she reached the stairway, he tripped and started to fall, but Allie moved quickly and caught him. Her voice was instant, "let me help you. Where are you heading?"

He seemed to look up right into her eyes, and Allie could tell instantly how ill he was. Yet he looked a lot like Archer, and Allie knew instantly this had to be his other brother. His voice sounded strong and powerful as his eyes twinkled over. "In your arms seems like the best place, but I need to make it to the dining area."

Allie was instant to frown as she thought that Archer's dad was most likely forcing his children to be at this dinner, and the one she was helping should be in bed. "You know what, if you rather go back up to your bed, I will help you, plus I will bring you your dinner. You don't have to dine with us, we understand."

He actually smiled at her as he spoke, "I like you Allie. You have fire. If my bonehead brother messes this up, I'd love to have you as mine. Your soul is even more beautiful than the woman I am looking at. However I will be fine, this too will pass and soon I will be myself again."

Allie let him use her has a crutch as he got them going in the direction needed. Her mother was silent as she followed them. It made Allie wonder what he meant but she didn't say anything until she got him in the dining room and him seated in a chair where he caught his breath. Just when she was about to ask, Kane's voice came out of nowhere. "Allie it is good to see you again. I see you have met Price."

Allie looked at another doorway to see Kane dressed all in black but smiling at her. In fact his smile looked a little evil as it slid over her and then moved to her mother. Price's words were instant as they drew Allie's attention. "It's ok Allie, I will protect you from him," he said with a wink to her.

It made Allie smile at him as she spoke to him. "You get too tired, and I will help you back to your room. Just say the word," she said back with a wink.

Price was instant to laugh which had Allie smiling as she looked back at Kane. His dark eyes looked shocked but his lips tilted up in a smile as he moved closer to her. In fact he stopped on the other side of Price and held his arms open like he wanted a hug. Allie didn't think, she moved right over to him and hugged him as his arms closed around her. One of his hands drifted right under her dress and cupped her butt as he held her tighter shocking Allie a little before he let her go with a big grin on his face. "I've actually missed your company," he said as she stepped away.

"Well you can continue to miss her company," Archer's voice came out of nowhere as he sounded extremely mad to Allie.

Allie turned to see her mother's shocked face and Archer's heated glare behind her. However Archer wasn't alone, his father and what Allie assumed his sister was with him. Archer's father was instant to take Allie's mother's hand and lead her to a seat towards the head of the table. Once her mother was seated, he spoke. "It is nice to meet you officially Allie. I see you met Kane and Price, and you know Archer. My only daughter," he gestured to the girl that looked stunning as she took a seat, "Lacy."

Allie looked at her and gave her a little smile as she noticed everyone moving to a seat. It dawned on her in seconds that her seat was next to Archer, and on the other side of the table. Archer seemed to watch her as she moved slowly closer to him and taking the seat next to him. Once seated, Kane sat across from her and seemed to have a huge smile on his face. His stare was also making her uncomfortable, until it seemed the cooking staff walked in and started to place dishes on the table. It didn't take long for everyone to dig in as it was silent while they all ate. Once the food was cleared and everyone finished, Allie found herself staring at her mother and Archer's dad. Her mother wore a smile, and for the first time Allie could see that she was happy.

Looking down at the table cloth, Allie took a breath realizing this was what was best for her mother. Her hand drifted up instantly as her fingers stroke the locket. Kane's voice caught her attention, "what is wrong Allie?"

Allie looked back up at Kane to notice his strange look and Price's look of wonder. Her face looked in deep thought as she answered. "Sometimes you have to except things for what they are because nothing is going to change it from the coarse it is on."

Kane's fist hit the table hard as his glare became heated making Allie jump. His voice was instant making Allie jump again, "bullshit." He was instant to stand up and walk out of the room without looking at anyone.

Allie's eyes were big as she looked over at her mother who was staring at her looking shocked. Price on the other hand started to laugh drawing everyone's attention. Allie's head snapped towards him as his eyes twinkled looking at her. "Allie would you be so kind and help me back to my room," he said next.

Without even responding Allie stood up only for Archer to reach out and grab her arm. His voice was instant, "we need to talk afterwards, its important."

Allie just nodded her head as she made her way to Price and helped him out of his chair. He really seemed to use her as a crutch as they slowly made their way out of the dining room. Once they started up the stairs he spoke, "Kane isn't mad about your mother and my father dating, he got mad over your comment to him."

"Why," Allie asked as they made it to the top of the stairs.

This made Price chuckle, but also gave him a series of coughs with it. It also took him a few minutes to respond as he pointed her towards a hallway. Allie continued to help him down the hallway as he responded. "As a joke Kane went and talked to a woman that claimed to be a witch and could tell him his future. He told me what she said, and Allie your word for word at the table was part of it, except she told him the one that told him that would be the one he would never be able to have because she would bring him his destruction. This door here Allie," Price directed her as Allie opened the door and helped him towards his bed.

"That is crazy Price and no reason for him to get upset," Allie responded as she helped him to his bed.

"Would you be so kind and go into my closet and get me the flannel pants please," he said instantly as it looked like he really needed to lie down and sleep.

Allie moved without thinking as she walked into his huge closet and grabbed the first pair of flannel pants and headed back out. Within that time Price had removed his shirt and Allie actually stared for a minute over his pale skin that was almost a light green color. Granted he was skinny, his body was tone and he actually had a six pack. "Thank you Allie," he said instantly as he held out his hand for the bottoms making Allie blush a little and start heading towards the door to give him privacy to change. His voice was instant again has he realized she was leaving. "Wait Allie," made her stop but not turn to look at him. "Give me a minute to place these on, and then I would really like to chat a little longer with you." Allie didn't respond as her cheeks were heated but waited until he spoke again. "Ok it is safe for you to come back."

Allie turned around slowly to see Price in his bed not looking too well at all. He patted to a spot next to him with a smile on his face making Allie slowly walk towards him. She sat but wasn't comfortable with it as he actually smiled at her. His voice was instant. "You really surprise me Allie. I can see why my brothers will fight over you now." Allie felt confused about his words and was about to comment on it when he continued to speak. "No one embraces Kane like you did down stairs. It is the first time in my life that any one has willing walked into his arms not afraid. Not only that you helped me without thinking of yourself and not knowing if you can get what I have. You're brave Allie. You also passed my test, so you will have my blessing next year. Something tells me Archer will have his hands full next year."

"What?" Came out of Allie's mouth as she really felt confused about what Price was talking about. She even shook her head. "Price, I think you really not feeling well. Your words don't make any sense. Archer always has his hands full because he is a nosey jerk that likes to pick on me. The difference is I fight back and hand it back to him as he dishes. Other than that we have no relationship and we never will."

Price started to chuckle as a series of coughs had Allie patting his back and rubbing it as he got it under control. His eyes closed briefly, as he laid his head on his pillow with a smile on his face. Allie was about to get up and leave as his hand reached out and grabbed her arm. His words were instant. "You're wrong Allie I know what is between you two. I can see it as clear as day. Soon you will see it too, but for the time being you will not understand his reasoning. It is so simple on why he keeps you at an arm's length now, but in the future it will take just one kiss and you will know how long he has bottled it up."

Allie blinked as Price released her arm to realize he had fallen asleep. She shook her head and pulled his covers up tucking him in. She wasn't going to think about his words as she got up and headed towards the door. She walked out slowly turning to shut the door quietly deep in thought. When she turned back around, Archer was standing there with a scold on his face. Allie was instant to raise an eyebrow up at him questioning him silently. He shook his head and spoke, "your mother is ready to leave."

Allie nodded her head and started to walk down the hallway when Archer suddenly grabbed her arm and spun her back around. She was instant to fall right into his arms and nearly mold to his front. Her hands rested on his chest as she looked up at him with big eyes. Her breathing even increased as his green eyes looked a shade darker and a little grin formed on his face. "You're going the wrong way," slipped out of his mouth as he continued to hold onto her so tight against him.

"Oh," Allie said next as she couldn't tear her eyes away from him.

It seemed Archer also couldn't let go of her has he seemed to lower his head a bit closer to her. Allie's heart started to pound as she wondered if Archer was going to actually kiss her this time. Price's words really started to run through her head as slowly she began to panic inside. What if all this time Archer had been pining for her? She wasn't going to let this be easy for him when he would deny it tomorrow and make her sound insane. She found her voice instantly. "Archer, if I am to go in the right direction, you need to let me go."

Archer's eyes looked like they sparkled for a minute. A smile formed on his face as he spoke. "I think you are afraid to be alone with me Allie, and you should be."

He let her go instantly with a smirk and walked down the hallway she almost went down. It left Allie stunned as she watched him walk away and suddenly knew this was far from over. They had just entered a new level of mind games and he didn't even tell her what he wanted to talk about before she took Price up to his room. Tomorrow she would need to be on top of her game, or she would be going down.

CHAPTER FIFTEEN
THE LAST STRAW

If school could have been any weirder for Allie the next day, she would have stayed home. Archer was back to his normal self of picking and tormenting her as each minute passed. Aaron seemed to be grumpy about something, that it made Allie worry about him. Josh seemed to smile every time he caught her eye and gave her a wink like he had a secret. It was frustrating to Allie as she watched Janice and Matt walking hand in hand to his car. Deep down she didn't want a relationship with anyone, she just wanted to be left alone.

Allie knew what she needed to do in that instant. She needed to find Josh and tell him not to bother about tonight. She was in no mood to go out and watch a movie. She rather park by the river and watch the fish jump. Turning around, Allie headed toward the gym knowing Josh was most likely hanging out there. No one seemed to stop her as she made her way towards the gym in fact the school seemed empty to her. She heard Josh before she saw him.

"Tonight Allie will be screaming my name. I'll give you all details and you can pay up with the bet." She heard Josh say right as she rounded the corner to see him with his back to her.

Thinking quickly Allie moved back around the corner before any of them saw her. She listened as she heard Steven speak. "I bet she is not a virgin. I think Allie and Tyler went at it, and she was horrible."

Suddenly she heard Archer's voice. "Allie is a virgin, and I bet none of you will ever get in her pants. In fact Allie will be a virgin until she marries."

Allie's jaw dropped as she heard Archer as clear as day. Her heart was pounding in her chest and then it stopped as she heard Aaron speak next. "I'm in agreement with Archer. She is too much of a prune to put out."

Josh was laughing instantly as he commented, "oh poor Aaron, you haven't been able to score have you. You're stuck in the friend category. However after tonight I will tell you how sweet it is to sink inside her."

"Well that will be hard since she asked me and my cousin to go with her tonight," Aaron replied smoothly.

"Oh the more the merrier," Josh laughed. "I don't mind if you want to watch, you might learn something."

Allie was beyond shock now. In fact her temper was ready to shoot the next one that spoke. She didn't think as she rounded the corner and stared a hole in the back of Josh's back. She even crossed her hands over her chest and waited until Steven noticed her and got Josh's attention. Soon she had all four of their eyes on her as she spoke before any of them could. "Well it seems like Archer will win the bet since I'm cancelling on you Josh. By the way Archer I expect half of the winning or you will lose as Aaron will be the first to score." She noticed the smile on Archer's lips as he remained silent, but her eyes looked right at Aaron feeling betrayed by him. Did he really see her as a prune? Slowly she shook her head letting him see the disappointment in her eyes. She turned and started to walk away fed up with them all, and at the moment she wanted nothing to do with any of them.

Archer started to smile real big as his planned worked perfectly in cancelling Allie's date with Josh. Aaron actually laughed as he spoke, "oh so sorry Josh it looks like your date is never going to happen now, better luck next time."

Josh looked like he was sizzling as he glared at Aaron. "Oh no the date is still on. I told her that I wouldn't take no for an answer, and I meant it. Besides no telling what all she heard and I'm smooth with words. You on the other hand Aaron, she is pissed at. I know for a fact she heard you call her a prune and most likely thinks you only became her friend because you were after her tail. I'm the lesser evil and much easier to forgive. I'm just a stupid jock after all."

Archer watched both of them walk away. He could feel wraith inside him wanting to kill them, but he couldn't kill all of his problems. Greed on the other hand told him to find Allie. Something was off with the demon and he couldn't figure out why the demon seemed like it was life and death. Then War's voice moved in his head, and suddenly Archer knew. "Aaron, Nathanael is here. We need to get to Allie now." Aaron took off without even asking in the direction Allie went. Archer wasn't too far behind he knew they needed to hurry.

Allie was sizzling with anger as she made her way to the parking lot to walk home. She wasn't even paying attention to anything around her, that she was surprised when a hand reached out and stopped her. She turned suddenly ready to deck whoever stopped her not caring who they were but was really hoping it was Aaron. So she was more surprised to see Nathan and surprised even more when he grabbed her other hand to stop her from actually decking him. His stare pierced right into her eyes, and Allie felt like she couldn't even look away from it. His lips slowly curved in a smile, and then everything changed. Allie was no longer at the school. She was suddenly in the forest next to a stream. Her hand shook as she realized what had just happened couldn't be, and Nathan knew it. His voice was instant as he spoke, "it is alright Allie, and you know I would never hurt you. I have plans for you in the future. You're our hope and the one that will save everyone."

Allie's lip trembled as she spoke. "How did we get here?"

Nathan smiled at her as Allie's breathing increased. "I could tell that you were upset, and I knew this spot would calm and relax you. Besides it is time we talked." Allie seemed to take a breath to relax thinking that maybe this was a big a dream, this couldn't be real. It made Nathan smile bigger at her. "If it helps to think that way, I will return you to your bed when we are done." Allie gasped shocked that Nathan had read her mind. She had to be dreaming now. This only made him laugh as his eyes twinkled.

"Ok so I have finally lost it. What is next? Am I dead," Allie said in a bit of outrage not knowing how to deal with this.

Nathan was quick to lead her to a boulder and sit her on it. His eyes were still twinkling as he spoke. "I'm afraid to tell you Allie that in a little over a year you will change. You will be very powerful, but you have never been trained for this type of power." Allie was quick to raise an eye brow in doubt. This made Nathan shake his head as he continued. "So much to tell you Allie and you will not understand. I'm an angel Allie, but not any angel, I'm an arch angel. I rule over fire and vengeance. The children in my line have the power over fire and control it like they are breathing. The last two children in my line that were born, only one was to be granted those powers and become the element of fire to protect humanity. The fates tampered with that, and well the other child's powers were made dormant. Those powers are starting to come out, and I no longer know which will become the element of fire."

Allie was instant to reach down and pinch herself. She had to be dreaming, but the pinch hurt like hell. "Why are you telling me this?" Came out of Allie's mouth as she realized she was not dreaming but she was losing it.

Nathan seemed to take a deep breath. He knew she wasn't taking this well. "Allie, a war is coming for humanity. The four horsemen are born and growing as each day passes. You know who they are, but you will refuse to believe it. Those around you are not what they seem. Demons and angels exist and walk among you daily. You have to be open. If you focus you will see who they really are and know their names instantly. You need to connect to the other elements, together you will be strong. Allie, I want you to brace yourself for this, but you are of my line and I'm counting on you to break the curse."

Allie blinked and suddenly she bolted up in her bed not even sure how she had got there. She was also fully clothed from what she wore to school that day. Sweat covered her from head to toe and her heart was pounding. Her cell phone was also going off. She was quick to pick it up to see that she had twelve missed calls and thirty messages. She jumped instantly when her bedroom door opened and Aaron was suddenly there. His stare was piercing as he spoke. "Allie what the hell I've been calling and texting you like crazy. You scared the living hell out of me." He was instant to move in and wrap his hands around her in a hug. He let go instantly and looked at her as he realized she was covered in sweat. "What's wrong Allie you're trembling?"

Allie couldn't speak. The dream was too real and she had no clue how she got home. Aaron was staring at her really concern now as he was quick to pull out his cell and dial a number. Allie watched him as he continued to look at her and speak into the phone. "I found her. She was at home in her room, but something is off. She is trembling and covered in sweat. She even looks like she might toss her cookies."

He closed his phone instantly as Allie blinked at him wondering who he had called. It seemed like seconds passed, and then suddenly Archer was in her room looking worried. Allie was instant to hold her head wondering if she bumped it. She was instant to pinch herself to see if she was dreaming again, but ended up crying out because it hurt. Archer was also instant to slap the hand that was pinching her as he spoke sounding so angry. "What the hell Allie? You're not dreaming, but you have had everyone worried sick when you just vanished. One minute we could see you and the next you just disappeared. What the hell happened?"

Allie blinked she couldn't even get her mind to wrap around what had happened. She didn't know what was real and what wasn't. She couldn't understand why both Aaron and Archer were in her room. Then she remembered she was mad at them. "Get out of my room, both of you," Allie told them in a normal voice.

"No," Archer said instantly as he glared at her.

Allie was about to really give him a piece of her mind when Aaron spoke. "Allie you're not acting yourself. I think a shower and maybe some herb tea might help you a bit. Do you remember how you got home?"

Allie blinked at Aaron as his words made her want to answer. Finally she did answer him. "I think your right Aaron a shower will wake me up." Then she looked right at Archer and glared at him. "I don't want to deal with you right now, so please leave."

"Not until you tell me where you went," Archer demanded of her.

Allie felt outraged as she looked at Archer. She then decided why not tell him what Nathan told her in the dream. "Fine, I was teleported to a creek in the woods by the arch angel Nathanael. Why because he wanted to tell me I was of his line and he was counting on me to save all of humanity by breaking a curse. He then told me I would wake up soon, and hence I did in my own room. Does that meet your curiosity?"

Archer's heart was pounding in his chest from Allie's words. Angels do not make it a habit to lie, and normally almost always tell the truth. The fact that an arch angel had stolen Allie to tell her this must mean that his father and her mother had a huge secret. Allie suddenly threw her hands up at him clearly frustrated. She made jerky movements as she ignored him and started to grab a change of clothes most likely hoping that he would leave. Aaron had the same look on his face that Archer knew he had on his. Neither of them was moving and neither of them wanted to leave her alone. Allie voice was instant, "I expect you gone when I get out Archer."

Archer watched her walk into the bathroom across the hall and closed the door. His voice was instant as he spoke to Aaron, "you know what this means. From this moment on, one of us is always with her. I don't care if you have to sleep on her floor as a roach we are not leaving her alone. I have no doubt that the angel told her that so I would hear it and destroy my bride."

Aaron's comment was instant. "What if Allie is part of his line? She could be half or a fourth angel. Your children would be stronger than you are now. Her arm will bruise where she pinched it."

"What," Archer said instantly as he realized that Aaron had told him that Allie had hurt herself. Without thinking he marched to the bathroom where Allie was and opened the door. She was completely naked and just turning on the water as she turned to notice he was there. She was instant to grab a towel and scream at him. Archer couldn't help the smile that formed on his face as he toned her out. His voice was instant as he spoke, "if you want me to leave let me see your arm where you pinched yourself."

Allie was embraced and mad. She clutched the towel around her body thinking this was it with Archer. After today she wanted nothing to do with him. This was indeed the last straw. She was quick to flash him her arm to get rid of him, however Archer surprised her and grabbed held of her arm. His eyes were instant on the new little bruising she had given herself. Allie watched as he lowered his head and kissed her bruise. The move shocked her as his lips felt like fire on her skin that her whole body flushed. Instantly Allie knew this was another one of Archer's head games. She pulled her arm from his grip as if he burned making Archer's eyes focus up at her. They were darker than normal as Allie spoke, "get out of my bathroom Archer and out of my house."

His lips twitched in a smile, and before Allie could speak, Archer grabbed her hand and pulled her right up against him. The whole move caused her to drop her towel, so she was literally unprotected against him. His eyes bored right into hers as Allie could smell his cinnamon breath with a hint of mint. He smelt way too good for Allie. His forehead touched hers slightly as his eyes kept focused in hers. His words were instant, "soon Allie, but not yet. Tonight I will follow your request, but no promises tomorrow." His hand drifted down her backside and rested right on her butt. Allie's heart started to pound as she couldn't look away from his heated stare. His hand squeezed her butt a little making her gasp and him smile more. His eyes even twinkled. Then he started to lean in like he was going to kiss her, yet something inside Allie told her not to let him.

Thinking quickly, Allie pushed at his chest with her hands making him break contact. She succeeded in getting him out of the bathroom, and then grabbed the door. As she closed it she spoke, "go away Archer. I'm not playing your mind games no more. This is it. I'm done with you."

She heard Archer chuckle on the other side as she heard him say that they would see about that. Allie's heart was pounding in her chest as she knew Archer was at a new level of head games now. She listened to him walk away before she released a breath. She was losing her mind, and Archer was helping her. Allie was quick to lock the door this time and moved to stand under the rays. Tomorrow she would be polite but would ignore each of Archer's barbs to get to her.

She could do it, and it would drive Archer insane. Allie took another breath as she told herself only another year of this and she would escape Archer.

CHAPTER SIXTEEN
A KISS

It had been a rough year and half for Allie, as she sat in her room looking at her senior yearbook. She had her backpack by her door as she waited for Janice to come pick her up so they could head camping with the girls. It made her smile knowing this was her last outing with the girls before each of them headed to colleges in the fall. Sitting on her bed, Allie started to reflect events of her senior year. Granted she avoided Archer as much as she could, it became harder her senior year when she had every class with him, and he sat next to her in each one. Aaron was always her friend and took her to dances, but he never made a move on her. He was just her friend and nothing more. As easy as it seemed that Allie could say that Archer haunted her days, Nathan had haunted her nights. Every dream she had Nathan was her drill instructor training her for something she had no idea what. In each dream it seemed like he was trying to pull something from within her, but it seemed she failed each time. The dreams were strange, and many times seemed impossible to believe, so Allie was thankful they were only dreams. Too many times she had gone to school tired to have Archer staring at her. Only a few times she had fallen asleep on one of his ongoing arguments, which ended up having Archer waking her up by yelling and making her jump. Aaron seemed in tuned when she was tired and would kidnap her at lunch from her friends so she could sleep against his chest for an hour. Her friends hinted at her relationship with Aaron, but the truth was he was just her friend.

Flipping through the year book, Allie smiled as she had taken most of the pictures in there. Her classmates had left little remarks all over it. Then suddenly she lost her smile when she came across the photo of Archer that she had taken. Granted it was a good photo of him, what shocked her was that somehow he had got a hold of her yearbook and wrote in it. His words were simple, 'Allie my love, I look forward to this year where we can finally be together.' Allie blinked as he had clearly made little hearts next to his name. This had to be a sick joke or something, but Allie knew for a fact that it was Archer's handwriting. It made her heart pound in her chest as she wondered what he meant by his simple words, and knowing Archer it could be anything.

Closing the yearbook, Allie was tempted to toss it across the floor. His words in the book might ruin her whole trip, and something Archer was good at was ruining things for her. Slowly she got up and checked herself in the mirror. Her skin was still too pale for her liking, but for some reason no matter how much sun she got, she never tanned or burned. Her hair was almost to her butt, and for several minutes Allie debated if she should cut it. The thought made her laugh, but she just couldn't bring herself to cut it too short, maybe only a trim before she headed off to college. She smiled big with that thought as she glanced at her acceptance letter from Oregon State. Two months and Allie was going to be a Duck. She smiled bigger as the next thought of no more Archer to pick on her made her feel like she was finally escaping.

The sudden beeping of a horn made Allie jump as she realized Janice was here and she had been spacing the whole time. Quickly she grabbed her backpack and made her way to the door. Her mom seemed to appear suddenly right as she opened the front door. "Have fun on your camping trip dear, but be careful in the woods. Keep your cell phone with you and call me if you girls run into any trouble."

Allie waved at Janice signaling her to give her a minute. She walked over to her mom and gave her a hug knowing that Mel, Archer's dad was taking her out tonight. "I plan to have fun, and I will be careful. I have the cell with me and will call you if we get in trouble. Mom, you go out and have some fun too. Mel seems like a good guy to me, and he worships the ground you walk on."

Her mother hugged her tighter for a second and then let her go with a smile on her lips. If Allie was paying closer attention she would realize that her mother was holding back tears. Instead Allie smiled at her and headed back towards the door. She didn't look back but continued on out in the sunshine and climbed into Janice's jeep. Janice was quick to flash a smile as she spoke, "We have to stop at the store before we meet up with Melissa and Rebecca. Seems Rebecca forgot a few items on the list, and she called me once they were already at the cabin. So pit stop before we can start our girl thing."

Allie just nodded as Janice took off in the jeep. She was surprised her father let her even use his jeep, but he most likely thought that she would tear up her car on the back roads to get to the cabin. Within minutes Janice pulled up to the only market in town that was open twenty four hours a day. Janice had a frown on her face as Allie knew instantly why Janice was frowning. "I take it Matt is working, and you are still avoiding him."

Janice gave Allie the look. The two of them had broken up right as school ended, but it was mainly because they were heading different ways. "I just don't want see him right now and he is working in the bakery. One of the things Rebecca forgot was bread. Will you get that while I get the other things?"

Allie smiled at her friend, "no problem Janice."

This made Janice smile as she released a breath. "Thanks Allie you are the best." With that said both girls got out and headed towards the entrance.

Allie was heading directly to the bakery without a thought in the world. The bread was across the counter from where Matt worked making cakes and stuff. Allie always liked Matt, so she didn't mind waving to him if she saw him. Rounding the corner to the bakery, Allie nearly skidded to a stop. Within thirty feet of her was Archer with his back to her chatting with Matt, and neither of them had yet to spot her yet, she thought. Thinking quickly Allie turned her back to them and though to herself to grab the closest loaf of bread and run before they did notice her. Her heart was pounding in her chest as she grabbed the first loaf she saw. She was mentally telling herself to move quickly before she was spotted, and was getting ready to do just that when suddenly she jumped to Archer's voice, "hello Allie."

Just the way he said it sounded like a purr to Allie that she cringed as she slowly turned around to face her tormentor. "Hi Archer," she started. "I didn't know you would be here," came out next sounding very lame to her.

Archer smiled as the look on his face seemed like he was amused which told Allie that he most likely planned to run into her. His eyes drifted down and suddenly a laugh escaped his mouth. "Grabbing the first loaf of bread and running I see," he stated as Allie was ready to protest, but Archer reached down and grabbed it. "Allie," he said next as he shook his head. "You realize that you grabbed a loaf of rye bread, and even I know you hate rye bread." He placed it back on the shelf and then walked down some grabbing a different loaf. He walked back slowly and held the loaf out to her as he spoke. "If memory serves me right this was our favorite."

Allie looked down at the loaf to see her favorite type of bread, but it was Archer's words that really stunned Allie. "Why are you here Archer? This is not your normal hang out."

Archer's eyes looked like they were twinkling as he spoke, "I needed to talk with Matt." The way his eyes were twinkling made Allie think there was more to it as he continued. "Seeing you here is an added bonus of not having to look for you."

Allie knew she was frowning as she spoke, "why would you need to look for me?"

Archer's eyes were twinkling now that Allie couldn't look away. What he was about to tell her would be something that could most likely ruin her whole weekend. "I figured we should talk about the school we are attending in the fall, and look for places to live together."

Allie didn't think she was hearing Archer right. In fact he had to be pulling her leg. She nearly snorted a laugh as she spoke. "Oh that is a good one Archer, you almost got me.

206 Sara Wilson

However I didn't get into Yale or Harvard or whatever Ivy League school you did. Nice try."

Allie was about to turn and walk away when Archer spoke still wearing a smile. "Quack, quack Allie. State of Oregon is where we are heading."

Allie felt herself paling. "Why would you want to go there?"

Archer stepped closer to her as he spoke, "because you will be there Allie."

Allie felt her breaths coming and going faster as she thought she would never escape Archer. His plan was to torture her until she broke. For several minutes Archer only stared at her with a smile as he was letting this all sink in. Allie couldn't think and then it dawned on her that he was doing this all on purpose to ruin her weekend. She suddenly laughed deciding to call his bluff. "Ok Archer when I get back from the weekend, we can find a place together. Maybe we will find some old frat house with a picket fence and not too far from the campus. I will paint your toenails while we chat about it. I think I have pink polish, which will look great on you."

Allie was rambling as Archer was narrowing his eyes at her. Suddenly he reached out and grabbed her hand as he spoke, "Allie." One simple word and Allie looked at him confused. Archer was quick to pull her up against his body as he stared down at her. Allie was totally off balance as she was now nearly molded to Archer's chest looking up at him as he continued. "Shut up Allie," slipped out of his mouth as suddenly as his mouth lowered to hers capturing her lips.

At first Allie was stunned as his lips touched hers. Then something inside her came undone. She felt heat rising up as she opened her mouth and really started kissing Archer back. It felt like she was breathing him in, and she didn't want to stop as his hands became tighter around her. His tongue slipped right into her mouth and Allie was sucking it as she tasted the mints. Her tongue then went in his mouth tasting more of him. She couldn't get enough of him that she nearly whimpered when he slowly pulled away.

Allie's eyes opened quickly as she looked at Archer, who still had his eyes closed, trying to catch his breath. His forehead was resting on hers as he was slowly regaining control, and all Allie could do was stare at him. She knew her heart was pounding like his was, but all she really wanted to know was why he stopped when that kiss was everything she had ever wanted to feel. His voice was instant even though he kept his eyes closed. "You are so lucky we are in a very public place right now with your friend staring at us in shock. I think that is the only reason why I was able to stop myself." He opened his eyes looking at Allie. Allie blinked as his green eyes were so dark, but she couldn't look away either. She was lost into his eyes. A smile lifted up on his lips. "We will be continuing this Allie, but next time we will be alone. I will be seeing you tonight."

He let go of her and turned around walking away without so much as to look back at her. Allie stared after him watching him walk away. She had no clue what had just happened, but deep down she wanted to kiss Archer again. The hand moving in front of her face broke the spell and made Allie blink. She was instant to turn and face Janice's shocked face. Allie was speechless as she stared at her friend, no way could she explain what had just happened. However Janice was full of words. "Oh my god Allie, that was like the steamiest kiss I have ever seen. I've never seen Archer melt like that. He looked like he wanted to devour you, and would have if the two of you were alone. Now how long have the two of you been faking the whole hate relationship? And how long have the two of you been dating behind my back without telling me?"

Allie blinked as she looked at the loaf in her hand, it was completely crushed. She blinked as she looked up at Janice as words failed her because she was now so confused. "I don't know what you are talking about Janice." Her friend's mouth dropped in shock as Allie continued understanding that this was so like Archer to pull something like this to make her think of him all weekend. "Archer and I have no relationship. That was just Archer trying to make me think of him all week, hopefully I gave him something to think about too. Besides that I think he wanted to tease me about the two of us going to school together in the fall and moving in with me, well if that is even true," Allie was staring back at the bread ignoring the look on her friend's face. "This got completely crushed we will have to buy two loaves."

Janice blinked at Allie completely shocked as Allie walked over and grabbed another loaf of bread. Allie couldn't let Janice see just how undone she was by Archer this time. Like the crushed bread, Allie knew that would be her with any relationship with Archer. She had to school her face as she looked back at Janice and smile. "Did you get the rest of the stuff?"

Janice shook her head at her and rolled her eyes as she spoke. "You Allie, you have some explaining to do, but I will let it slide for now. Yes all the rest is up front you were taking so long I decided to come find you."

Allie took a breath as she was glad her friend was dropping it for now. She needed to sort this all out first and not be under the third degree from Janice. With luck, Janice might forget about it and Allie would avoid the topic completely. Following Janice, they both headed to the front to pay for their items. However Allie was still trying to calm her nerves as all she could think about was Archer.

Archer's heart was pounding as he watched how Allie had handled the whole thing with Janice. Janice alone had been a thorn in his backside as she pestered him all year about the relationship between him and Allie, and what he was waiting for. The little she demon had even told him all about Allie being accepted into Oregon State and asked him if he was going to follow his heart, or stop her from going. It almost felt like Janice knew something and wasn't telling him, a little secret. He knew that Janice knew who his family was, but none of them knew who or what she really was. His sister tried to find out, but Janice was too clever. Allie was playing it off smoothly as Janice tried to get her to spill the beans, but he knew Allie. Right at the moment he knew she was thinking of nothing but that kiss, that he was smiling knowing that she didn't know how to respond to Janice's questions and that she wouldn't until she could figure out why he had kissed her. He was also thinking of that kiss, and he really wanted more of them. War was pretty much in control of him now, and he was persistent about Allie. War really wanted to conquer every inch of her, and then do it again. His other two demons did nothing but sit back and agree. They didn't want to pull away from Allie in that kiss, they wanted to teleport her to his bedroom, and keep her there for days. He had to make them a promise that by tomorrow Allie would be theirs and that is where she would always be once the crowning was complete. He had made it this far, no way was he letting Allie go now.

Teleporting back home was easier said than done for Archer. He had a lot to do just so he could be with Allie tonight. She had no idea he was planning to crash the girl's camp fire, and he was planning to keep it that way. In truth he needed to know how she really felt about him, and he would find out tonight.

CHAPTER SEVENTEEN
CAMPING

Allie should have been dragging after hiking for miles with the girls. Instead she was thinking of Archer. Her mind would not shut off, and just once she actually wished he was there so he could say something that would ruin what had happened earlier. Instead she was thinking on how right it had felt to kiss him, almost like she had been waiting for it. The whole thing was making her nuts that she was missing Rebecca whining that she wanted to head back. Melissa was going off and collecting wood for a fire, and Janice was surprisingly quiet. That alone should have made Allie stop and look at Janice, she was never quiet.

Looking at her friend, Allie noticed she was instant to smile at her. For the first time in hours she spoke, "so you ready to talk about it?"

"No," Allie said instantly as Janice narrowed her eyes at her. "We should head back and gather some fire wood while we are at it."

"About time someone is listening to me," Rebecca stated as Melissa snickered.

Within minutes they turned back around gathering some wood as they hiked back to the cabin. It felt a little too déjà vu to Allie, but she remained silence as the girls talked with each other. Mentally Allie was swearing to anyone in general about Archer ruining her weekend because she was indeed thinking of him. Rounding the corner, they walked by the river knowing they were almost to the cabin. Melissa was talking about roasting marshmallows, while Rebecca was talking about boys. Yet Janice seemed to be humming a tune that sounded like the country tune this kiss. Allie's eyes went big as she realized Janice was indeed taunting her and wanting to know what was going on. Allie knew that Janice would wait, but she wouldn't wait forever. She was going to be spilling by the end of the night, and at the moment Allie had no idea what she would be spilling.

About two hours later they had the camp fire going and were sitting around laughing and joking. For several minutes Allie actually forgot about Archer as Melissa started to tell jokes. Then Janice spoke up. "Ok let's play a game. Let's play truth or dare." This had Rebecca laughing as she stated she had nothing to hide, and Melissa laughing. Allie felt dread as Janice smiled at her and continued. "The rules are simple, no back peddling or changing to a dare because you don't want to answer. If you call truth, you must tell the truth of the question asked. Do we understand the rules?" Everyone nodded but Allie knew what Janice was going to ask. "Good, let's start with Allie, truth or dare?"

Allie blinked twice as Janice stared at her with an evil smile. She was going to make her talk no matter which she picked. "Fine, I pick truth."

Janice smile got bigger as Rebecca rolled her eyes hoping for a dare. "So is it true that in the store this morning you and Archer were kissing and planning on moving in together in the fall since your both going to school together?"

Melissa was taking a drink of water, and ended up spraying it out over the fire as she turned and looked at Allie with big eyes. Rebecca laughed as she spoke, "no way that is true. If it is I want proof."

Janice was still smiling big as she gestured for Allie to answer while Allie glared at her. "Archer and I were in fact kissing in the store this morning. He caught me off guard and did it on purpose so I would be thinking of nothing but him this weekend." Rebecca stopped laughing and leaned in as Janice gestured for Allie to continue. "He did bring up that we would be going to school together in the fall. Even said we should get a place together. However who knows if that is true or not? Why would he want to be a duck?"

"Oh gosh Allie, you're next on the Archer radar," Melissa said instantly.

Allie tried not to roll her eyes at Melissa for that comment. Instead she stuck her marshmallow in the flames to cook ignoring the round of truths or dares from the others. Her arms and legs felt achy as she watched the marshmallow and then slowly pulled it out to blow the flame out. "Allie, truth or dare," Rebecca asked her.

Shrugging, Allie gave a response. "Truth," slipped out again.

"Is it true that you have always secretly wanted Archer?"

Allie was glad that she didn't have the marshmallow in her mouth or else she would have choked. It took her a minute to form words from her mouth, but she did feeling a little angry about her friends ribbing her over something so trivial. "Let me set the record straight for you all. Archer cannot stand me. He does things to me on purpose to get a rise. We have no relationship beyond that, and I have never secretly wanted him." The minute that slipped from Allie's mouth, it felt like a lie. It made her stop in the middle of her speech to her friends to wonder if she had secretly always wanted him. She shook her head instantly and continued. "That's it no more talk about Archer. I just need a break so just stop asking about it."

"Touchy," Rebecca said instantly as Melissa was looking at her funny.

Then instantly Melissa asked, "How long have you been in love with him?"

Allie blinked at her friend shocked that she had just asked it. Janice and Rebecca leaned in wanting to hear her response as Allie shook her head. She was defeated so why not confess it all and get it off her chest. "You really want to know, I fell in love with him when I first met him. I looked forward to seeing him every day that it put a jump in my skip. Then we started high school and he wanted nothing more to do with me. I was hurt, but deep down I still loved him."

All three of them were shocked by Allie's confession. They sat back all quiet as Allie bit into the marshmallow. Melissa was the first one to find her voice, "you still love him, but how do you think he feels about you?"

Allie was wishing for a different subject but answered anyway. "It doesn't matter what he thinks about me, it won't change how I feel about him."

Rebecca spoke suddenly drawing Allie's attention, "so how mad would you be if I told you that Archer is right behind you, and listened to your whole confession with a knowing smile on his face."

Allie couldn't breathe and refused to turn around. She dropped the stick holding the marshmallow as she noticed Janice glaring behind her. Janice was the one that spoke, "why are all of you here?"

It was Matt's voice that spoke, "I wanted to see you, and we knew where you would all be."

Janice was quick to stand up and walk off towards the cabin as Allie saw Matt running after her. Allie refused to turn around, and she really didn't have to as Joey moved and took a seat next to Rebecca being all flirty and Joel moved next to Melissa snagging a marshmallow. Allie had four sets of eyes on her, but it was nothing compared to the ones she felt behind her. She was trying to remember how to breathe when suddenly she felt two arms go around her and just picked her up. She panicked and wrapped her arms around Archer twisting in his arms and ended up looking him straight in the eyes. They were very dark as they looked at her and his lips were tilted up in a smile. Allie's heart was pounding as she couldn't look away from him. She heard Joey speak so suddenly but she refused to look away from Archer. "Hey Archer truth or dare," Joey's words seemed to echo in her mind as she watched Archers lips tell him dare. "I dare you to kiss Allie like you did this morning, I heard it was steamy."

Joey laughed at his words, but Archer smiled bigger. "Oh my pleasure," he purred as he lowered his head and connected with Allie's lips.

Within seconds Archer felt Allie's response to his kiss. Her lips parted instantly letting him in to taste the sweet cinnamon taste. Her hands were at his neck to hold him close to her so he could devour her lips. Her kiss was sweeter this time as her tongue darted in his mouth being bolder than she was. He was the one moaning, as she was making him come undone. If Janice and Matt were not in the cabin right at that second, Archer would have lifted Allie and took her there so he could explore her kiss more. It took everything in him to stop kissing her and just to let her breath.

Allie verily caught her breath as Archer started to withdraw from her. His forehead was resting on hers as Joel spoke, "oh man that was hot. Who would have ever thought Allie could kiss like that? I'm turned on and I didn't even kiss her."

Archer's eyes opened instantly and Allie saw the anger in them as he addressed Joel. "You better not be turned on and you will never kiss her," came out like a growl from Archer's lips.

Joel laughed, but Allie was shocked. Archer's lips were smiling at her again as his eyes twinkled. Rebecca then spoke, "holy hell someone, fan me that was too hot for me."

That made Allie turn away from Archer and look at her friends and his friends that were staring at the two of them clearly shocked. Joey's grin was huge as he said, "I dare you to do it again."

Allie turned and looked back at Archer who didn't need to be told twice. His lips found hers again stealing her breath. His kiss was undoing her making her feel on fire. She felt like she was burning up inside as his hand moved and cupped her butt to pull her closer. She was losing herself in him until suddenly a pain raced up her arm making her break contact from Archer and gasp in pain. The noise she made had everyone concern as Archer was nearly demanding what was wrong. Allie felt embraced as she spoke, "I think I just pinched my hand."

Even though she said that, her hand was in pain. It really hurt as Archer seemed to focus on her hand. "Your hand is really hot we should head down to the river and dip it in. Might make it feel better too."

Allie couldn't help but look at the distance from the fire to the river. If Archer walked her down there, no one would be able to see them too well, and it would be easy for them to head upstream a little to be alone. That thought alone with the way he had kissed her had her afraid to be alone with him. She needed a minute alone to sort what had just happened. Her words were careful as she spoke. "It's not that far. Why don't you wait here for me and I will be right back? No reason for you to move away from a warm spot."

Archer's lips quirked in a smile as he knew it was Allie's way of saying that she needed a moment to pull herself together. "Alright Allie," he responded. "If you need my help just call out to me," he said next knowing that she would be too chicken to actually do that.

Allie actually released a breath she didn't know she was holding. Archer moved too quickly and kissed her lips making her melt against him before he sat her on her two feet. His hand even swatted her butt as he had a smile on his lips telling her to hurry back. Allie didn't look at anyone else as she walked slowly towards the river knowing that Archer was watching her. The moon itself was full and bright lighting her way as both of her hands tingled. Allie started to wonder what was wrong with her as she felt heat rushing up and down her arms when she should have felt the cool night air.

Reaching the river tuned out the voices of her friends at the camp fire. Allie bent down and dipped her hands in the cold water only for steam to come out of the water and in her face. She pulled her hands back instantly looking at them strange as they throbbed more. Looking over her shoulder, Allie noticed her friends laughing and talking. Archer was chatting with them, and seemed like he wasn't watching her, so he just missed what had just happened. Looking upstream a little, Allie decided to move out of her friends' line of sight. Carefully she went around a bush and to a little cove. Her hands were still tingling as she dipped them back in the water to have more steam come up in her face. Not understanding what was happening she kept them under the water until they stopped tingling and she saw a little blue glow bug moving on her right hand. She quickly pulled her hands out of the water to see the bug still on her. She was trying to swipe it off of her when she suddenly noticed more of them were all over her hands. Freaking out a little, Allie lost her balance and fell back landing in a puddle soaking her butt. Her arms were holding her up as Allie noticed that her arms were not covered in little glowing blue bugs, her arms were covered in little blue flames. Lifting up a hand she studied how the flames danced along her fingers. The flames did not hurt her at all, but seemed to caress her skin. Then as quickly as they appeared, slowly they sunk back in her skin like they were never there. Confused by it, Allie stood up not knowing how to explain how she had got wet when she heard a twig snap. Her eyes darted to the bush that was across from her as she hoped it wasn't a wild animal of some kind because her only option to escape one would be a swim in a cold river.

Watching the bush shake, Allie felt a little pain on her finger to notice only a single little flame. She held up her hand as a shadow of a man stepped out of the bush. Everything about the man screamed at her that he was evil. His eyes were so black that they did not appear to look human in the lease. He smiled showing pointy teeth that looked like something that she would see in a horror flick. She shook as the flame crawled back in her skin, and she noticed the man narrow his eyes and stare at her with his smile disappearing. "What are you?" Came out of him like a hiss as Allie noted a snake like tongue slip out of his mouth.

Allie took a step back into the water and almost fell backwards, but held her balance. She was starting to feel like she was in a bad horror film as the man stepped closer into the moonlight and smiled at her. "He doesn't know what you are, or else he would have killed you."

Allie took another step back sinking deeper in the water. "What are you," came out of her mouth too easy followed by, "Asmodeus."

The man smiled at her as he spoke, "ah she knows my name, so a touch of angel inside you. Surely you know what I am."

His tongue forked out as Allie took another step back and lost her footing. Within seconds she screamed out Archer's name as the current took her before the man could. She was fighting to stay above the water when two big arms wrapped around her suddenly and pulled her from the water. Archer was swearing at her, but then stopped when he saw her face. "What happened, Allie?"

Allie's teeth were chattering, as she noticed all of her friends including Janice were looking at her with worried eyes. Somehow she got the words out, "a man startled me, and then I slipped and fell." That comment set the guys off to go find the pervert, but Allie leaned closer to Archer so only he would hear her, "he wasn't human."

Archer was pissed that someone would dare attack Allie, let alone someone of his world. He pressed a kiss to her brow and told her everything would be alright. He cradled her in his arms as she spoke again. "It was Asmodeus."

Archer stopped and looked at Allie as she most likely thought she was going insane. She was shivering also that it made Archer worry. "It's ok Allie. A hot shower will make you feel better, and the guys and I will take a look around." She looked like she was about to protest as her eyes got wild for a minute but Archer stopped her from talking. "Everything will be fine Allie. I will be back before you know it."

He sat her down in a chair in the cabin as he told Janice to make sure she got a hot shower, and then told the others that the guys would handle this. Allie reached out and touched his arm as she looked so worried. Her voice was soft as she spoke, "be careful Archer, and come back to me."

His lips tilted in a smile as he leaned down and captured her lips in one of the sweetest kisses he had ever received. "I will be back before you know it," he told her as he walked to the door with the guys behind him.

Allie stared at the door after it had been shut for several minutes before Janice started to mother hen here and make her take a shower. She was worried about Archer and made the shower a quick one. She also dressed in warm sweat pants with a tee shirt looking ready for bed. She was running a brush through her hair when she walked out of the bathroom to see if they had returned yet. When Janice noticed her worried look, she just shook her head. Before Allie could start pacing, Melissa had pulled her into the back bedroom with Rebecca. Within no time her friends had her thinking of other things even though her mind keep hoping Archer would come back and tell her everything was alright. She was biting her bottom lip thinking about it when suddenly the bedroom door opened and Joel came in. He took one look at the four of them lying in bed, and then jumped right in to be in the middle of all the action. His words were instant, "ok girls worship your hero."

The move had both Rebecca and Melissa nail him with a pillow as Janice escaped off the side and Allie the other. Allie was instant to turn toward the doorway to see the guys there with smiles on their faces, but Archer was behind them with a frown on his. Without thinking Allie went to him, and instantly put her arms around him glad that he was back and in one piece. He was also instant to hold her and rest his chin on top of her head. His words were soft as he spoke, "we didn't find anyone out there. They might have got scared and ran off, either way I think you're safe for the night."

Allie released a breath as she held Archer a little tighter. "I'm just glad you made it back and in one piece."

Archer's demons were purring at Allie's words. He was having a hard time controlling them while thinking about Asmodeus. He had indeed found the demon and got his message, but the tale he told him about Allie seemed impossible. He smiled as he enjoyed holding her like this, but he really didn't want the others to be somewhat watching them. Slowly he lead her to one of the back bedrooms, and she went with him not thinking a thing about it as he directed the others to stay away. Once inside the room he sat her on the bed and then started to remove his shirt. Allie's voice was instant, "Archer what are you doing?"

Archer smiled as he could tell that Allie was nervous. He responded instantly back, "my clothes are wet from pulling you out of the river, and I'm a little chilled. I'm taking them off so they can dry, and I'm hoping you will continue to let me hold you as we lay down. You can keep your clothes on if you want."

Allie was blushing and felt so silly. She was instant to turn and pull the covers back so she would not be staring at Archer's body as he stripped down. She climbed in first and then turned to see Archer smiling at her as he moved in to lie down next to her. It wasn't awkward at all as Archer pulled her in his arms and held onto her. Allie's head was resting right on his chest listening to his heart as her fingers brushed right over his abs before his hand caught hers and held onto it. Looking up at his face Allie noticed Archer's eyes closed, and couldn't help but smile as it seemed that he had just fallen asleep. Carefully she leaned up and placed a soft kiss on his lips before resting her head on his shoulder. Several minutes later she also fell asleep feeling safe and right in his arms.

Archer opened his eyes slowly once he knew Allie was asleep. She had no idea what her little kiss moments ago had done to him, yet he was content with her in his arms. Asmodeus had told him that she carried the blue flame of the fire angels inside her, but she could call it back into her. That was something that an angel could not do, so now Archer was curious about Allie. He noticed the little blue lights moving under the skin of her arm as she lay with him in the bed. He couldn't help but trace over them with his fingers as they seemed to dance with his fingers. Slowly one came out and wrapped around his finger not even burning him, but more like tickling his finger. He felt War inside him smiling and pleased as the little flame soaked back in her skin. His Allie wasn't human like he wasn't and he could understand why Nathanael was trying to get her. He knew fire angels were mainly all male. Female fire angels were used for breeding to create more. They were not allowed out of a male fire angel's sight so they would remain pure. Yet here he held one in his arms, and the part he couldn't understand was why Nathanael hadn't tried to swoop her up again and why other fire angels did not know about her.

Greed seemed to whine in his head about protecting Allie. He had named her his fire after his talk with Asmodeus. This worried him too because the demon had wanted to kill her. He had a week before War was crowned and then to announce Allie as his bride which would make her safe from all demons. Wraith had somehow leaked out during that conversation and told the demon that to go up against her would mean his death. The demon had coward back from Wraith, but Asmodeus was sneaky. He would feel better if Allie was safe at home. War stirred again inside him talking to him. "When she wakes I claim her. She will wear my mark, and all will know she is my chosen bride."

Archer blinked as he looked down at Allie. He was smiling as she was still cuddled against him sound asleep. He closed his eyes with that smile on his face thinking he had waited years and finally he was going to have what he always wanted.

CHAPTER EIGHTEEN
LITTLE FLAMES

Allie was sure she was dreaming as she seemed to be back in that gym she saw Adam in. She felt confused as she walked farther into the building noting that it was empty until she saw Adam sitting on a barrel looking at his hand that was covered in a blue flame. He seemed amused with it as he twirled it around but then looked up right at her. His voice was instant as he spoke, "Allie, how…" He didn't finish his words he was looking at her hand.

Allie followed his gaze too easily to look down at her hand covered in the same blue flame. She brought it up not understanding what was going on as he jumped down from the barrel and moved to stand in front of her. He held his hand out to her as Allie slowly raised hers to his. Then Allie jumped as she heard a male voice speak, "Adam what are doing?"

Allie turned her head to see the same man she saw last time along with the guy that had challenged her in paintball about a year and a half ago. "Jehoel, don't scare her away this time,"

Adam said quickly. "Something is different, her hand is like mine."

Both men leaned in to try to see her, but she was only available to Adam's eye. "Why is she here and why is her hand like yours?" Jehoel seemed to demand.

"Forget the why Jehoel, her hand is like his which means she is a fire angel, and female. We need to find her before a demon does." Paint ball guy said as he turned his head suddenly to Adam. "Adam, where is she?"

Adam focused on Allie ignoring the two of them, and waited until she looked at him. "Allie let me protect you now, tell me where you are. You're one of us, and being female will attract demons to you like honey."

Allie blinked as she stared at Adam. She looked back over at paint ball guy and almost laughed. Jehoel was quick to speak, "what is she doing?"

Adam looked confused as he spoke, "she is looking at Seraph and laughing at him." This made both guys look a little confused as Adam looked at Allie and spoke, "what is so funny Allie?"

Allie believed this was one big dream so why not tell the truth. "I kicked his butt in paintball."

Adam blinked rapidly and then turned towards Seraph. "She knows you Seraph, she beat you in paintball."

"What does she look like?" Seraph demanded.

Adam nearly shrugged as he spoke while Allie darted looks at all of them amazed that Adam could hear her this time. "She has my hair color and eyes. She is shorter than me and too thin."

"The red head with the demon, Allie, she was too good at that game, but a very good sport." He smiled then as he continued, "I know what town she is in, and it is demon central. The horsemen are there too, she needs to leave, or they will eat her alive."

Allie felt her eyes go big for a minute as her dream felt like a nightmare now as she remembered the man out by the river. Her face paled a little as she started to feel weird, "Adam," slipped out of her mouth a little quickly as he started to disappear in front of her eyes.

Allie blinked slowly awake to have Archer staring down at her. It made her very uncomfortable as he spoke, "who is Adam?"

"Who," slipped out of Allie's mouth as she was slowly waking up but wondering if she was talking in her sleep?

Archer narrowed his eyes at her as they seem to darken. He had her pinned under him but yet wasn't putting any weight on her. It seemed like something had changed about Archer instantly as Allie stared up at him. His hand was touching her bare flesh making her shirt come up slowly. He spoke suddenly making Allie jump, "you're mine Allie. I will not share you with any other, even in your dreams."

Allie only blinked before Archer's lips were on hers robbing her of her breath. She couldn't think as she was drowning in his kisses, that she didn't realize that he was stripping all of her clothes off of her until he broke up the kiss to pull her shirt off over her head. Allie was scared because this was moving too fast for her, that she actually shivered. Archer had her pinned still, but it was flesh on flesh now. His eyes were very dark as he looked at her and he spoke. "It's ok Allie you know I would never hurt you. The first time there will be discomfort and a little pain, but I promise I will make it pleasurable for you. Your body is a temple, and I plan to worship it until I breathe my last breath."

Allie didn't get a chance to respond back to him. His mouth was back on hers making her forget how very real this was. She didn't even understand what was happening as Archer spread her legs wide open. She felt his fingers instantly rubbing her bud making her gasp in his kisses. Her body felt on fire as each gasp made Archer devour her more. She didn't even know when he removed his hand until something big entered her making her eyes water and her scream swallowed in Archer's kiss. He stopped moving as Allie felt whatever it was resting inside her, but instantly she knew. He was letting her get use to him inside her to ease the pain. He pulled back from the kiss and watched her face. He even wiped the tears from her eyes as he spoke, "it's alright Allie my love. Your body is adjusting to mine which will make the next time so much easier. The pleasure will start soon I promise you."

Archer was back to kissing Allie making her forget. That she gasped in his kiss when he started to move inside her. Allie's breathing increased with her pounding heart as Archer's nonstop kisses consumed her. She didn't want this to end as she felt the pressure build up inside her and spill over making her roll her eyes in bliss as Archer pushed her to the next pressure point. His speed was increasing with each pressure point until suddenly Allie felt it. She was instant to feel all warm and fuzzy as Archer collapsed on her. Allie's hands were wrapped around him as she still felt him inside her throbbing. Archer was catching his breath as his body was covered in sweat before he focused and looked her straight in the eye with a smile on his lips. He was also instant to turn on his side and cradle Allie in his arms. She felt him slowly slip out of her, but to be honest Allie couldn't believe how sore she suddenly felt. She also felt drained enough to want to sleep and forget where she was. Archer was instant to start kissing her again, and once again she felt consumed by him. He pulled back gasping for breath as he spoke, "Allie, I'm going to have to leave you or else I'm going to want to do that again, and your body needs time to heal."

Allie had no energy to even respond. She just watched Archer's eyes fade back to the green she knew. She just nodded her head and slowly closed her eyes.

Archer watched Allie close her eyes. It was the most beautiful thing he had ever seen. He wanted to take her again, but War was in his head laughing and telling him soon. She was sound asleep within seconds, and that alone made him smile. He started to slowly remove himself from the bed when he noticed the little blue light under her skin moving back and forth. He reached down and touched it tracing it slowly until a single blue flame popped out and raced along his fingers. He watched it slowly dance along his fingers without hurting him. Then the flame stopped like it was looking at him. He couldn't help but stare back at it like it was its own life form. Then slowly it sunk into his skin and disappeared. For the longest time he looked at his hand wondering, but then he looked at Allie and smiled. This was something he wanted to ask the witch about. He just needed to let Kane let him talk to her. His brother had nabbed the young witch a year ago after he learned she was transforming into an oracle. She would be able to explain Allie's flame. Hating to leave Allie, in the end Archer did just that.

Allie woke up reaching out for Archer, but he wasn't there. She was instant to sit up in the bed to realize she wasn't wearing a thing and her clothes seemed like they had magically disappeared. She felt confused now as she stood up on her wobbly legs and wrapped a blanket around her. She snuck her head out the door to find the cabin a little too quiet. Everyone was gone as she padded out to the living room. Then Allie saw the note in Janice's writing. She was quick to move over to it and read it loud. "Allie we all decided to head to the waterfall for the day. Archer told us to let you sleep in because you had a very long night. Join us if you are not too sore."

Allie stared at the wink and nearly snorted. No telling what her friends though happened between her and Archer, but she was sure it was all in the gutter. Deciding quickly, Allie located her bag with her clothes in it and headed for the shower, she would join her friends in no time.

Archer had been home for five minutes before he was able to locate the witch. She was in Kane's room on a chain covered in blood. As he walked into Kane's room he had the instant shivers knowing that his brother loved to torture souls. Looking at the witch named Ellie Archer could see her beauty through the busted lip and black eye. At the moment she was asleep, but he knew the minute Kane was back she would be awake and terrified. Moving quickly Archer walked towards Ellie as he watched her facial expressions change. She was awake but her eyes were closed. Kane had taught her not to speak unless she was spoken to first. Archer swallowed as he stared at her about to speak when she did. "I will only tell you what you wish to know if you will get me away from him."

Her eyes opened slowly and looked Archer right in the eye. Archer was spell bound looking into the witch's green eyes that seemed like every earth tone possible. Her eyes were a thing of beauty against her coco cream skin. "I will set you up in your own home, but I cannot promise to keep my brother away. What I can promise is to take you out of here."

Ellie snorted at him as she spoke, "your bride is his weakness as she is yours, I think you can make me a better bargain than that."

"I still have to negotiate with my brother for your release, that alone is hard to do you understand. Take the offer I am giving you," Archer replied back to her.

Kane's voice came out of nowhere making Ellie jump and coil into a ball. "Why do you need my witch brother?"

Archer stared at Ellie for a second longer than he should before he stood up and faced his brother. Kane was focused on Archer, and there was always truth between the two of them. "Something is wrong with Allie," came out of Archer's mouth too easy as Kane looked intrigued. "She controls a blue flame, but she can call it back into her."

Kane's intrigued suddenly transformed into worry. His eyes even got bigger as he yelled at Ellie. "Witch, you will tell me what will happen to Allie."

His voice echoed throughout the room as Archer stared at his brother that looked like he was coming undone so worried about his bride. "Grant me freedom and I will tell you some," Ellie responded.

Kane actually growled that it surprised Archer. Kane was upset that his body shook as he looked like he was about to kill the witch. Archer was quick to stop his brother with his words. "Brother the witch has requested her own place to live and her freedom."

Kane head snapped towards Archer, and Archer realized Death was in complete control of his brother as he spoke. "Ellie I will give you ten days of complete freedom from me. You will have your own place to live, but you are still mine."

Archer was quick to look at the witch. Her eyes were open as she stared back. "Undo my chain, you know it weakens me and set me free for the answer you seek."

Kane walked over to Ellie and touched the chain for it to dissolve off of her. Archer didn't imagine it, but the witch's skin seemed to glow like it was healing. She stood up slowly as she seemed to catch her breath and start healing right before his eyes. Once her lip looked normal again and her eye no longer black Kane spoke like he was losing patience with her, "answer my question Ellie."

"Nothing is wrong with War's bride she just has never been fully human. War must have triggered her powers somehow and they are slowly maturing." Ellie smiled at her words as her eyes suddenly turned white showing her a vision. Both Kane and Archer watched her carefully until her eyes went back to normal and Ellie seemed out of breath.

"What did you see witch," Archer demanded when he noticed how weak the vision had made her.

Ellie actually mumbled as she looked ready to fall. "I can't explain what I saw. It makes no sense. I will have to meditate on it, and try to figure out what it meant. However War, do not worry about the blue flame that entered you. She has accepted you as you have claimed her, however her heart is a fragile thing and so easy to break. You must be careful with your words or a war she will make."

Archer narrowed his eyes hating how all oracles spoke in a riddle. "Thank you witch, but if you see more, you will tell me."

The witch nodded her head towards Archer in agreement and then looked at Kane. Archer took this as his sign that he was now dismissed, so he didn't linger. The minute Archer was out of the room Ellie spoke again but only to Kane. "Is she worth betraying your brother for?"

Kane smiled at Ellie as he spoke, "you talk too much witch." Without a word more he held off and hit her sending her sailing across the floor. He was laughing as he spoke, "our agreement starts tomorrow, but in the meantime I will enjoy you one last time before your freedom begins."

Allie knew how to get to the waterfall from the cabin, and the fastest way was to follow the main road and then take the short path to it. It was less than a mile hike. She had on her green swimsuit top with a pair of tan shorts. Since she never burned, she never bothered with lotions to protect her skin. She was determined to join her friends and continue having fun regardless of what had happened between Archer and her. Almost to the path to get to the waterfall, Allie suddenly got the chills up and down her arms as her arms tingled. She stopped instantly knowing something wasn't right. She looked around feeling uneasy not knowing that little blue flames were dancing around her fingertips. A male voice came out of nowhere making her jump. "You're all alone and unprotected. He doesn't know what you are, but I do."

Allie turned towards the voice to see the same man she saw last night. Fear shot through her as she mentally recited a prayer of protection. His eyes darted to her hands and his smile looked so evil. Allie's voice came out sounding shaky as she spoke, "what am I?"

His smile got bigger as his sharp teeth showed a little. "He thinks you are part fire angel, but a fire angel cannot call their flame back into them. I know what you are even though he has yet to figure it out. To eliminate you now will make my kind lead in victory to take the souls. You are not use to your power and you have never been trained to use it, they have you weak fire." His laughter was sinister as Allie's heart pounded. "I will be reward by killing you, War's mark be damned."

He leaped to attack Allie, as Allie froze afraid lifting her hands up to block him from hitting her. Surprisingly fire shot from her hand nailing him in the chest and sending him flying back a few feet. His laughter echoed around her as he spoke, "fire doesn't hurt me, it only tickles. I will enjoy killing you fire."

He got up and started to run at her and Allie knew this was it. He took a leap at her with claws aiming at her throat as Allie's eyes went big. A sudden gust of wind came out of nowhere and instead of the man killing her with his claws, he was sent flying into a nearby tree. Allie's heart was pounding in her chest as she watched the man shake his head and get back up. He was glaring in her direction when suddenly his arms became flames. He lifted his arms and pointed them at her shooting a red flame at her. Shaking, Allie lifted her hands suddenly to have the blue flames create a shield blocking the red flames and slowly turning them to blue. Faster than Allie could blink the blue flames took over and sent the man on his butt again. A voice behind Allie spoke making Allie jump, "not bad for a rookie. However, game time is over and the demon needs to go bye so he can't report I'm here and all hell breaks loose."

Allie took in the man behind her with his black shoulder length hair and naturally tanned skin of an islander. She couldn't place his ethic, but defiantly from Asian descent. His eyes almost looked completely white if it wasn't for the slight shady of lavender in them. With a quick flick of his wrist, Allie watched the little twister form on the ground and race to the man that had attacked her. All Allie could do was watch as the twister swallowed up the man and then rip him to shreds before disappearing into the earth. Allie turned quickly to look at the other man with her heart pounding faster than it should. He gave her a smile that would melt the normal person, but at the moment Allie was very afraid.

"Hi I'm Ashley," he introduced himself. Allie continued to stare at him as he waited for a response. "Ok and you are?"

Allie blinked as she tried to grasp what had just happened, none of it made sense. "I'm Allie," slipped out of her mouth not even sounding like her.

Ashley cocked his head and looked at her funny. Then he shook his head and spoke, "didn't your angel guide teach you anything?"

"You just made a man disappear over there that was planning to kill me," Allie stated the fact as Ashley was looking at her weird.

"That was a small thing. He was a minor demon, and nothing important compared to what we are trained to do." Ashley stated like it was fact. "Look, I felt your pull for help. We can only do that with our kind. We are elements Allie, it is who we are, and I'm surprised your angel has not told you this."

"I don't have an angel," Allie told him feeling frustrated. "I have no idea what you are even talking about. I can't even explain why a blue flame came out of my hand."

Ashley stared at her in shock as Allie felt like she was losing it. Then he shook his head and spoke, "wow, my angel didn't even know you existed. He said the fire element was male. He also thought it was clever on Nathanael's part to have another, but fire angels would never risk a female. Why are you special Allie?"

"Nathanael haunts my dreams," Allie said more to herself.

Allie didn't get a chance to finish that statement because suddenly her friends emerged from the path helping Rebecca who was limping. Janice was quick to look at her and speak, "Rebecca got hurt, I think she twisted her ankle or something. We are going to have to take her in to get it looked at." Janice then looked right at Ashley and spoke, "oh hi, who are you?"

Melissa and Rebecca looked like they were drooling looking at Ashley, but he had a look of concern on his face as he was looking at Rebecca's foot. "I'm an old friend of Allie's. Her mom told me where I could find her, and I did. I will carry her she shouldn't be on her foot at all."

Ashley moved right in and swooped Rebecca off her feet. She looked at him like he was her hero as Janice glared at him like she didn't believe a word Ashley had said. Then she focused on Allie and gave her the look like she had some explaining to do. Allie actually threw her hands up in the air as she didn't know what to say at all but the logical thing. "Ash, the cabin is not too far and that is where the jeep is. I can always run back and get it while you all wait here."

"Nonsense Allie, she is as light as a feather. Besides by the time you got there and back, it would take too long. However please lead the way," Ashley said with a smile on his face that made Allie not trust him too well.

As they slowly started the walk back to the cabin, the girls introduced themselves to Ashley, but surprisingly it was Rebecca that asked Ashley the question they all wanted to know. "So Ash, tell us, how did you and Allie meet, and why has she not told anyone?"

Ashley's smile lit up his whole face making him look younger. Rebecca stared at him like the deer in the headlights she couldn't look away if her life depended on it. "Our dads are business associates, and Allie and her family would use the beach house next to ours in the summers. I would help her collect shells, and we hung out together."

All three girls looked at Allie as she arched her eyebrow up at Ashley wondering what his plan was. He seemed normal and harmless at the moment, but he had also created a little twister to rip a man apart. She actually wanted to get away from him, far away from him. The downfall was that Rebecca was in his arms, and in no time they were back at the cabin. Ashley was quick to place Rebecca in the front of the jeep as Melissa moved to the driver side. She spoke quickly, "I'll take her straight to the walk in clinic, follow behind me with all of our stuff."

Within seconds of moving out of the way, Melissa took off leaving Allie with Janice and Ashley. "How did you get here Ashley?" Janice was quick to ask making him smile at her.

He even winked at her as he spoke, "I flew." Janice rolled her eyes but headed in the cabin to grab things as Allie held back watching Ashley. He spoke again, "you don't trust me?"

"No," Allie answered him honestly. "I don't even know you."

Ashley actually laughed at her as he spoke and shook his head. Then he took a step closer to her and invaded her personal space as he looked into her eyes. His expression became hard as he spoke. "Well little fire, you better learn to trust me or else you will be eaten by the next demon that tries to attack you. We elements need to stick together or else all of humanity will perish. I cannot understand why your angel did not teach you this."

Allie was at her limit of insanity as she worked on controlling her temper as she spoke. "I don't know you. I don't trust you. I don't like you. I've also had it with your level of insanity. You're a complete nut job and you need to fly back wherever you have come from."

Ashley actually smiled at her as he looked down at her. "You're incredibly sexy when your temper flares, but Allie your hand is on fire."

Allie was confused by his words as she was most likely giving him a strange look when Janice's voice came out of nowhere. "Allie a little help would be…" she didn't finish that statement as she stood in the doorway looking at Allie and Ashley.

Allie was quick to lift her hand up in a gesture to tell Janice she was coming, but she saw what her friend was staring at. Allie's hand was covered in a blue flame, and that alone made Janice freeze in the door frame. Ashley actually laughed as he reached out and grabbed her wrist to twist her hand towards him. His eyes stayed on Allie's as he bent down and slowly blew the flames on her hand out. He was still smiling as he spoke, "I'll let you get use to the idea of being an element Allie, but our time is short. We only have ten days to the crowning and then all hell is going to break loose."

Allie blinked as she felt him let go of her hand. Then she watched him slowly evaporate into the wind as if he was never there. Taking a deep breath Allie turned to try to explain what had just happened to Janice, however Janice was lying on the ground. It was clear that she fainted and for once in her life, Allie was grateful.

CHAPTER NINETEEN
THE CROWNING

A lot had happened in ten days for Allie, but the only thing Allie was thankful for was the fact that her hands had not produced any more flames. Rebecca had only twisted her ankle, but for the pass ten days she had pretty much stayed home. Janice seemed to call Allie everyday and ask her about Ashley, but she always seemed busy to meet up later. Melissa would call and want details on what happened between her and Archer, but she was also too busy to hang out. Sad part was that Allie really needed her friends because it had been ten days, and she had not heard one thing from Archer either.

Allie was pouting to herself because she had no one to cheer her up. She was channel surfing wearing a pair of terry cloth shorts with a black tee while eating pop corn. Her mother was at work and she was all alone, yet she didn't want her mom to see her like this anyway. Allie couldn't help but think that Archer had finally won. Her first time ever having sex was with him, and he ruined it for everyone else. Her pity party thought was that it was a one night stand too. It angered her that he planned it so well so she would always remember him. Even now she was thinking of him and not even paying attention to the channel she landed on. She was quick to turn off the television and stare out the window. It was dark out, but the moon was full and bright, that Allie moved to sit in the window stile. She was lost in thought about all the strange things that had happened to her and thoughts of Archer that she jumped when her doorbell rang.

Taking a minute to catch her breath, Allie rose up slowly and made her way to the door. It rang again right as she reached it that it made her a little irritated as she jumped again. Opening the door while controlling her temper for the rude person behind it, Allie received the shock of her life. She didn't even have a chance as a hand snaked around her body and pulled her into a strong body followed by a pair of lips that took hold of hers making her forget why she was mad. Allie was lost in that kiss that she didn't even care who it was that was kissing her. When the kiss ended, Allie was trying to catch her breath that it took her a minute to open her eyes to look up in a pair of dark green ones. Archer's voice was instant as he spoke, "I've missed those kisses and I've missed you Allie."

Allie blinked as she thought she should be furious with Archer because ten day without a word was a little cold. The main part of Allie was thrilled to be in his arms right now relieved that it wasn't a one night stand. "Where have you been," came out of Allie's mouth smoothly as she stared up at him.

Archer smiled still holding her tight to him. "I've been working Allie, but tonight I will be promoted, so all worth it. I want you to be there with me while I'm promoted. I want you by my side always."

Allie blinked not thinking she heard Archer right. Was Archer declaring that she was the only one for him, and when did he get a job? Allie actually started to pull back to realize that Archer was in a very nice black suit with a red tie. He was stunning. "You're all dressed up and I have nothing to wear," Allie stated as she nibbled on her bottom lip unsure of herself and afraid of where this would lead with Archer.

Archer's eyes twinkled as he spoke, "well I planned for that Allie." With his other hand he pulled out a designer garment bag. He finally let go of her to open the bag to reveal a stunning red dress that matched his tie. Allie was speechless as Archer spoke, "will you wear this for me Allie, and I've always wanted to see you in red."

A smile started to grow on Allie's lips. She reached out and took the bag from Archer feeling like Cinderella. "I'd love to," slipped out of her mouth as she took the bag.

Archer smiled big as he grabbed Allie and kissed her again. He didn't want to stop kissing her, but time was against them tonight as he spoke. "Hurry up and change, we only have an hour before I have to be there."

"Only an hour," Allie replied feeling panicked as she moved out of Archer's arms and back inside heading up to her room to change while telling Archer to come in and she would make it quick. She even called out to him while she was changing to call her mother so she would know where she was. An hour wasn't much time to get ready, and she had less than that if they had to be there in an hour.

Thirty minutes later Allie emerged out of her room feeling like a princess. The red dress was strapless, but so tight around her chest that it made her not need a bra. It also pretty much molded to her every curve until it flared out by her knees. Allie only had half of her hair up as the rest hung loose behind her. She had also placed on a pair of red pumps that she had worn for Christmas a year ago. She was glad that they matched. Heading out to where Archer was, Allie was nervous. Her heart was pounding as she rounded the corner to see him standing in front of the window looking out at the moon. He was waiting patiently for her but something about him told Allie that he was nervous. It made her smile that she wasn't the only one as she cleared her throat to get his attention.

Slowly Archer turned around to look at Allie to suddenly have his heart stop. She was stunning. Wraith and Greed both wanted her on the spot, but it was War that made him smile.

"You look beautiful Allie," came out of Archer's mouth easily as he felt his heart jump start again.

Allie blushed as she looked down. A second had to pass before suddenly she felt Archer's fingers lifting her chin up. She looked up into his dark green eyes and smiled at him as he leaned in and stole a kiss. Allie was melting against him that she was surprised when he pulled back and shook his head. His voice was instant, "we got to get going Allie, or else we will be late."

Within minutes they were out the door and driving away in Archer's car. Allie couldn't help but watch him as he drove. He was holding onto her hand, but focused on the road. Allie didn't even realize they stopped until Archer turned and smiled at her. "We're here," he stated as the car door opened for Allie.

Stunned Allie noticed the valet service waiting to take the car as Archer got out. They were at Archer's house, but it looked like a huge party was going on. Getting out of the car slowly, Allie verily shook the shock off of her before Archer was next to her helping her. His smile became her focus as she couldn't look away from him as he led her inside. The music was the first thing Allie heard that woke her up. Her head turned away from Archer to notice all kinds of people eating and dancing. Most stood in groups talking, but it seemed like most of them turned their heads to look at her and Archer.

"This is some party Archer," Allie stated glad she was dressed right.

His hand was around her waist as he was leading her in the room, that she looked back at him feeling that together they could conquer the world. He came to a stop suddenly and Allie noted that Archer's dad was looking at her with a smile. "Allie I'm so glad Archer brought you here for this. Tonight is his and his siblings' greatest accomplishment."

"I'm glad to be here Mel," Allie said politely. "You must be very proud of him and the others."

"Allie you look stunning, and you're on the wrong brother's arm," Kane's voice came out of nowhere making Allie turn.

Allie was instant to smile as she thought Kane looked handsome dressed in a black suit. He also held his arms open for a hug, and Allie moved right in them giving him a hug. Price's voice was next making Allie peek out from between Kane's arms. "Wow brother, share already, I've missed Allie."

Allie laughed as she escaped Kane and moved to Price to give him a hug as well. "Your health is much better I'm so glad to see."

Price laughed as he held her tighter, "all thanks to you Allie."

"Allie!" Archer's sister Lacy stated in shock making her look at his only sister. She also had a mirror out powdering her nose, but she gave her a wink anyway as she continued to speak. "They are trying to mess up your hair and what little make up you have on. We girls need to stick together anyway or they will outnumber us."

That statement made Allie laugh, and it surprised her when Lacy held out her hands for a hug as well. Naturally Allie hugged her as well feeling like Archer's family had accepted her for who she was, and it didn't matter that the room was full of people she didn't know. Archer was quick to move her out of his family's arms and into his own as he seemed to always be touching her. Allie's eyes darted across the room looking at the people all dressed amazingly. She saw both Aaron and Fred looking just as sharp as Archer did and she smiled at them to only have them bow to her. That made Allie confused on why they would bow to her. She had a confused look on her face when a guy dressed in a sharp grayish blue suit walked up to their group. "Mel it has been too long," the man greeted Archer's dad as he continued to speak. "You must be so proud of your children, but who is the treat that your youngest has brought?"

Mel smiled at the man as he looked at Allie. Allie didn't imagine it she saw pride in his eyes as he looked at her.

"Allie I would like you to meet Paymon, he is the master of ceremonies. Paymon with luck, Allie will be Archer's bride."

Allie's heart started to pound in her chest as she couldn't believe what Archer's dad had just said. She even thought that she had to mishear him clearly he wasn't planning on Archer and her getting married. This was only the second time they had been together without fighting. That thought was weird to Allie too as Archer seemed to mold her backside with a hand around her waist. Paymon was smiling at her as he spoke, "I would be honored to host that ceremony when the time comes. Will you both think of me?"

Archer was instant to comment, "It is us that would be honored to have you."

Paymon smiled big and then made an excuse to move on. Within minutes another man walked up. Allie couldn't turn away from his face that looked angelic, and he seemed to ignore everyone in the group but her. In fact he spoke only to her, "hello young one."

Allie blinked as Archer's arm became tighter around her. "Hi," she said feeling awkward.

He smiled at her as he spoke, "ah she even has the voice of an angel." His eyes closed for a moment like he was savoring what had just happened and then he spoke again. "War I'm tempted to steal her from you, she is much too beautiful to be on your arm."

"Your way too old for her to be on yours Arrael," Archer told him through clenched teeth.

Arrael laughed at Archer's comment, but his eyes stayed on Allie. "Your name little one," he asked her next.

"Allie," came out next as she stared at him to suddenly see him frown and look at her funny.

"Allie McAlister," he said instantly.

"Yes," Allie responded as Arrael shook his head like he couldn't believe it.

Arrael laughed so suddenly that several others around him stopped to stare at them. "Oh Allie you have been on my list before to vanish before I could get you. I'm sure it was their doing," he stated as he pointed at Archer's siblings. "I'm sure I will get to see you again," he said as he reached for her hand and placed a kiss on it. However his eyes lingered on the ring she wore. His words were instant, "I see you have been blessed by the red witch. She protects you even now."

Allie slowly took her hand back as he stared at her one last time before turning and walking away. She couldn't help but watch him walk away as her hand felt tingly. Allie didn't get to linger on his behavior long before a man with a beautiful girl came up. Allie felt herself drawn to the girl with the long blond hair with blues and purples in it. Her eyes were like the brightest emeralds she had ever seen, that Allie wasn't aware that she was staring back at her just as hard. The man's laugh drew Allie's attention as he saw him giving Archer's father a hug. "Mel you old dog, you must be so proud of your children. Tonight is the beginning of the end."

Archer's dad laughed as he spoke, "Cal it is good to see you old friend, and what a beautiful creature you have on your arm tonight."

Cal's eyes lit up as he spoke and wrapped an arm around the girl. "Oh yes this is my pet Melody. The boys fight over her for some unknown reason. Would you believe that I won her in a card bet against her father when she was a baby, it was the best bet I ever made."

Archer's dad laughed at this as Allie suddenly felt confused. "Yes humans are so foolish sometimes," Archer's dad said as he turned and looked at Allie. "This is Archer's future bride, Allie," he said next as he gestured towards her.

Allie felt shocked by Archer's dad's statement, and wasn't surprised that Archer's grip became tighter. It dawned on Allie then that he was afraid she was going to bolt. He knew her too well, because she turned to look at him about to say what was going on when he suddenly kissed her. She was lost in that kiss that it took her a minute to realize where she was. Pulling back slowly she heard Lacy speak, "I need to find someone to make me feel like that."

Price's comment was instant, "you won't Lacy, and they wouldn't be able to compete with your mirror."

It was a funny comment that Allie watched Lacy stick her tongue out at Price. Then she looked back at Melody that was now glaring at her like she instantly hated her. In fact if looks could kill, she would be dead. Cal on the other hand smiled at her before he ushered Melody away. Allie was frowning as she watched them walk away, confused why the girl decided to hate her. She jumped instantly hearing a voice she knew, "oh my Allie you look stunning in red."

Allie turned the other direction to see Ashley standing there in a suit that seemed made just for him in white. Next to him a man stood with long white hair and white eyes wearing a black suit as he was cocking his head at her like he was curious until he smiled at her. Allie spoke instantly, "Ashley I'm surprised to see you here."

Archer nearly growled as he moved her behind him and glared at Ashley who was smiling with a twinkle in his eye. "How do you know this trash Allie?" Archer growled at Allie making her jump as his grip on her arm became tighter.

"Archer you are hurting my arm, let go." Allie responded as she tried to twist it out of his painful grip.

Kane was suddenly next to her as he spoke, "Samael why did you bring trash?"

The man with the white hair spoke, "I brought my air with me. He's cocky and I like him. Besides the elements have to be present for tonight's crowning. I can't wait to see the other elements I heard they are all girls, except my air."

"He looks like a girl to me," Price's words came instantly like he wanted to fight.

Ashley actually laughed at Price's comment, but his eyes were on Allie as he spoke. "You do look beautiful Allie, but you're surrounded by a bunch of assholes. Shame that they have you in their clutches, I'm sure that will change after tonight. Catch up with you later, and save me a dance Allie," Ashley said with a wink before turning and walking away with the man with white hair.

Archer turned around glaring at Allie as his grip on her arm became tighter. Allie nearly protested in pain as her hand was instant to try to get him to release her. Archer was furious as he spoke, "how do you know him Allie?"

"Let go of me Archer now," Allie replied back just as furious as Archer was.

Kane's voice was the voice of reason as he spoke, "brother your grip on her arm is hurting her." He slowly let go of Allie's arm as Kane's voice made him relax a little. Then Kane focused on Allie once Archer let go and she was rubbing her arm. "Allie how do you know him?"

Allie responded instantly, "He's the one that saved Rebecca when she twisted her ankle."

Archer looked like he was going to hit something as Allie could feel his anger. She was still rubbing her arm and knew she would bruise. Archer's voice was instant. "I forbid you to ever talk to him again Allie."

Allie was instant to look up at Archer and lift an eyebrow up at him. "You forbid me?" Allie responded thinking she didn't hear him right.

"Damn right I forbid you. I don't want you nowhere near him," Archer said through clenched teeth.

Allie almost snorted at that as she started to lose her temper. "You have no right to forbid me in anything Archer Stevens. Last time I checked I was free, and if I want to stand next to an asshole I will."

Allie was outraged. Her arms were throbbing now. Archer took a step closer to her and invaded her personal space looking down at her with a heat stare. Allie looked up at him with the same heated stare as his lips slowly spread in a smile.

Within seconds Archer was kissing the breath out of Allie. Allie forgot where she was and why she was so mad to begin with. She was lost in that kiss that seemed to go on forever until someone spoke, "wow, does War need a time out before we get this crowning going?"

The kiss ended that suddenly as Allie felt her cheeks go red and Archer's grip pull her in closer to him. Archer's father was the one to speak, "Duma, we have been waiting for you to arrive so the crowning can begin. Archer will claim her afterwards."

Allie couldn't help but look at the new comer to notice that his eyes were almost the same shade of purple as hers, and he was staring at her in wonder for several seconds before he shook his head and spoke. "Alright then let's get this thing started and over with, I'm a very busy angel."

Allie blinked at his words thinking she didn't hear him right. Duma was the angel of dreams Allie remembered her mother telling her when she was little. It made her feel protected when she went to sleep, that she was shaking her head thinking it couldn't be. Duma's eyes lingered on her for a minute longer, and it made Allie feel awkward. Archer seemed to notice it as well, and moved Allie behind him as if to shield her. The action made Duma smile at him and nod his head as he spoke, "You're lucky to have her War, but the trick is how to keep her." He clapped his hands together so suddenly as he continued, "well I will get this thing started."

Allie watched him from behind Archer turn and walk towards a stage that seemed to suddenly appear. She noticed four pillows on pillars right next to him as he suddenly spoke into a microphone. "Ladies and gentlemen, it is time for the crowning of the four horsemen. So without farther delay, let's begin."

Allie felt the color draining out of her face as Duma said those words. Mentally she thought that she had to be asleep and needed to wake up. There was no way she had heard him right. Archer moved her into his arms easy enough, but he was not looking at her but looking at Duma on the stage. Duma's voice rang out as he walked the first pillar and picked up a single ring that was silver with a white stone. "In my hands I hold the ring of death. Death I call you forward now to claim your ring and your powers." Allie watched Kane walk forward to claim the ring as her heart pounded. Duma didn't hand him the ring, he placed it on his finger as it glowed, and then very suddenly Allie notice a shadow that reminded her of the grim reaper with wings enter inside Kane as he smiled.

Duma moved to the next pillar as Kane stayed on the stage. Duma's voice made Allie's heart beat louder. "In my hands I hold the ring of Pestilence. Pestilence I call you forth now to claim your ring and your powers." Allie looked at the ring that was gold with a pale green stone for a second as she watched Lacy move towards it. She wanted to shake her head at what was happening, but seeing Archer's sister on the stage now with a strange white glow behind her told Allie too well that she had indeed received those powers.

Duma moved to the next pillar and picked up a silver ring with a black stone. His voice spoke loud again. "In my hands I hold the ring of famine. Famine I call you forth now to claim your ring and your powers." Allie watched Price move forward to claim the ring as she turned and looked up at Archer with panic in her eyes. She knew he was next and felt like she had to stop him, yet she didn't know how. He turned his head down and looked at her, and Allie noticed how dark his eyes were as he smiled. Allie watched him as Duma spoke again. "In my hands I hold the ring of war. War I call you forth now to claim your ring and your power."

Allie was instant to shake her head as words failed her. Archer just smiled at her and then leaned down placing a kiss on her temple as he spoke, "everything will be alright my love, I promise you this."

He moved away from Allie without a second look as Allie felt the lost. Her hands were shaking as she watched him walk up for Duma to place a plain gold band on his fingers. Her heart stopped as she saw the shadow behind Archer enter inside him. She felt the first tear leak from her eyes as she suddenly thought she had lost Archer forever.

Archer finally felt complete as War merged with him. He felt strong as Duma announced his siblings and him as the four horsemen to the crowd that came to witness the crowning. He had a smile on his lips as his eyes searched for where Allie was, and then his heart stopped as his smile vanished. His heart started to pound in his chest as Wraith and Greed cried out a no. Allie was crying as she stared at him shaking her head like her heart was just broken. However she wasn't crying tears. Allie was crying little blue flames that were running down her face and along her arms claiming her as an element of fire, in which made her the enemy. Archer felt a breath escape him as he felt a little deceived now however War was smiling inside him as he spoke directly to him in his mind. "She is my bride, fire is mine. I will claim her now."

Allie didn't notice the flames she was staring at Archer as he started to move directly towards her. She didn't even notice the look on Mel's face or any of the others. She couldn't stop crying knowing that Archer was one of the horsemen that would bring the end of the world. Archer was heading directly towards her as his father tried to stop him, and Allie didn't know why. Archer moved his father aside keeping his eye on Allie. Allie had to look down to break the eye contact and that was when she noticed that her arms were on fire along with part of the floor around her. It was strange that the flames were not burning, but more like circling around her in protection. Archer's voice is what made her look up from her scared panic, "Allie." Just him saying her name made her look at him to notice that his hand was reaching out to her for her to come to him. "Allie everything will be alright let me in love."

"Archer," Allie choked out with a sob. She couldn't speak as all words failed her as she felt like she couldn't stand up much longer.

"It's ok Allie, take my hand. I promise you I will protect you always. No one will hurt you ever. You are my heart and you always have been."

Allie's hand was shaking as she slowly lifted it up reaching out for Archer. She heard several no's around the room, but only one person hushing someone. She was scared and the truth was Archer was the only one she trusted. Her fingers shook bad as she spoke, "you've always been my heart too."

Archer smiled at her as she slowly placed her hand in his trusting him completely where her flames did not hurt him. Her words melted his insides. Her words alone told him that she had always loved him, and she always would. He was quick to lean in and kiss her lips loving the taste of her. He pulled back from the kiss feeling her flames now dancing along his skin yet not burning him. He stared directly into her eyes as War spoke out of him. "Allie, I freely share my powers with you, for my heart I can't defend against you, I must protect you first. What is mine is now yours and always will be. Marry me Allie."

"No Archer," Archer's dad said from outside of the flames. "She is your enemy," came next as Archer turned and glared at his father to silence him.

Archer took a minute to look at every one by his father the only one not shocked was Kane. It made him wonder if he knew all this time about Allie and understood why he was doing it. His brother seem to nod at him for to continue as Archer felt a smile on his lips and looked back at Allie who never took her eyes off of him. She seemed so lost that he knew she was having a hard time excepting this. The whole room was in silence watching the two of them as Allie had yet to respond. She seemed to close her eyes for a minute and take a breath as Archer watched her closely not knowing that he was holding his breath. Slowly Allie opened her eyes. Archer couldn't believe how beautiful her amethyst eyes looked swimming with little blue fire tears. She opened her mouth to speak but nothing came out at first. She closed her eyes and slowly shook her head making Archer think she was turning him down. Then suddenly Allie looked him straight in the eye and found her voice. "I love you Archer. I always have. You've been my heart from the first time I saw you, and you always will. Any power I have will always protect you first, as my power is half yours. I will marry you."

Joy spread through Archer. He was instant to wrap his arms around Allie and kiss her deeply that he missed the gasp around the room. He didn't even realize that Allie's little blue flames were soaking into his skin. He started to slowly pull back from the kiss when his father's words broke the silence. "What have you done?"

Allie turned and looked at Mel's shocked expression. In fact he didn't look too good at all, and Allie wondered if he was having a heart attack. His eyes were darting back and forth between the two of them like he couldn't believe his eyes. A tingling on her left hand made Allie look down at her hand to suddenly notice a gold band on her finger. She lifted her shaky hand feeling like none of this was real when a man suddenly spoke, "the marriage has been approved it seems."

Allie's eyes darted to the man who spoke. He looked like a model with very dark eyes with white hair. She knew instantly he was a demon, but he was the king of demons, Abaddon. He bowed to her as if he approved of what he had just witnessed before he suddenly just disappeared before her eyes. Archer's father then spoke grabbing Allie's attention. "You have betrayed us tonight Archer, all for the enemy. I shall rip you apart with my bare hands."

Archer's father lunged for them, and Allie's first instinct was to protect Archer. Without knowing how, flames leaped out of Allie's fingertips creating a wall around them. She had moved herself between Archer and his father who stopped in his tracks knowing he could not go through the wall to get them. He stared at Allie with a glare as Archer suddenly laughed sounding evil. "Oh father, you need to calm down and realize how great this is. Allie and my children will be so much stronger for the next line of horsemen that they will be unstoppable. Not only that, but she has betrayed the elements by choosing me. This round goes to the horsemen as claiming fire as one of our own. She is already one of us, and accepted by the rest of my siblings, together we will wipe the rest of them out."

Kane stood next to Archer's dad and spoke, "you tied your life forces together. To kill one kills the other. They can't hurt you without hurting her and vice versa, very clever." Kane then looked down at Allie and smiled as he spoke. "Little sister, I welcome you with open arms like I always have."

Allie blinked as she felt something she had never felt before. Her eyes moved around the room in her little protective circle. It felt like a calling coming from two people in the room. Her eyes landed on Ashley as she could feel his power ready to attack if needed, and then her eyes moved to the girl named Melody. She was glaring daggers of hate at her making Allie feel guilty for choosing love. Archer's voice was instantly next to her. "Allie kill any of the elements in the room, they threaten us."

Shock made Allie wake up as deep down she felt the pain in her chest. She looked at Archer feeling torn between love and duty. She slowly moved away from him as the flame wall slowly went down and raced back to her. Everyone was watching her as she shook her head and spoke, "you're using me Archer. I gave you my heart and already you have ripped it out to feast on. I will kill an element in the room, but not the one you think."

Allie turned to the table next to her and picked up one of the knives. She looked at Archer feeling like it would be finally over as she closed her eyes with a smile on her lips raising the knife. She could hear Archer call out a no, but it was Ashley that spoke as he knocked the knife out of her hands. "I'm sorry Allie, but not going to let you kill an element tonight. However War should know that I plan on having his bride tonight so the marriage will never be consumed."

Ashley's lips were very soft as they came down on Allie's. Then suddenly she felt him sucking the air out of her mouth as darkness made her black out and the pain go away.

CHAPTER TWENTY
REALIZATION

Archer felt everyone closing in on him as the element of air took off with his bride. His whole world suddenly seemed destroyed in seconds and it was all Air's fault for touching Allie. Wraith was roaring in his head to get her back as Greed seemed to be pissed that the element of Air would kiss lips that belonged to him. He wanted to fight, he wanted to maim, and mostly he wanted the element of Air's blood to drink for breakfast. Before anyone could move his head snapped in the direction of his father's friend Cal and his female guest named Melody. For some reason War inside him wanted to take it all out on her because part of this was her fault. She thought she was clever and going on unnoticed, she was dead wrong about that, he knew who she was. Her eyes met his as she stared at him from across the room, and then slowly her lips curved in a little knowing smile, as if she was accepting the challenge from him and taunting him. That smile confirmed that she was part of this somehow and responsible for Allie being abducted by Air, so she would pay.

Rage ate at Archer as he suddenly grabbed the nearness table and flung it in her direction like it was nothing more than a rock. Cal was quick to move, but the girl did not move an inch. Instead she raised her hand up and blasted the table with water of all things sending it flying up and to the right. Archer felt more rage as he suddenly created an illusion of several of him. Each one of him surrounded the girl who suddenly laughed. Her laugh made him pause in his attack, because in his current mood she had to be insane to taunt him like this. "I'm much stronger than you are War. Unlike the other elements, I learned long ago how to control water demons among other things."

Her eyes darted around the room as he felt others moving in, and then suddenly Archer was under attack. Several demons were in fact attacking him and the other images of him, as he felt his siblings joining in to help him. It seemed like every water demon in the room attacked them, and by the time the mess was cleaned up and they were winning, the girl named Melody was still laughing as she spoke. "Fool. You tied yourself to the element of fire, and you did it before any of us elements joined forces. This time we are much more powerful, and you shared your powers with her. So like she said, an element will die tonight, no regrets. I kill her, you die. I have no regrets, just one less horseman to deal with."

She seemed to melt into a puddle of water and then suddenly disappeared before his eyes as the water evaporated. Panic hit Archer hard as most of the water demons seemed to snap out of whatever spells the element of water had placed on them. His eyes darted around the room to land on Samael. The angel of death stared back at him and then suddenly spoke. "She meant her vow War and she is far from weak not to be able to stand alone against anyone. I will admit I never saw that coming and never has it happened before. For her alone, I will send someone to guild her and teach her how to use her powers if you will allow it once you have her back. However you should learn your words better, you have no idea how much you have just wounded her. She was willing to kill herself to be free of your tormenting and take you with her if I didn't have Air stop her. You are her weakness War, but the question is she yours?"

Archer screamed instantly in frustration. His fist slammed into the closest wall and destroyed it as his breathing was heavy. Kane was the only one that dared to touch his shoulder as he spoke calming him some. "We will find her brother. Air wouldn't dare touch her as you have touched her. Nothing can hide from Death. We go now and we bring her back, even if it is kicking and screaming."

Why suddenly the kicking and screaming part made Archer smile he had no clue, but he felt both his demons smiling inside. He would have Allie back tonight and consume the vow they had made to each other.

Allie was slowly waking to a voice that didn't sound too happy. In fact the voice was sure laying into someone as it took her a minute to get herself to focus to notice she was in a very basic bedroom with nothing on the walls. "You're a complete idiot Ash to bring her here. I've only been free of that monster for ten damn days and you know how many visions I have had? Let me tell you it has been the same damn vision over and over again, and it surrounds her, the one that is in my bed. You do realize that they will be able to track her, so they will come directly here, and guess what will happen to me."

"Ellie calm down, I didn't know what to do, and I panicked. She was going to kill herself. She couldn't except that the guy she was in love with was the bad guy and planned to use her to destroy us. Even I felt her heart breaking over that. You should have been there to see it Ellie, she had no clue what he was and he had no clue what she was."

"It doesn't matter Ash, they will come here soon and you will have to leave. If that monster comes I can kiss my freedom good bye. If she leaves here I will be punished, and either way I will be the one that pays. Have you forgotten that my power has yet to surface and according to my vision it will not emerge until I die? I'm the weakest of the elements."

Allie heard something move and suddenly she knew that Ashley was holding the girl in the other room. Even lying in the bed she knew that they loved each other and it made her heart throb. Slowly she opened her eyes to have the girl named Melody in her face. It made her move back instantly that she nearly fell off the bed as the girl snorted. She spoke instantly, "you have done us a great favor tonight. We kill you, we kill War, and the horsemen will be easy to take out."

Melody suddenly had a dagger in her hands, and Allie had to move fast off the bed as the dagger landed in the mattress cutting it deep. She laughed as she pulled it out and walked around the bed. Allie was backing up against the wall with nowhere to run. She was bracing herself to die at this girl's hands when suddenly Ashley was in the room knocking the dagger out of Melody's hands. Melody had no problem glaring at Ashley as she spoke. "Don't stop me in this Air. We kill her and we take out a horseman. She is not the element of fire the element of fire is a boy. She is the fake lure to cover for him."

"Melody, we will not kill Allie even if it would make us in the lead. I will not risk my loves life because you never asked for this gift to save humanity. I'm even sorry that you hate humanity because of what your father did to you, but don't take it out on her," Ashley said gesturing to Allie.

Melody seemed to puff as she glared hard at Allie. She spoke instantly, "I don't trust you Allie. You're screwing War of all people. If you make me regret not killing you tonight, I will make you pay in the most painful of ways, do we understand each other?"

Allie nodded at Melody as her back was against the wall. She didn't know if she should be scared or thankful. Melody seemed to nod at Allie's response and got up walking out of the room. That was when Allie noticed the other girl standing in the doorway watching Allie. For several minutes she found the girl to be beautiful as she could not place her ethic. Her strongest features looked African American, but she could see Native American as well. The girl moved closer to her as her hand touched Ashley before she kneeled next to her on the floor. Her voice was instant as Allie looked her straight in the eye. "I've seen you in my visions Allie. In fact visions of you saved my life more than once from Death. I owe you one for that, but I must tell you that we will not have much time before they will be here. War will be coming for you as he has marked you for his bride, and he will not be stopped until he has you back. He won't care if you go willingly or not, he will take you."

Allie seemed to nod not trusting her voice. She was still trying to understand everything that had happened, and believe that none of it was true. Ashley kneeled down next to the girl as he too spoke, "I'm sorry Allie for what I did back there, but you were losing it. No way would I hit you either to make you realize it was all true, but I will have to say it was fun to kiss the breath out of you with War watching. He was beyond pissed with what I did."

The girl rolled her eyes at Ashley as he smiled at her. For the first time Allie found her voice, "you shouldn't have stopped me."

Both of them stared at her in disbelief about her words. The girl was the one that spoke, "Allie you do not mean what you say."

"Yeah I do mean it," Allie was quick to say. "I love him so much that I hate him for making me feel this way. I'm broken and useless and I don't know my purpose in all of this. If you wouldn't have stopped me, I would be at peace right now," Allie directed at Ashley.

The girl's eyes seemed to film over with a white spooky look. Her voice was instant as she spoke, "they are here. Ashley you and Melody need to leave now. They do not know I am Earth."

Ashley's voice was instant, "Ellie, I'm not leaving you here knowing you will be at risk to that monster. Come with us."

"No," Ellie said instantly. "I need to stay with Allie, she needs me."

Ashley looked like he was about to argue when Melody reappeared back in the room with someone pounding on the door. Kane's voice was strong as he spoke, "Ellie undo the wards to your door now and let us in."

Allie blinked at the way Kane sounded as she slowly stood up thinking that Kane would hurt Ellie. Ashley wrapped his arms around Ellie holding her like he was protecting her as Melody hissed in a quiet voice at Allie, "Protect her."

Allie walked slowly towards the door that Kane was pounding on and swearing through. She couldn't believe that the apartment didn't have much in it and everything was white. It seemed like if Ellie was to leave, she wouldn't need to take anything with her because nothing in her place was personal. Then suddenly Allie did see one thing that did stand out in her apartment, it was a rosary made with agate and jade. Some reason it gave her strength and Allie knew she had to protect Ellie as she found her voice. "Go away Kane, and tell Archer to drop dead."

The banging on the door stopped and it was followed by silence for several minutes. Then suddenly Allie heard Kane's laughter on the other side. His voice was nearly a purr on the other side as he spoke. "Oh little sister, we have been worried sick about you. I'm surprised Air brought you to my witch."

Allie snorted thinking yeah right Ellie was his witch. Her temper exploded a little as she spoke. "She is not your witch Kane, she doesn't belong to you, and she is not an object. On her behalf you can drop dead too, geez I can see where Archer gets it from. I'm sure your father is the same way."

He was laughing on the other side of the door as he spoke, "oh come on Allie tell me why Air brought you here to the witch?"

Ellie was suddenly next to Allie as she unlocked the door and opened it. Kane was nearly framing the door as Ellie spoke. "He knew it was the only place you could not see until you came to me to look for her. I have kept her safe for you my lord."

Kane's eyes narrowed at Ellie, and Allie did not like the way that Ellie would not make eye contact with Kane. She was scared of him, and Kane was enjoying scaring Ellie. Without thinking Allie stepped between the two of them and glared up at Kane. "Knock it off you oversized bully."

Kane blinked at Allie's words really surprised that she was bold enough to go against him. "Little sister I'm not someone you wish as an enemy."

Allie glare became more intent as she spoke. "I can say the same big brother."

Flames lit up along Allie's arms as she blocked Kane from entering to get to Ellie. He watched her amused as he spoke. "You still have lots to learn little sister. It will be fun to teach you as the days come and go. I will make you one promise tonight. Tonight I will not harm the witch if you come willingly back with me to Archer. He needs you Allie."

Allie didn't even hesitate as she responded. "No, you will leave her alone period, or you can just jump in a lake with Archer."

Kane's smile formed so fast on his lips that Allie verily had time to blink before he moved. Within seconds he reached in and grabbed her pulling her out of the witch's apartment. Allie couldn't help but gasp at the move as he didn't stop there but lifted her up and toss her on his shoulder like she was nothing but a rag doll. Allie started to kick and scream only to have Kane swat her butt as he spoke while walking down the hallway. "Calm down Allie or you'll rip your dress. Besides I made a promise to my brother to find you and bring you back even if it is kicking and screaming."

Archer paced the living area of his home as his father stared at him. He was worried about Allie more than anything that it over rode his anger at Air. "Archer, Kane will find her," his father said instantly trying to calm him.

Archer stopped pacing and looked at his father as he felt War come to life. "You doubted my choice of bride, thinking I did not know who I was choosing. Your doubt made me explain my reasoning to you and hurting her because she doesn't understand everything yet. The fact that Air would dare touch her makes this very personal between the two of us, so don't try to calm me. I will not be calm until she is back here in my arms."

Archer's father blinked as Archer went back to pacing the living room waiting to hear anything from Kane. It had been hours, but it felt like years to Archer as each minute passed by. Fury suddenly walked in the room with a huge smile on his face as he spoke instantly, "Kane has her."

Archer stopped his pacing as his father stood up. He found he couldn't talk as he felt relieved that Kane had her now and she would be back here very soon. Archer actually closed his eyes and took a breath as his father spoke, "how long before Kane returns?"

Fury didn't answer as Archer suddenly heard Allie calling Kane every name in the book. Kane walked into the room within seconds after Archer heard Allie. She was kicking and yelling over Kane's shoulder to be let down as her arms were on fire. Kane's backside showed exactly how dangerous her arms could be if she seriously wanted to hurt him. Kane slowly sat her feet on the ground as she glared at him hard.

Kane's voice was instant. "Allie you wound me by calling me all of these names, however you should know fire doesn't hurt me when I am part fire demon." Kane then looked at Archer and spoke again. "She was with my witch. Good hiding place since it was the only place I could not see. However Allie is mad at me now for bringing her back to you. I think she even told me to join you as we jump in a lake."

Archer stared at Allie hard. Even now she was beautiful as she had her hands crossed over her chest with her back towards him. She was refusing to look at him, but Archer didn't mind because she would be looking at him very soon. Her voice came out not directed at anyone, "I demand to be able to go home. I have no desire to be here."

Archer smiled at her stubbornness. His voice was full of charm as he spoke, "Allie you are home."

She spun around so quickly and glared at him as she spoke in anger. "No Archer this is your home. My home is the normal one where the four horsemen don't exist, and people can't appear and reappear in thin air. I want no part of this world or anything that has to do with you."

Archer moved quicker than he ever had before. Within seconds he had Allie in his arms as his mouth came crushing down over hers. She started to protest at first but slowly she was melting. Within seconds she wasn't fighting him, but moaning in his mouth. Not wasting a minute, Archer picked up Allie to where she was cradled in his arms. Allie was catching her breath as she stared at him and he smiled at her. His voice was instant as he left the living area ignoring the smiles from the three inside it. "Allie you can't escape my world when you are my world. I love you Allie."

Allie stared up at Archer not fighting him at all now. He was taking her somewhere private, but that didn't matter to Allie. What mattered was what he had just said and how he was looking at her. She felt her insides melting slowly as he looked at her and at that moment Allie knew. "I love you too Archer."

Archer smiled down at Allie as he opened the door to his and Allie's room. He kissed her instantly planning to show her how much he did in fact love her.

CHAPTER TWENTY-ONE
REALITY

Allie was slow on waking up, but she felt warm and safe. Slowly she opened her eyes to be looking into Archer's dark green eyes. He was also smiling at her which left Allie staring at him with a smile of her own on her lips. She was sore all over from last night, but she wouldn't have changed the outcome. As happy as Allie was at the moment she suddenly started to frown as several thoughts crossed her mind. Archer was quick to speak not liking the fact that Allie was frowning after the night they had shared. "Allie what is wrong?"

Allie half smiled as she looked up at him. "Several things just ran through my mind, but I think it will work out."

This time Archer gave Allie a look she was use to as he spoke. "Allie I want you to be able to tell me anything that is on your mind no matter what."

Allie bit her bottom lip for a moment as Archer watched her cheeks heat up a little. She looked even more beautiful to him in his arms and in their bed with that blush coloring her cheeks. "I think my mom might start to worry about me since I never came home last night."

That wasn't what made her cheeks red, and Archer knew it. "Actually my father is breaking the news to your mom this morning over breakfast, and she knew you were with me last night. What else is on your mind?"

Allie was instant to bite her bottom lip as she thought for a moment not too sure how to go about the thought that was really on her mind. Then she took a breath and just said it. "You know you were my first, so you should know I'm not on birth control."

Allie was instant to stare up at Archer afraid of what he would say to that. He was wearing a huge smile on his lips as he knew this is what was bothering Allie the most. Without giving her a moment to wonder about his smile, he pulled her in closer to him and started to kiss the breath out of her. His hands even started to explore as Allie moaned. This made Archer smile in his kisses as Allie was about to be very sore. She had no idea that he knew all of those things about her, and that was what pleased him the most. Allie would only know him and no one else like this. Archer planned to mark every inch of Allie as his alone.

Allie woke up for the second time sore all over. Archer was no longer in the bed, but a single red rose was on the pillow where he had been. That alone made her smile as she stretched before she sat up thinking a shower would be nice. Within seconds she was up and padding her way into the private bathroom looking forward to that shower without a care in the world.

Archer was listening to his father talk to Allie's mom. Granted he was relieved when his father said he would take care of Liz, he wondered how she would take the news. Right at the moment they had finished breakfast and were sitting out on the back deck drinking coffee. So Archer was surprised to hear Liz start the conversation, "Alright Mel, I'm assuming you're trying to break something to me gently, but I already know about Archer and Allie secretly dating. I also know that Archer picked her up last night and she didn't come home. I assume you must want me to discourage Allie in having a relationship with Archer so he can pick his bride to recreate the next line of horsemen."

The fact that Liz knew all about that shocked Archer a little, his father must have told her a lot about them for her to be so calm about it. Mel was quick to hold her hand as he got right to the point. "Archer chose Allie to be his bride last night, and she accepted it." Liz gasped hearing this as Mel continued quickly. "Also you should know that Nathanael lied to you all those years ago. Allie is the element of fire."

"No," came out of Liz's mouth. She was even shaking her head in disbelief. "He said I only had to give up one child. He said my son was marked and took him. All these years not knowing my son and now he wants my Allie too. He can't have her too!"

Liz was crying, but Mel was quick to place his arms around her and just hold her. "It's ok Liz. I'm not sure how this will play out with Archer chosen her as his bride and her being an element. Either way the horsemen cannot hurt Allie without hurting Archer, and vice versa."

Archer listened more closely and then nearly jumped out of his skin when he heard the arch angel of death Samael speak. "Liz is one of the fallen, but she is also Nathanael's only daughter. As punishment, he took away one of her children for disgracing him. She cried for over three days in the hospital not letting anyone go near Allie. That was where she meant Allie's father he was trying to help her get her son back. I got to admire a mother's spirit to protect her child."

Archer stared at Samael shocked that he had snuck up on him so easily. Samael had a cup of coffee in his hand with a spoon stirring it like he was bored. He also smiled at Archer as Archer found his voice, "why are you here?"

Samael's smile got a little bigger as he took a sip of the coffee. After he took a drink he answered. "I told you that I would bring people to train Allie to use her powers. Funny part was that they were lining up on both sides. I thought it would be only fair to pick one from each side. The two of them had to agree to get along before I brought them with me."

Archer felt surprised hearing this news as he spoke. "Alright I will bite, who is here with you to teach my bride?"

Samael smiled as he spoke giving his eyes an unnatural glow. "Duma and Flereous will be teaching Allie, and they might already have begun."

Archer blinked surprised as he spoke, "an angel of dreams and a demon of fire will teach Allie without hurting her."

"Well I will be supervising to make sure they don't start fighting as well. However I expect that Allie will wipe the floor with both of them if they do fight. She is a lot stronger than she seems." Archer blinked at Samael and then nearly went into panic as he realized he had left Allie in their bed, and she had no clue she was about to have company. He moved quickly with Samael laughing behind him.

It took Allie several minutes to locate something she could wear. Lucky for her someone was thoughtful and left a small pair of terry cloth shorts and a tee shirt for her to wear. She suspected that Archer might have raided his sister's room for her, but either way she knew she needed to head home.

Everything she owned was there and she needed to talk to her mother.

Leaving the bedroom, Allie adventured into the hallway not really sure which way to go. She rounded a corner suddenly to be grabbed and tossed on the ground. Shocked, Allie turned her head to see who had grabbed her. A man with dark skin and red eyes looked at her with a smile on his lips. When his smile started to show teeth that were pointy, Allie started to scramble quickly away from him making him laugh. She heard another male voice speak instantly, "time to strip you of reality and see what you can do."

The walls seemed to darken around Allie until they faded away. She kept her eyes on the glowing red eyes as she was panicking inside. The minute the red eyes disappeared, Allie's breathing increased. She was scared out of her mind as she heard a voice nearly slither in front of her sounding like something out of a horror movie. "You're weak fire. You shouldn't be allowed to be his bride. Not fit to save yourself fire."

Allie was scared but suddenly something clicked inside her. It was a sudden calming as her skin started to tingle. She closed her eyes and took a breath as she spoke, "this is not reality. I'm in a lighted hallway. You're not here."

Laughter echoed around Allie as she opened her eyes to find herself still surrounded by darkness, however something was different. Her arms started to tingle like little electric shocks and Allie found herself slowly rising up. Her pale white skin started to glow lighting up the room like it was a beating heart. The glow became so bright that she saw the man with the red eyes just staring at her. His voice was instant, but it was directed to behind her. "That is not a fire element quality, this is something different."

He was staring at her like he was fascinated as he seemed to watch her, but the voice behind her made her turn to see Duma. "I'd like to know who your sire is Allie, but let's test this too for all I know this can be some weird side effect."

Before Allie could respond, both men seemed to disappear as she was the only light in the darkness. Her heart was still pounding in her chest as she felt the first chill enter her body. Suddenly she heard Archer's voice, "Allie where are you?"

His voice was suddenly cut off with a scream making Allie call out for him. She heard laughter around her as she kept calling out for Archer searching for him with just the soft glow of her skin. The man with the dark skin was instant to speak in the darkness. "Oh poor Allie can't even save her love. He will taste so good when I start eating his flesh."

Allie heard the sick noise of what sounded like something tearing into flesh followed by Archer's scream. Panicking Allie did something that was not expected. An energy shot out of her body lighting up the whole room with blue flames sending both men flying back in the air. She turned towards them ready to blast them with her flames as she suddenly saw her reflection in the mirror behind them. Her white creamy skin was glowing as her red locks looked like a breathing flame, but it was the set of blue fire wings behind her that made her stop. Her hands were trembling as she could hear Archer telling someone to let him go. She turned searching for him thinking he shouldn't see her like this, but she had nowhere to hide. With her heart pounding she looked back at the two men on the floor staring up at her knowing that someone was stopping Archer from getting to her. Her voice was instant, "don't let him see me like this. You two did this to me, so don't let him see me looking like this."

The man with the dark skin spoke first, "we cannot stop him, and he thinks you are hurt and in danger."

Duma then spoke as he seemed to be studying every inch of her, "why would you not want him to see you like this? You are very beautiful Allie with your magic invoked around you."

"Beautiful," Allie glared at Duma feeling anger and slowly being able to tell that he was looking at her a little too hard.

"Take a good look at me Duma. I'm covered in flames! How can this be beautiful? I'm horrid."

"You're right you're not beautiful," the man with the dark skin and pointy teeth said with a smile. "I'd say you are so horrid right now that you don't realize how sexy you are to me, but you should call in your flames before they burn the hallway to the ground along with your clothes, not that I don't mind a show, I just think I'd like to stay in tack without War ripping me to pieces."

Allie sucked in a breath. She tried to focus, but nothing happened. She tried again but still it did no good as Duma started to lean in closer looking at her with sharp eyes. "I can't," slipped out of Allie's mouth too quickly as she dropped to the ground feeling the tears escaping her eyes for something she had no control over.

Archer had to fight his way around the corner to get to Allie. Samael had blocked him every inch of the way, but all it did was slow him down. Even Kane and Price had joined in to help Samael and keep him from reaching Allie. Never had Archer been more upset with his brothers before, that they deserved those punches to the face. Having Lacy appear suddenly and tell them all to let him go seemed like a blessing. She only looked at them all and told Archer directly that he needed to see his bride to believe it. That was the only reason they let him go.

Archer raced to Allie knowing they were all directly behind him, but he skidded to a stop when he rounded the corner and saw her on her knees with Flereous and Duma also on their knees on the floor. Duma was also staring at Allie a little too intently that an instant distrust to the dream angel formed in Archer's mind. Archer stared at Allie feeling shocked to see her hair looking like a breathing flame as her porcelain skin glowed. Attached behind her were the most beautiful blue fire wings he had ever seen. His heart stopped as he took her in. He felt pride in War as he looked at her and wanted to claim every inch of her right at that moment not caring if the wings would burn him or that everyone would be watching. She slowly turned her head in his direction and he saw that she was crying little blue fire tears. Her voice was instant as well, "no Archer, please look away, I'm hideous. I don't want you to see me like this."

Archer's heart was tearing in two watching Allie fall apart. War glared at Duma and Flereous for making Allie feel this doubt about herself as Duma looked up and stared back at him. Something was off with the angel, and Archer didn't trust him. He started to walk closer to them slowly as Allie's tears continued to fall and she turned away from him. Duma was quick to speak even though Archer did not want to hear him. "Easy War, she cannot focus and retreat the wings back inside. Fire wings can be deadly to some demons, and these are the most powerful fire wings I have ever seen."

Archer stopped as Allie's head snapped up to glare at Duma. Within seconds she lifted her hand and shot a white light from it sending Duma flying back into a wall. This had Flereous laughing until she did the same to him, and had him next to Duma wearing the same shocked expression. Kane's voice came out of nowhere from behind Archer stating the oblivious, "that is not a fire power."

Kane's words were enough to make Allie look back at Archer. He could tell that she was scared. Her voice trembled as she spoke, "Archer I'm afraid. I can't make it stop. It feels like it is taking over."

Archer was lost. He didn't know what to say or do, he just wanted to reach Allie, however Samael stopped him. "Don't be foolish War. Only three types of people can go near her when she is like this, and you are not one of them." Archer was ready to attack Samael, but he spoke quickly. "Kane I think you will be the only one she will trust. Get her to take her wings in before she destroys everything here, including us."

Archer looked at his brother as he moved forward closer to Allie. Death was in complete control as he moved pass Archer and closer to Allie. Allie seemed to watch Kane move closer as it seemed like she was unsure of herself. Archer knew his brother was smiling at Allie just by the look on Allie's face. When he reached her she was left looking up at him as he held his hand down for her. Slowly Allie accepted his hand as Kane helped her to her feet. Then before Archer could blink, Kane was kissing his Allie.

Allie was stunned as Kane's lips came crushing down on hers robbing her of breath. His hands even moved to her backside cupping her butt as he pulled her closer to him. His kiss felt like he was absorbing her into him that Allie started to feel weak against him until suddenly something ripped Kane away a little too fast and caused her to lose her balance. Allie fell to the floor to notice instantly that her skin was no longer glowing. She also didn't feel the wings no more and a quick look at a piece of her hair confirmed that she was back to normal. Turning her head to see what had happened to Kane, she was shocked to see Archer pounding his fist into Kane's face. Granted it looked like Price was trying to stop him, Allie could not believe the amount of rage in Archer's face. Her voice was instant as she called out to him, "Archer."

Archer stopped with his bloody fist raised ready to hit his brother again with Price trying to stop him. He knew his eyes were most likely completely black as he looked at Allie, but he saw her worried look instantly as War demanded that he claim every inch of her. He blinked as his eyes returned to normal and he realized that Allie was back to normal. He was quick to look down at Kane who wore a satisfied smile on his bloody lips that were healing slowly. His words even taunted him, "oh she tastes so good brother that you might need to share her with me."

Kane was laughing even though he was the one on the floor that Archer was about to hit him again until he heard Allie again. "Archer," her voice came out like a tremble of need to him.

Archer pushed Kane hard against the floor as he got up and made his way to Allie. She seemed scared as he moved towards her and she seemed to be breathing heavy. Right before he could reach her, he felt the rush behind him knowing it was Kane about to attack him. "No," he heard Allie say as he turned to face his brother knowing the hit would hurt.

Archer saw Kane's fist sailing towards his face, but it seemed to stop in mid air like someone had grabbed it. This made Archer pause feeling confused, and he was not the only one, Kane was confused as well. Then suddenly Allie was between them, almost like she materialized between the two of them. It was another power the element of fire should not have. Allie stood there brave as Kane looked down at her and smiled as he spoke as his face was completely healed from Archer's hits. "Allie, you're turning me on with these new powers of yours. I can still taste some of them in my mouth."

Within seconds Kane went sailing into the wall behind him making a nice little dent, and making Archer smile. Allie spoke with the anger he knew and loved. "That is for taking advantage of me and trying to attack Archer from behind."

"Mm, foreplay Allie," Kane said as he rose up away from the wall brushing the dust and plaster off of him and started to move back towards Allie and Archer.

This time Archer moved Allie behind him to stand between her and his brother, making Kane stop and smile. Archer didn't need to say anything as Kane tilted his head to look at them. Kane's voice was eerie as he spoke, "for now little brother I will let this pass."

Kane then turned and walked away without looking at anyone else. Archer watched him as his hand still held Allie behind him. She was nearly molded to his backside. Price and Lacy was looking at him funny. Price spoke instantly as his bruising was also healing from being in the middle of the fight between Kane and Archer, "I will go talk to him."

It was all he needed to say before he just vanished. Lacy was staring hard at Archer. Her voice was hard as she spoke. "That was not a fire quality and you know it. I'm not even sure I know what that was."

She also seemed to vanish before Archer's eyes as he felt the threat decrease around him. Samael was watching him taking a sip out of his mug as both Duma and Flereous still sat on the floor both looking shocked at what had just happened. Duma was the one that spoke before anyone else, "who is her mother Samael?"

Samael smile as he swallowed whatever he was drinking. "Her mother is Elizabeth, Nathanael's only daughter."

Duma paled before Archer and Allie's eyes. In an instant, both Archer and Allie knew that Duma knew something about Allie's mother, but they never got the chance to question him about it. He vanished as well as Flereous started to laugh. "What is so funny?" Allie seemed to ask him.

Flereous stopped laughing as his grin was huge. "You Allie have Duma's abilities and he knows it. Which means, he might be your sire, and the reason why Elizabeth fell to begin with? He had no clue, and that alone is funny."

Flereous was laughing as Allie felt shock all over. Archer was quick to turn and hold her looking down into Allie's shocked face. His voice was instant as he spoke to Flereous and Samael. "This is more than enough training for Allie for one day."

"I agree," Samael said instantly. "We will continue tomorrow, but I might have to find another to replace Duma."

Allie felt her knees shaking. This was too much to take in for one day, it couldn't be true. Archer didn't wait for Allie's knees to buckle he swooped down and picked her up. He got her back to their room as quickly as possible and planned to distract her for the rest of the day.

CHAPTER TWENTY-TWO
UNCONTROLLABLE URGES

Duma was bent out of shape as he entered Nathanael's private home without knocking. Anger ate away at him as he walked into Nathanael's place as if he owned it looking for the angel. Searching the whole house, he was surprised that he couldn't find the angel at home. Instead he found a beautiful woman sitting on a bench sipping some tea looking up at the sky. He was about to speak as he stared at her long black raven hair when she beat him to it. "Hello Duma. It is nice that you have finally stopped in to visit." Another girl with blond hair appeared from nowhere refilling the woman's tea. Duma couldn't help but stare at her thinking she was very young as the woman spoke again, "thank you Janice that will be all at the moment. Please go back to being my eyes as I will expect a report later." The blond gal smiled as she bowed and vanished.

Confused as to why the woman was there, Duma moved to where he stood in front of her. The first thing he noticed was the woman's bright green eyes shimmering at him like a flame from a fire pit. She was a lot older than she looked and Duma couldn't help but smell the magic on her skin marking her as a witch. "Where is Nathanael?"

She shrugged her shoulders as her eyes casted a white field over them like an oracle would do. She smiled as she spoke, "oh I see you discovered the truth about Allie. She is perfect you know for my Archer. It's a shame I was never allowed to know him. Every time I do get to see him, I have to shield who I am from him and try to guide him as best as I can. It is what parents do for our children." Duma was instant to look at the woman in disgust as he realized she was the mother of one of the horsemen, but why was she in Nathanael's home. She smiled at him as her eyes returned to normal. "Your anger is not towards or for me. You are the one that betrayed Nathanael and made him cast out his only daughter. He had to punish her he had no choice when Michael made him do it. As to why I'm here, well that is between Nathan and me."

Anger spilled out of Duma when he spoke, "my daughter should never have been picked to be the element of fire, nor War's bride. He condemned her to an unjust crime. The fact that you are here confirms that he has betrayed us. You're nothing but a whore."

The woman started to laugh and then suddenly stopped as she stood up. Anger filled her eyes looking like green flames as she spoke to Duma, "I want you to listen to me well Duma.

In the war, Fire was cursed by one of the horseman before she took his life. He cursed her to be stuck loving her enemy until she birthed his child and the spell breaks. Fire was smart and added to her curse. She added that if she birthed more than one child from her enemy after his spell broke because she loved him, the war would end and the curse would be broken from both sides. In which entails that good would win over evil and the challenge to take over humanity will end as well. You know who that fire element was? She was my grandmother or better known as the red fire witch. None of the fire elements have been able to break the curse as we have to watch our child die before us from the hand that should save us." Duma blinked at her words feeling stunned by them. "This time it will be different. I know Allie can do it, and she will not kill my son or I will kill her. It is why Janice has been her friend for so many years, I've been watching them. Hmm now I can't let you leave here Duma knowing what you do. However no one will know you are missing either."

Allie stared at her plate of food as it felt like all eyes were on her. Kane sat across from her just glaring with no facial expression at all. Price was next to him cutting up a piece of meat, but also staring at Allie. Lacy for once wasn't looking in a mirror but sipping on a glass of wine while looking at Allie. Archer's dad was missing from tonight's dinner as it seemed he had other plans. Allie had talked to her mother over the phone for a few minutes telling her where she was.

Her mother had only asked if she was planning to pick up some clothes, and didn't bother to ask why she was there. The thought left Allie playing with her food while being stared at by Archer's siblings.

Archer was quiet as well, but seemed to be eating his food rather quickly. Allie found herself watching him as he ignored everyone else. Then it almost seemed like he could sense her watching him as he turned and looked at her. His voice was instant as he spoke, "eat Allie, you will need your energy later."

Allie looked back at her plate, but she could not eat what was in front of her. At lease she couldn't eat with the way Kane was staring a hole at her. Her voice was instant as she pushed her plate away. "I'm not hungry."

Kane's lips tilted up in a small smile as his eyes looked a little too smug to Allie. Price set his food down and spoke, "the cook can bring you something else Allie if you do not like it."

"It's not that," Allie said instantly as Archer gave her a funny look. "Excuse me," she said instantly getting up and heading out of the room.

Archer watched Allie walk out, but did not follow her right away. His eyes turned to Kane as he glared at his brother that was suddenly wearing a smile. "You are making her uncomfortable here," Archer was quick to state.

Kane rolled his eyes as he spoke. "Relax little brother, I will go and talk with her. Just give me a few minutes to make things right."

Archer watched Kane follow Allie out of the room wondering how his brother would fix this. He would give them a few minutes, but that would be all.

Allie was sitting on the staircase by the door. She couldn't explain how she felt or what she was going through. The little hallway mishap as she called it kept playing in her mind starting with Kane's kiss. She was now uncomfortable around Kane because all she was thinking about when she saw him was the fact that he had kissed her and almost started a war between the two brothers. Maybe it was guilt eating away at her however for some reason she didn't know that she was suddenly being watched until Kane cleared his throat.

Allie looked up startled as Kane smiled at her and held out his hand to her to help her up. She let him pull her up not trusting him a hundred percent. His smile grew bigger as he spoke, "I must admit Allie I've been thinking about something all night."

Before Allie could ask him what it was, he pulled her right against his body and kissed the breath out of her. Allie was melting against him for several seconds until she realized that it was wrong to be kissing Kane like this. She found herself suddenly jerking away from Kane and landing on her bottom on the stairway. He was looking down at her with a big smile on his face. His voice was instant as he spoke, "now I know Allie, now I know." Without another word he turned and walked away from Allie as her heart was racing.

Allie verily had time to calm down from what had happened before Archer rounded the corner. He knew something was wrong, but Allie shrugged it off telling him that today was too much for her to take in, and she really wanted to go to her home. For once Archer felt at a lost and agreed to take Allie back to the home she knew.

Kane watched Archer take Allie back to her home. He could still taste Allie on his lips, and he wanted more. He felt that satisfied smile on his lips as he walked to his room and opened the door to see Ellie sprawled out on his bed wearing nothing. Ever since he had kissed Allie he had been releasing his sexual desire with Ellie. Poor Ellie looked tired on his bed as she turned and opened her eyes to look at him. Kane had been going nonstop sexually since that kiss, and it felt like he could continue all night. Tonight he would be picturing Allie as he took Ellie, and he planned on it lasting all night.

Archer was worried about Allie as they pulled up to the house she had lived in. Her mother was waiting at the door with a worried look on her face that seemed to mirror Allie's. "Archer do you mind if Allie and I chat alone for a bit," her mother asked him. Archer nodded as Allie and her mother headed towards her room. He waited for the door to close, and then followed to overhear what was bothering Allie.

Allie was instant to sit on her bed as her mother closed the door behind her. She was instant to move against the headboard and grab a pillow to clutch as her mother made her way over to the bed and took a seat looking worried at her daughter. Allie was the first one to speak as it seemed her mother was waiting for her to begin. "I don't know what I should think no more. Too much has happened today for it all to be real. I keep thinking that I will wake up at any minute and things will be back how they use to be. Why didn't you tell me any of this?"

"I was hoping that you would never have to go through with any of this Allie, and would have a normal life. That was what was promised to me by my father the day you were born." Allie's mom told her point blank. "However he lied," she said in the next breath. "I will tell you something that will shock you now Allie, however I think it is time you should know." Allie stared at her mother thinking all she needed was a cherry on top of her day to make it so perfect. Yet Allie waited for her mother to tell her what would shock her. Allie's mother schooled her face and then just said what would shock Allie. "You have a twin brother. When you were both born, my father came and said your brother was marked to be the element of fire and he needed to be trained and protected. He took your brother when I was too weak to stop him, and I have not seen your brother since that has taken place. Now I think your brother was taken from me as punishment for embracing my betrothed, yet I don't think Michael is satisfied. I think he learned about you as well, and now are making you suffer."

Allie stared at her mother without blinking as several thoughts roamed in her head. She might have been in shock as she spoke, "mom who is my real father?"

Allie's mother was quick to look down, but she spoke. "When I was your age, I fell in love with the angel of dreams. He was fun, but I was only a moment to him and nothing serious. I learned later that he couldn't stand Michael, and had a reason for seeking me out. He destroyed my relationship with Michael, and I let him. Your real father's name is Duma."

Allie stared at her mother in shock as her mother slowly looked back up at her meeting her eyes. It took her a minute to get out of her shock, but she did. "Mom I think I need to know everything about your old world, so I know what I'm up against."

Archer moved away from the door to go take a seat. He knew the conversation was going to take a while now. His mind was processing the fact that Allie had a twin brother. He knew Allie, she was going to want to find him, and it would mean trouble. Archer still kept within earshot so he could hear everything being told to Allie. He couldn't help but smile at how well Allie was taking all of this as he heard her mother talk about fire angels and her past. Their conversation was interrupted by the phone ringing in which Archer was asked to answer. He did so, but hearing Janice on the other end made him wish he didn't. Within seconds she was grilling him that Archer thought of hanging up on her, but he knew she would call back. So he fed her something she would never forget. He told her that they had eloped and they were trying to break it to her mom, but promised that Allie would get back to her later if not tomorrow. This satisfied Janice, as Archer was able to get off the phone and listen to the conversation that mattered most.

Allie couldn't believe the words out of her mother's mouth. Fire angels were the worst type of control freaks and her poor twin brother was raised by them. She was surprised to learn that female fire angels were not allowed to roam around without a male fire angel with her at all times. Not only that her mother's first sexual encounter resulted in life for Allie and her brother. Her mind instantly thought of Adam. All these years she reached out to him, and he had no clue she was his twin. He needed to know and he should know who his father is as well. She was about to reach out to him with her mind when her mother's words stopped her. "Allie I still would like to talk about this marriage between you and Archer. It's important that you two follow the old way ceremony or it will be insulting to me for you two to be living in sin."

Allie blinked losing focus on trying to contact Adam. "What is the old way ceremony?"

Allie's mother actually smiled. "It is the ceremony where you wear a dress, and walk down the aisle to make your vows to each other in front of many witnesses. I did that with the man you believed was your father and in many ways he was, he raised you. I would like you to do that as well, and the sooner the better," she said a little louder hinting to Allie that Archer was listening.

So it wasn't surprising to hear Archer suddenly speaking loudly from down the hallway. "Anything for Allie, and to please you Liz," he responded.

Knowing that Archer was listening, Allie didn't feel like she could really talk to her mother about what else was bugging her. She didn't know what to make of Kane. Granted his first kiss helped her to control her uncontrollable urges of her new power, the second kiss made no sense to her. It was almost like something about him wanted her, and it scared her a little bit. Her mom's voice was instant, "what else is bugging you baby?"

Allie shook her head. She couldn't tell her mother what was really bugging her with Archer listening, no telling what he would do. "I guess it is the pressure of it all. I most likely need time alone without anyone around me. I just feel like none of this is real and at any moment I will wake up."

Her mother was looking at her strange as it seemed like she was thinking about something. "Maybe you need your own place, well maybe just until the wedding."

Archer was suddenly in the doorway with the door wide open just staring right at Allie. Within seconds he was knelt in front of her and looking up into her face. His words made Allie stop breathing. "Allie I can't live without you. I need you next to me always, or nothing will matter to me anymore. You are my strength and reason for going on. The past two days have been bliss in your arms, and I crave you unlike any other. Don't leave me behind Allie, it will kill me."

Allie couldn't tare her eyes away from Archer. She didn't even notice that her mom got up and walked out the door closing it behind her. She felt tears in her eyes just swimming but not falling. She couldn't speak as she was deeply touched. So instead Allie leaned in and kissed Archer's lips pulling him closer to her. He was all over her in seconds kissing her like she was the air he was breathing. Allie had to stop him before things went too far as she remembered they were in her mother's house. He stared at her with a smile and whispered at her to collect what she needed so they could finish what she started here. He even started to help her pack to help move her along. Allie found herself watching Archer with a smile on her lips as he was dumping drawls into a suitcase. He looked up and caught her smile at him and was on her again in seconds. His kisses were searing her brain and she knew that she couldn't keep stopping him, yet she did with a laugh as she spoke. "I love you Archer, but you need to behave."

He smiled back at her as he spoke, "I can't help but be under your spell Allie. Can you really blame me for losing control when you look at me and nearly beg me to touch you?"

Allie couldn't help but laugh as the blush crept in her cheeks. Her eyes even twinkled as she spoke, "then we better hurry."

Archer moved quicker than before not realizing that they were being watched. Seraph was invisible, but he watched the two of them through the window shocked. He moved away and back to the others before he was spotted. He moved directly to where Jehoel was and spoke instantly, "we have a problem." Jehoel looked directly up at Seraph as Seraph noticed Adam next to him. "I found Allie, but she is with War. He can't keep his hands off of her."

Adam's fist slammed instantly into the wall next to him cracking it. Jehoel looked at Adam for a minute and then back at Seraph. "We need to know the minute he leaves her alone so we can make our move."

Seraph nodded at this but then continued. "One more thing, Allie's mother, it's Elizabeth."

Jehoel seemed to stop breathing his hand even shook for a moment. Then he nodded at Seraph dismissing him deep in thought.

CHAPTER TWENTY-THREE
A SINKING FEELING

For the past three days, Price had been keeping an eye on Allie. Something about her seemed to be missing that it had perked his demons up to be secretly watching her. Flereous seemed to be with her most of the day working with her in the private gym to get her to unleash her powers again. So far he was unable to coax anything out of her, so he was looking like a drill instructor more than anything. Furfur or better known as Fury for short was also there. He was teaching her basic hand to hand moves. Xaphan or better known as Aaron watched her with a worried expression. Out of everyone Xaphan knew Allie best and could most likely tell Price what was wrong with Allie.

Price didn't wait to be invited in, he moved silently next to Aaron as he waited for the demon to acknowledge him. It didn't take long before he did as he continued to watch Allie sparing with Fury as Flereous was instructing moves. "Yes Price," Aaron said instantly.

Price never beat around the bush, so he went straight to the point. "Why is Allie acting so weird around us now?"

"She has a lot on her mind and most likely doesn't realize she is acting standoffish. However I notice her and Archer act like lovebirds, and I find it hard to believe how they always seem to be together except when she is in here training. What is she doing that is bothering you?"

A small smile was on Price's face as he watched Allie nail Fury in an unexpected move sending him on his butt. Her eyes darted over to him making her lose focus and allowed Fury to take her down. In which cause Flereous to call it all to a stop and look at him as well with a scowl on his face. Price was quick to answer Aaron. "It seems like something is bugging her, and I would like to know what it is."

To his surprise, Aaron called out loud to Allie. "Allie what is your problem? You noticed Price was in here, and you lost focus. What are you thinking?"

Allie was catching her breath from having the wind knocked out of her. Fury was still on top of her pinning her to the mat with a satisfied smile on his face. He even leaned down and whispered in her ear that she was lucky they were not alone. She also heard Aaron as clear as day, and the action made her growl out a response. "Right now I'm thinking that Furfur weighs a ton and he is crushing my pelvis."

This caused Fury to laugh as Allie noticed his flaming tail behind him. His voice was also instant, "bring out your wings baby and we really can dance."

This caused Allie to growl as the little blue flames made her hands glow a second before they sent Fury flying back in the air and slamming into the other wall. He was still smiling at her, but so was Flereous as she got up and the blue flames danced along her hands. Then almost instantly the flames sunk back into her skin making both Fury and Flereous scowl instantly. Aaron shook his head as he spoke, "that is not what I'm talking about. I know you Allie, and I know your body language better than anyone. What is bugging you?"

Anger seemed to spill out of Allie as she spoke, "what are you saying that I have a huge chip on my shoulder? Well you would be too if you realized that angels and demons existed, and you were in love with the one person who you have been in love with your whole life that turns out to be one of the horsemen. So why don't we throughout some more like the fact that my birth father is the angel of dreams that hasn't bothered to come back after finding out that I'm his daughter, and most likely doesn't even know about Adam."

Allie stopped her ranting instantly as she realized she said what exactly had been bugging her. It was the fact that she had not even started to connect with Adam. Price's voice was instant as he ceased the last thing she said, "Who is Adam?"

Allie blinked as she stared at Price. He wasn't Kane and she had no idea how to act around Price since he was no longer sick. Then again, Allie had made sure she was never alone with Kane because she didn't trust what he would try to do to her since the last time he had kissed her. Allie was quick to shake her head at Price as she looked down at the ground. Within seconds her chin was being lifted up as she found herself looking Price straight in the eye. "Allie I have always liked you and I am thrilled my brother has picked you to be his bride. However the past couple of days I have found myself worried about you since you unleashed your wings. I know this is a lot to take in, but I want you to be able to talk to me. Trust me Allie."

Allie sighed as she took a breath. She had always liked Price too. "My mother told me that I have a twin brother, who was taken away by my grandfather the day we were born." The room went silent as Price stared at Allie with wide eyes. Allie met Price's stare not knowing what to make of it. "I would see him in visions and we could talk with each other. He was being taught by fire angels. I don't trust them."

Price blinked as he took a step back clearly shocked by Allie's news. He didn't have to communicate with the others to know what they were thinking too. A pen could be dropped in the room from the silence and be heard from someone outside of the room. Price's mind was telling him it could be possible for there to be two elements of fire, but he wasn't sure if they shared the powers equally or if one was stronger than the other. Allie's mood was suddenly understandable as he spoke, "do you want to try to find him?"

Archer was in a jewelry store of all places looking for a ring for Allie. He had a simple smile on his face as he was looking for one that would surprise Allie. His eyes landed on a ruby surrounded by diamonds. It seemed perfect in every way that it called out to him. He was quick to turn to look for the sales girl to help him, but the shop seemed to be empty. Instantly Archer's senses went on high alert as something felt off. Someone was watching him. War stirred to life inside him and he felt the smile on his lips as he spoke, "I know you are here."

A male laugh seemed to echo all around Archer. Within seconds it felt like a gust of wind nailed Archer and slammed him into the wall making him gasp for air. He was pinned against the wall struggling to get free when suddenly he noticed Ashley in front of him with a cocky smile on his lips. "Oh please struggle away, but you will not be free unless I let you go. Besides I wanted to have a little chat with you."

Archer growled making Ashley smile bigger. "What do you want," came out of Archer's mouth sounding like venom.

Ashley ignored him for a minute and then opened up the case Archer was looking in earlier. He pulled out the ring Archer wanted to get Allie with a smile on his lips. "I'm so amused how Allie has you wrapped around her little finger. Shame that it is all a spell, the minute it wears off, she will be the one to kill you."

Archer blinked twice at Ashley not thinking he heard him right. It had to be trick to make him doubt the love between him and Allie. "You're lying," came out so easy.

Ashley laughed at him clearly amused. "Oh I'm lying, that is rich, but I'm not War. See a horseman cursed Fire, when she defeated them. The only reason she won was because that horseman fell in love with her and could not destroy her. However she destroyed him, but not before he laid a curse on her, and you know what he cursed her with? He cursed her to fall in love with him the minute they met up again. She would not be able to resist him, and he could not resist her, until a child was born from between them. Then the spell breaks, and all hell will break loose."

Archer could not find the lie in his words, and his demons were silent. "Why are you telling me this?"

Ashley lips smiled in a mocking way as he spoke, "because you tied each other life forces to each other. When the spell breaks, and it will, you will end up killing each other. So in a way I'm thanking you for making this easy on us. Also just wanted you to know we can feel another Fire to take her place."

Within seconds Ashley was gone as Archer's heart was pounding. The curse couldn't be true, but who could confirm it? If it was true, how could he change the outcome? Instantly Archer's thoughts went to Ellie, he needed to find her and talk with her.

Allie found herself sitting next to Price in front of a computer with Aaron, Fury, and Flereous behind her. Price was pulling up birth records, and other records on Adam. He pretty much lived off the grid. None of the information seemed to tell Allie where he was. Frustrated with the search online, Allie got up and started to pace when she suddenly thought she heard a voice. Stopping suddenly she noticed Aaron watching her and the look in his eyes told her that he heard it too. His voice was instant, "I have an idea, Allie sit still and think of him. See if you can connect mind to mind."

Allie moved to the soft chair across from Price's desk and closed her eyes. She was thinking of Adam, that suddenly she started to see images. She knew instantly that he was seated in a room somewhere, and it seemed like he was doing the same thing she was. Her voice was instant, "Adam."

His eyes opened quickly and locked on hers, however it wasn't his voice that spoke. "We can see her."

Allie suddenly saw the others in the room. Six others seemed to be staring at her and the look in their eyes made Allie pause. Adam's voice was instant. "Allie I'm within arm's reach to you. I want you to come to me, without the demons. You're not safe there."

"Where are you," came out of Allie's mouth as her eyes stayed focused on the fire angels? Something about the way they were looking at her made her think that they meant her harm.

Adam leaned over and picked up a coffee cup. It was a Starbucks cup. He spoke instantly, "I will meet you here alone. Just you and me, no one else," he said with a smile.

Allie nodded her head as she spoke, "I will be there in thirty minutes."

The connection ended instantly as Aaron was the first one to speak. "No way in hell we are letting you go alone to meet him. You might trust him, but I don't trust fire angels. They want to lure you out alone."

Price's words were almost instant as he spoke, "no Aaron she will be alright. It's important for Allie to connect with him, and no fire angel would dare interfere."

Everyone in the room seemed to look at Price strangely as he smiled at Allie. She didn't think twice and headed out of the room. The minute she was out of the room, Price picked up his phone and dialed a number. It made everyone else in the room unable to question his motives. The line was answered instantly as Price spoke. "Allie is heading to the Starbucks to meet her long lost twin. I think it is an ambush, and need you to be inside waiting. They wouldn't dare try anything in your presence."

Price hung up the phone and looked at the others. "One of you should secretly tail Allie to protect her from them trying anything before she gets there."

Flereous nodded his head and then vanished. Aaron stared at Price and then slowly started to laugh as he shook his head as he spoke, "well played Price. She will most likely think you are on her side."

Price smiled at him and then slowly stood up. He could feel his demon stir to life inside him, and knew he needed to feast on a soul soon.

Archer found Ellie in his brother's room of all places, yet something was different with the witch. She seemed to be staring straight ahead at him as her eyes had the white effect over them. He noticed quickly that her hands were chained to the bed and her body looked stiff. He walked slowly towards her unable to look away from her as she suddenly spoke, "he did not lie to you."

Archer blinked at her words as he moved next to her and took a seat on the bed. He had a sinking feeling knowing it was all true. "I love her, I always have," Archer confessed to the witch. "Somewhere deep down I know she loves me too. It is not a spell on her part. I want you to break the spell." Ellie blinked thinking she did not hear him right. Archer was quick to speak again, "I would give and do anything Ellie. I would even give my own life for hers."

Slowly Ellie reached out and touched his hand shocked by his words. A simple touch and suddenly flashes of the future and the past flashed in Ellie's mind. Her hands started to shake as her mind went on overload. Her breathing even increased suddenly as the room started to fade out. What Ellie saw shocked her to her core. In the vision she saw a woman that was breathtaking looking into a basket. She spoke to someone that was in the room. "Ellen, take the other child and hide her. I want you to raise her as your own and teach her the gifts I have gifted her with. Their uncle will be here soon, and he will take Archer as his own son."

The woman stepped forward and Ellie knew the woman who had raised her instantly. She had called her mother her whole life until she was killed by Kane's hands, and Kane claimed her as his. Instantly Ellie's heartbeat increased as it made her chest hurt and the images move forward. Then she saw the same woman again as she was looking into a crib. "Hello my little one, you have my eyes. I knew you could create the bond needed to save them. You are very powerful, and never doubt that."

"What the hell is going on in here?" Kane's voice came out of nowhere ending Ellie's visions and making her let go of Archer's hand shaking a little.

Archer spoke instantly as Ellie was lost for words. "Allie has a curse on her to hate me after we have our first child. I asked the witch to break the curse, and I'm sure she was seeing if there was a way before you came in and ended her vision."

"Well that will have to wait for another time. Allie is skipping off to go have coffee with her brother, and we need to head that way before she gets there. Price got her to open up to him, and well needless to say we have several fire angels in our yard that need to be taught a lesson."

Archer was on his feet instantly. No way was Allie going alone to meet her brother. He walked out the door without looking back at Ellie. Ellie watched both brothers walk out of the room knowing one truth. Her heart was pounding in her chest as a single tear rolled down her check. "What is wrong my love," was instantly in her head as she heard Ashley talking to her mentally.

"He's my twin brother. My whole life is a lie and so his is."

CHAPTER TWENTY-FOUR
NOT AS PLANNED

Allie was surprised that she was able to make it to the coffee shop in thirty minutes. She was looking everywhere for Adam, but he didn't seem to be there. She was instant to take a seat looking out the window as she waited. Within seconds a female voice spoke drawing her attention. "Well I'm surprised to see the traitor here alone. Are you waiting for someone?"

Allie turned to see Melody standing next to her. Melody stared at her like she had every right. Allie's words were instant. "You call me a traitor and then want to know if I'm waiting for someone, maybe I should ask why you are here?"

Melody actually cracked a smile as she took a seat. Melody's whole vibe put Allie on high alert. "I was actually told to come here and give you a warning. Personally I don't think you deserve a warning, but it was either you or your lover." Melody actually smiled as she spoke. "Your warning," Melody said as she made quotes in the air, "is for you to know that you are under a spell. What you think you might feel for your lover is not real. After you bare him your first child, you will hate him, and you will try to kill him. However he has tied your life forces together, so you kill him, and you kill yourself." The smile disappeared from Melody's face, "I delivered your warning to you, but something else you should know." She looked down for a minute before making eye contact with Allie again. "You walked into this with a choice. Some of us had no choice and did not ask for it. We know you are not the only fire."

Melody rose up then as Allie stared after her. Not once did she turn around as Allie's heart felt like it was pounding. Allie watched her walk out the door and then her eyes moved to the left to see a man sipping on coffee staring at her. She remembered him instantly as his lips tilted up in a smile. Her eyes darted around to notice several other guys just staring at her and watching her with a smile. Instantly Allie knew they were fire angels, and this was all a trap.

Melody was steaming as she walked out of the coffee joint. She couldn't believe how stupid Allie was. She didn't even know she was being used and the first to fall. Cursing to herself she rounded the corner to nearly collide into a small petite blond girl. The blond was instant to smile at her as something seemed to nag Melody about her. "Oh I must be heading the right way if I'm bumping into water, but you might want to leave quickly, War and Death are heading to the coffee shop. Allie is in there with a bunch of fire angels, and well it is almost show time." Melody's eyes went big as guilt attacked her knowing she left Allie in there alone to face them all. She was going to turn and head back towards her when the little blond grabbed her pretty fast slamming her into a wall. "You are not allowed to interfere, Melody. If you do, Ellie will never be set free. This must play out and my girl needs a five minute head start. Do you understand me?"

Melody blinked shocked as she spoke, "who are you?"

The blond smiled as she responded. "I'm Janice, Allie's best friend, and I'm not going to let you mess this up besides I know you made a deal with the fire angels." Within a second Janice nailed Melody in a cold punch as she slipped to the ground. Janice knew she was in a safe spot as she was out cold, and she only needed to be out cold long enough for everything to fall through as planned as when Melody woke soon, she would think that Death had planned this little trap and be ready to fight.

Adam watched the girl that had haunted him for years suddenly appear. She looked so much like him that it made him fell paralyzed. Jehoel had told him they needed to bring her away with them so the demons would not follow. It would be the only way to protect her because he knew demons would show up. Seeing her knowing that it was a trap made Adam step out of the shadows and move toward her. She watched him as her eyes darted around at the others. She knew it was a trap and somewhere deep down he knew he needed to comfort her.

Allie watched Adam emerge out of the shadows. It seemed like time had stood still for her as all the noise in the coffee house faded away and he moved towards her. He took a seat in front of her and smiled as he spoke, "this is much better than using my mind to contact you."

"I'd thought you would come alone?" Allie stated as her eyes moved around nervously to the others.

"They wouldn't let me. The girl you were just talking to, why did I feel a pull to her?" Adam asked suddenly feeling the fire angels moving closer.

Allie blinked as she spoke. "That was Melody. She is the element of water, and I'm afraid she hates my guts."

Adam arched an eye brow at her and looked about to speak when suddenly he seemed to stare over her shoulder. Allie felt two hands come to rest on top of her shoulders making her jump at first before she could tilt her head back to look up. Archer stood behind her with a smile on his lips looking down at her like she was the only thing that mattered in his world. His voice sounded rich as he spoke, "hello love. Kane and I saw you in here and decided to join you."

Archer leaned down and placed a tender kiss on Allie's lips. Then he grabbed a chair and placed it next to Allie as he sat. He looked away from Allie to stare right at Adam. Allie stared at Archer feeling a little shocked that he was even here. However she received the shock of her life when another chair pulled up on the other side of her and Kane took the seat boxing her between them. His look at Adam was not friendly as he spoke. "Are you planning on taking Allie against her will rodent?"

"Kane," Allie said instantly.

Kane turned and looked at her with a smile on his face as he spoke. "Allie my sweets, you are surrounded by fire angels that are planning to take you. He is their rat leading you into the trap, your twin or not, he is going to betray you."

Allie felt shocked as she felt Archer's hand slipping into hers. She looked back at Adam who sat back looking at them as a whole. His words were sudden as he spoke. "I would never betray Allie, but one thing for sure she doesn't belong with you."

Within a blink of Allie's eye, the attack happened so quickly. One second they were all sitting there and the next flames engulfed around them as Kane and Archer seemed to be engaged in a battle with Adam and several others. Allie didn't know what to do as she seemed frozen in place. People were running out of the building in panic as the flames grew. She noticed that Adam's wings were not blue but a reddish orange as were some of the other fire angels. Kane seemed to be all over Adam as Archer was fighting off two other fire angels. Some of the ceiling started to come down as Allie heard fire engines in the distance. This did not go as planned, and Allie knew she had to stop it, but she didn't know how. The choice was taken from her suddenly when she felt two arms circle around her and pull her back. A scream cut through her drawing Archer's attention, but the whisper in her ear made her panic. "You belong to me Allie, none of the others matter."

Allie started to struggle in the arms that felt like steel bars that were slowly pulling her out of the building. In a panic she looked towards Archer in time to see him get nailed in the chin and sent flying in the air. Her eyes moved to Kane who had a sick smile on his face as he pulled the same move on her brother and took out another fire angel with him. Kane then looked right at her as his eyes were a pitch black. His smile was sinister as he spoke, "come on Allie I know you can take him. His plan is to take you somewhere to rape you and then place you in a cage."

Everything stopped for Allie after hearing that. Her eyes moved to Archer that was lying on the ground not moving as three fire angels circled him. Her thoughts were of Archer alone that she didn't realize that her skin was starting to glow and Kane's smile grew bigger. Those arms around her suddenly let her go as Allie turned to look at the angel that planned to take her. It was Jehoel, and he stared at her shocked. Blue flames covered her arms like a well fit glove as Allie felt the heat behind her knowing her wings were out. Her eyes darted back to Archer to see the paintball angel tossing him over his shoulder with a smile on his face. His words taunted her, "you want him, come get him."

Suddenly he had wings and took off in flight blasting through the burning ceiling. Allie didn't think she was instant to follow as her wings focused with her mind and gave her flight. Allie didn't know how to fly it felt more like she was running after them in the sky. To her surprise the angel looked over his shoulder and smiled right before he dropped Archer. Allie's heart stopped as she saw Archer start to fall. Her first thought was to get to him, but the plan was spoiled as she was suddenly knocked sideways by an unknown force. Her eyes stayed on Archer as she spotted another angel catch him that she felt relieved instantly before realizing the danger she was in. She was spun quickly around that she smacked into a hard chest. Her eyes met amethyst eyes like her own as the paintball angel was smiling at her. His words were instant, "we are keeping your lover our prisoner Allie, unless you come with us willingly. Only then will we let him go."

Before Allie could speak, Kane did from behind her. "Afraid we are not going to do that. Allie will stay with me and you will return my brother, or else I kill Adam."

Allie's head turned to see Kane flying with velvety black wings holding Adam limp in his arms with what looked like a blade to his neck. Torn for several minutes Allie couldn't speak as she saw Kane smile and slowly cut into Adam's neck as Adam's blood slowly tickled down his neck. The angel let go of Allie instantly as Allie started to fall forgetting her wings were holding her up. She sunk down instantly to suddenly falling on something or someone. Jehoel had caught her and slowly started to take her to the ground in the middle of nowhere. Within seconds Kane landed as his wings sunk back into his skin. He still held onto a limp Adam, but the blade was no longer cutting. He spoke again, "my brother Jehoel."

Jehoel spoke while holding in a laugh. "He will be returned in due time Death. Release Adam or the deal is off."

Kane released him, and Adam dropped to the ground like a hard brick. Allie moved to check on him, but Jehoel grabbed her quickly as he spoke, "so foolish."

Allie blinked and suddenly she saw a gust of wind grab Adam and move him away until he disappeared. Kane growled as a blast of water nailed him knocking him off his feet. Melody's laughter came out of nowhere as she spoke.

"Water always beats Death. Every war, Water defeats Death. I'm the one that can kill you, and I will now for that little trap you set up for me earlier."

Kane was up on his feet as Allie notice the darkness around his eyes glow giving off a dark fog. Within seconds she couldn't see five feet in front of her, but Allie could hear the water rushing towards them. Her gut told her to get out of there before it was too late, but what surprised her was Kane wrapping his arms around her and taking off skyward. Allie felt her legs getting soaked as they went up a little higher but still in the fog bank. Melody's laughter was all around them as Kane whispered in her ear. "She is too strong, and with the fire angel's help we are sitting ducks. We will regroup and you will find Archer with your mind. They will not hurt him because they want you."

Archer woke suddenly to find himself in a cell of some kind. He could tell that it was magical, and knew he wouldn't be able to escape it. He turned his head to lock eyes with Jehoel, who stared at him like he was disgusted. "She doesn't belong with you," came out of Jehoel's mouth.

Adam's voice was next, "what spell did you cast on my sister?"

Archer felt his lips twitch as a smile grew on his lips. "It is no spell. Allie loves me more than anyone. She will never be with any of you."

Jehoel spoke again looking like he wanted to rip Archer apart. "Then why was she making out with your brother?"

Archer stared at Jehoel feeling stunned as Jehoel started to smile at him knowing doubt was in his mind. Before Archer could respond, a cloaked figured entered the room. Archer could feel the power coming off of the figure to know it was an arch angel of some kind. The voice was female and sounded musical as she spoke. "I saved your fire Jehoel, and now you owe me so I am calling in my debt. You will release War when Fire brings me my Earth."

Jehoel looked like he was about to argue, but Adam spoke. "Why do I want War to be free or better yet why do you?"

The female laughed as she pulled the hood back. Archer went instantly pale as he recognized the oracle he had killed as a young boy. Her bright green eyes looked right at him as she smiled, but she spoke to Adam. "I want my daughter returned to me. She is Death's prisoner, and only Fire can give her life. You will give your sister the message, and you must tell her that she cannot tell the other horsemen."

Archer found his voice instantly, "If Allie gives life to Earth they will see her as a trader and try to kill her. Release me now so I can protect her and I swear I will return your daughter to you."

The woman smiled bigger as she spoke her eyes gazed over with a white. "Allie can do it, but to make it fair, after she gets my Earth out of the house, I will have you set free to save her, but a spell will be on you. You will return back here after your flesh touches hers."

Archer looked at the woman worried over Allie. His threat came so easily to his lips. "If Allie is hurt in any way from this because of what you will make her do, I will kill you all over again make no mistake about that."

The woman smiled at him as she stepped closer to his cage. Her words were instant as she spoke in a whisper to him. "I know you will my son. I know you will."

CHAPTER TWENTY-FIVE
BIRTH OF EARTH

Allie wanted to throw everyone out of the room as she couldn't focus on Archer or Adam. Granted Kane had left the room twice, but each time he returned Allie became more uncomfortable around him. Price gave her a look a few times that gave her the shakes, but Lacy just stared at her like it was all her fault. Lacy was also the one to break the silence, "where is he?"

Just her voice made her lose her focus, making Allie want to strangle her. Kane must have noticed because he was suddenly amused as he spoke. "Why don't you two leave the room so Allie can focus?"

Allie felt relieved by his comment and surprised that the other two followed his orders. Thinking that she would be alone in the room, Allie was surprised to see Kane stay behind. He turned and took a seat right next to her on the couch. His hand was instant to take Allie's as he stared at her. "Kane you are distracting me," Allie was instant to voice as she felt panic settling in.

Kane smiled as he leaned in closer to Allie making her lean back. His arms went around her as he spoke, "I think you need motivation Allie. So I plan to screw your brains out unless you can connect with either Adam or my brother and find out where Archer is." His lips smashed against hers leaving her nowhere to escape and making Allie feel trapped.

Within seconds' energy course through Allie's fingers as her blue flames leaped to life blasting Kane off of her. He went flying backwards crashing into a table shattering it as Allie leaped up putting distance between her and a laughing Kane. He started to rise up, but suddenly it seemed like Adam stood between them in a ghostly figure. It made Kane come to a complete stop as Adam spoke. "An earth witch saved my life in which I owe a debt and she has called in. War will be released to you Allie if you bring Earth to me. She is Death's prisoner."

Adam disappeared so quickly that Allie blinked and looked at Kane's shocked face. It took Allie several minutes to think of what to say, but she knew what she needed to do for Archer. "Kane where is she?"

Kane stood there motionless as Allie stared at him waiting for a response that never came. Shaking her head, Allie moved towards the door and opened it before Kane could move. Price was on the other side as was Lacy, both took one look at her ready to speak but Allie beat them to it. "Get out of my way."

"Where are you going?" Lacy asked instantly as Price stepped back looking at Allie with different eyes as she knew something had happened.

Allie didn't respond she moved pass them up to Kane's room with both of them on her tail. She burst into his room thinking it was the only place Kane would keep a prisoner to suddenly stop in her tracks. Ellie was chained to the wall looking like she wasn't breathing. Her skin didn't even have a healthy glow to it as it seemed like it was covered in bruises, and suddenly Allie feared she was dead. Allie's heart dropped right as she was suddenly spun around. Her eyes moved up to meet Kane's intense eyes. Before she could demand what Kane had done to her, his lips came smashing down on hers again making Lacy and Price both gasp. Allie didn't think as she brought her knee up and nailed Kane in the privates. Kane slumped down shocked by Allie's move as he winced in pain, and Allie raced over to Ellie to note she wasn't breathing. Letting the blue flames grow on her fingertips, Allie touched the metal bars around Ellie's slender wrists to burn them off of her. Ellie fell to the ground in a dead heap as Allie tried to catch her. On the floor holding a non moving Ellie, tears fell from Allie's eyes as she spoke, "what have you done Kane? She was the only one that would get us Archer back."

Allie closed her eyes as the tears spilled all over Ellie's non moving body. Price and Kane stared at Allie's actions shocked as Lacy leaned in closer noticing how each drop of Allie's tears was soaking into Ellie's skin. Her words were instant, "Allie what are you doing to her?"

Allie looked up at Lacy blinking back tears as she slowly noticed Ellie's skin glowing. Price spoke next realizing what was happening, "she is creating Earth."

Kane finally got over the pain from Allie's blow to him and spoke, "we have to stop her, no matter the cost. She is betraying us."

Ellie saw the look in their eyes as they were all in agreement. They moved as a unit making Allie start to panic as her heart raced knowing she needed to act to save Archer. She felt her wings burst from her body as flames leaped out knocking the three of them down. Ellie was light in her arms as the wings moved lifting her up. Allie only looked at the wall before she suddenly burst through it. She heard Kane behind her snarling knowing that he was coming after her as the others would be putting out the flames. A sudden pain in her side almost made her drop Ellie as Allie turned her head a little to see a black arrow wedged into her side and blood leaking out.

She felt herself weakening as her eyes started to close on her and her breathing became shallow. All Allie could think was that she needed to reach Archer and bring Ellie to them. So hitting the hard chest of someone not only nearly knocked her out, but made her drop Ellie. Allie felt herself falling thinking she welcomed death if it meant saving Archer, so more pain really woke her up when she felt someone grab her hitting the arrow to sink deeper in her. Archer's voice was in her ear as he spoke, "I have you Allie, and I have Ellie too, we are about to be transported back to the cell. They better be able to heal you or I will kill them all."

Archer was back in his cell with his side bandaged up that seemed to match Allie's wound from the arrow, but both Allie and Ellie were on the table on the other side of the bars from him. Raphael was in the room treating their wounds as everyone else waited outside. Archer's eyes were glued to Allie's eyes which were closed. So he was a little surprised when Raphael spoke, "your brother used an arrow that only he can heal. I can heal her as best as I can, but you will have to return her to him and hope that he heals her, the rest of the way."

Archer blinked not thinking he heard him right. "What type of arrow is it? I'm healing so I know she is."

Raphael picked up the arrow and showed it to him through the bars. Archer suddenly felt the smile on his lips from his brother's fast thinking. It was a beacon arrow, and right at the moment, his brother was tracking him to this location. His pleasure was short lived as Ashley suddenly burst into the room and raced to Ellie's side. His eyes seemed frantic as he scanned her over, but then his eyes looked right at Archer as he spoke, "your brother will die by my hand alone for what he has done to her."

Archer raised an eyebrow at Ashley as Adam walked in and sat next to Allie. Adam suddenly had Archer's full attention as War raged inside him as his hand came up and stroke her cheek. His voice was directed towards Raphael as he spoke, "were you able to cut the ties between the two of them so their lives are no longer joined?"

Archer felt shocked as he darted a look back at Raphael. "I have, but only Death can heal her since he is the one that poisoned her. You will have to let War take her back to him, or she will die."

That thought made Archer smile in a smug way as he stared back at Adam feeling his despair over the idea. However Adam's words surprised him. "I wish to stay with my sister and get to know her. Can you promise me that you or the others will not hurt me so we can get to know each other?"

"I can't promise for my siblings," Archer said instantly as he stared back at Allie noting that her chest was moving which meant that she was waking up. "You need to let me get her back to my brother now, since you cut our tie, I don't know how else to help her."

Adam seemed in deep thought for severally minutes, but then he got to looking at the arrow Raphael was holding. He was instant to move closer and look at it. His snort was instant as he spoke, "I want your word War that you will not interfere when I see my sister, nor let your siblings in on it. In return I will make sure I am not being tailed by fire angels. The place we meet will be very public, so no worries that I will escape with her once she is healed. Plus I don't care if you sit in on the meetings. Do we have a deal?"

"I don't want you nowhere near my Allie," Archer spit out at Adam. "Doesn't matter anyway you only have seconds to get away before they reach me."

The boom came out of nowhere shaking the room and making pieces of the ceiling fall. Adam stared Archer down as Ashley gathered Ellie in his arms and left the room. Adam then looked at Raphael as he spoke, "the earth witch I made the deal with, she can take Allie's poison out?"

Raphael looked a little shocked as he spoke, "yes she can and I'm sure she will do it as a reward to Allie for saving Ellie. However it can cause Allie to have memory lost. She may not remember any of this or any of us."

"So we can plant new ideas in her head and make her forget all about him," Adam said pointing at Archer who was looking at him with panic in his eyes.

"You could do that, but I strongly urge you not to tamper with her mind." Raphael replied back as another explosion made the walls shake.

Jehoel was suddenly inside the room as he spoke, "Adam we have to leave now. Somehow they found us."

Adam glared at Archer as he spoke, "you lost your chance with me War, and in the end you lost the girl." Adam then turned and looked at Jehoel. "Allie is coming with us the witch will be able to heal her."

Jehoel moved right in and scoped Allie up as Archer watched fighting against the bars trying to stop them. It was pointless as he watched them all walk out of the room, they were taking his Allie and he couldn't stop them. His roar alone echoed around the room in pain until he suddenly noticed that Kane stood in front of him looking down at him. His words were instant as he spoke, "they took Allie. They took her memories of us. I want to kill them all."

Kane's lips twitched in a smile as he opened the cell up his words were instant. "Oh we will kill them all little brother. Two fire angels died today, and that is only the start. It's time we start taking out the elements."

Allie's eyes fluttered as she slowly woke up. She had no idea where she was or who she really was. She sat up in the dark room as moonlight leaked in the window. Something felt off to her, but she couldn't place what it was. As soon as she blinked, someone moved from within the room drawing her attention. They reached over and turned on a light blinding Allie for a minute before she could focus on who was in the room with her. Once she could see again, she noticed the tall man with the shoulder length blond hair. He was smiling at her as he spoke, "I'm glad you have awoke love, you had me worried."

His words alone confused Allie. She had no clue as to who he was. "Who are you?"

A look of concern crossed his face as he moved and took a seat at the end of her bed taking her hand in his. "Allie I am your soon to be husband. I am Jehoel."

Allie blinked feeling like it was a lie. It made her shake her head as this all seemed unreal to her. She even frowned as she spoke, "why can't I remember then?"

He seemed to move closer yet as he spoke. "I'm afraid you took a serious blow to the head after the explosion my love. We were under attack by the horsemen, as we were housing the elements. Your own brother is the element of fire, and you demanded that we help them."

Again it felt like a lie to Allie as she tried to except his words. "I want to see my brother," Allie said next.

Jehoel nodded his head and then helped her up. Allie noted that she was in a long white gown of some kind, and her body felt like it had been through a ringer. She used Jehoel's strength to help her out of the room and into the next that seemed full of people. Her eyes darted around the room instantly to land on a blond with blue and purple in her hair. Her glare was heated with hate and she was the first to break eye contact. The action alone made Allie wonder what she had done to the girl. The girl with the natural tan skin and brown hair smiled at her warmly. She was also the first to speak, "I owe you my life Allie. The debt I owe you is beyond what I will be able to repay."

Allie seemed to nod at this not understanding why she had said it, but then her eyes moved to her brother. He had a genuine smile on his lips as he crossed the room picking her holding her tight against him. "I'm so glad you're ok Allie. I promise you I will never let them capture you again."

Somehow the words rang with the truth.